Murder [...]

"Charming characters [...]
have readers cheering."
—*Kings River Life*

"This series has appealed to me from the first book. The mix of characters and their friendships were what first attracted me. The stories and the mysteries captured me as well . . . I hope this series lasts a good while."
—*Fresh Fiction*

"What a fun mystery series this is! Fifield's writing gets better with each book, and I very much enjoy how carefully she plots out her stories. If Keyhole Bay were a real place, I'd love to visit, mostly to see Bluebeard and buy a souvenir or two."
—*MyShelf.com*

Murder Hooks a Mermaid

"A whodunit with a dose of the supernatural, *Murder Hooks a Mermaid* is a worthy successor to the series opener and showcases Fifield's talents for plotting, characterization, and humor."
—*Richmond Times-Dispatch*

"Author Christy Fifield creates the kind of characters that stay with you for a long time. Fifield's new Haunted Souvenir Shop mystery, *Murder Hooks a Mermaid*, has it all: a sunny, relaxed setting; captivating locals; delicious food; and—of course—murder! Delightful amateur sleuth Glory Martine is back with her wisecracking parrot and charming group of friends in this thoroughly entertaining adventure. Don't miss it."
—Julie Hyzy, *New York Times* bestselling author of the Manor House Mysteries and the White House Chef Mysteries

continued

NO LONGER
PROPERTY OF PPLD

"Quirky and unique, a heroine for whom you can't help but root. The story sucks you in." —*The Maine Suspect*

"With a lovable cast of characters, good conversations, and a great setting, this well-written book is a terrific read."
—*Dru's Book Musings*

Murder Buys a T-shirt

"A cantankerous parrot, a charming heroine, and a determined ghost vanquish a villain in Christy Fifield's appealing debut mystery."
—Carolyn Hart, *New York Times* bestselling author of the Death on Demand Mysteries

"A businesswoman, a parrot, and a ghost inhabit a souvenir store. That's not the setup for a joke, but for Christy Fifield's debut, *Murder Buys a T-shirt*, which packs a paranormal punch. Fifield expertly shifts the focus among the possible culprits and establishes Glory as a charming protagonist, sometimes impulsive, sometimes wary. And she invests the small-town setting with Southern spirit (and at least one spirit), as well as numerous recipes for traditional Southern food. A traditional mystery with an offbeat angle, *Murder Buys a T-shirt* will have readers, like Bluebeard, greedy for more." —*Richmond Times-Dispatch*

"An entertaining and clever Florida whodunit."
—*Midwest Book Review*

"Fifield offers a nice blend of the cozy and contemporary with a hint of the paranormal. I look forward to getting to know Glory and her friends better. Good writing, an appealing ensemble cast, and a tightly woven mystery; definitely a series that's a promising addition to the 'cozy' genre."
—*Once Upon a Romance*

"A fun book that will make the dreariest of days a little brighter! Socrates' Great Book Alert." —*Socrates' Cozy Café*

"Very enjoyable . . . [A] delightful cozy mystery, and I will definitely be reading more of the series. Yummy recipes of traditional Southern dishes are also included."
—*Novel Reflections*

"A great murder mystery with well-written characters, an unpredictable villain, and a nice setting."
—*Paranormal and Romantic Suspense Reviews*

"A thoroughly Southern atmosphere with a dash of Cajun spice provides a nice backdrop, with plenty of great-sounding food (and recipes), making readers feel at home and anxious to learn more about Glory, her family, and friends."
—*The Mystery Reader*

Berkley Prime Crime titles by Christy Fifield

MURDER BUYS A T-SHIRT
MURDER HOOKS A MERMAID
MURDER SENDS A POSTCARD
MURDER TIES THE KNOT

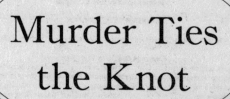

Murder Ties the Knot

Christy Fifield

BERKLEY PRIME CRIME, NEW YORK

THE BERKLEY PUBLISHING GROUP
Published by the Penguin Group
Penguin Group (USA) LLC
375 Hudson Street, New York, New York 10014

USA • Canada • UK • Ireland • Australia • New Zealand • India • South Africa • China

penguin.com

A Penguin Random House Company

MURDER TIES THE KNOT

A Berkley Prime Crime Book / published by arrangement with the author

Copyright © 2015 by Chris York.
Penguin supports copyright. Copyright fuels creativity, encourages diverse voices,
promotes free speech, and creates a vibrant culture. Thank you for buying an authorized
edition of this book and for complying with copyright laws by not reproducing, scanning,
or distributing any part of it in any form without permission. You are supporting writers
and allowing Penguin to continue to publish books for every reader.

Berkley Prime Crime Books are published by The Berkley Publishing Group.
BERKLEY® PRIME CRIME and the PRIME CRIME logo are trademarks of
Penguin Group (USA) LLC.

For information, address: The Berkley Publishing Group,
a division of Penguin Group (USA) LLC,
375 Hudson Street, New York, New York 10014.

ISBN: 978-0-425-27924-3

PUBLISHING HISTORY
Berkley Prime Crime mass-market edition / March 2015

PRINTED IN THE UNITED STATES OF AMERICA

10 9 8 7 6 5 4 3 2 1

Cover illustration by Ben Perini.
Cover design by Sarah Oberrender.
Interior text design by Kristin del Rosario.

This is a work of fiction. Names, characters, places, and incidents either are the product
of the author's imagination or are used fictitiously, and any resemblance to actual persons,
living or dead, business establishments, events, or locales is entirely coincidental.

PUBLISHER'S NOTE: The recipes contained in this book are to be followed exactly
as written. The publisher is not responsible for your specific health or allergy needs
that may require medical supervision. The publisher is not responsible for any
adverse reactions to the recipes contained in this book.

If you purchased this book without a cover, you should be aware that this book is
stolen property. It was reported as "unsold and destroyed" to the publisher, and neither
the author nor the publisher has received any payment for this "stripped book."

This one is for the fans, who make it all worthwhile.

And especially for Dru Ann, the patron saint of cozy writers.

Acknowledgments

To the usual crew of crazies:

Michelle, amazing editor;

Susannah and Rich, extraordinary agents;

Colleen, first reader, friend, gym pal;

Jan and Jeri, sisters who really know how to celebrate a birthday;

and most of all Steve, who's kept me sane for the last thirty years.

Thank you all!!

Chapter 1

I STOOD IN THE CENTER OF MY SMALL LIVING ROOM,
struggling to remain motionless. I wore a dark green satin
dress that clung to me in an unfamiliar way, and tottered
on a pair of matching heels far higher than anything I had
ever owned.

The sliding door to my miniscule balcony was open a
crack, letting in a cool, late afternoon breeze. It was early
November, and in the Florida Panhandle that meant seventy degree days. The temperature was dropping and I
would have to close the door soon, but for now I welcomed
the slight chill. It helped soothe my nerves, and I wasn't
the only one with an attack of nerves.

My furniture had been pushed back to clear the center
of the room, and Keyhole Bay's radio star, Karen "The
Voice of the Shores" Freed, paced like a caged animal.

"Glory! Stand still," Karen snapped. Normally I would
find the contrast between her actions and her words amusing. But this wasn't a normal day.

I sighed, not even trying to hide my exasperation. Ever since I agreed to be her maid of honor, my so-called best friend had started channeling every bad bride I'd ever seen. And as the owner of a gift shop in the Florida Panhandle, I'd seen plenty of them on "destination" weekends, bossing their bridesmaids around and generally acting like what my memaw called "donkeys in horses' harness."

"Seriously, Martine?" Karen said, her chestnut curls shaking in disbelief. "This poor woman is trying to mark the hem of your dress, and you can't stop fidgeting." She waved at her former and future mother-in-law, on her knees in front of me.

To her credit, Mrs. Freed just laughed. "Easy, Karen," she cautioned. "Glory already did this for you once, if you'll remember. Not many friends would do it twice."

Karen reached down and hugged the older woman. "And not many women would be lucky enough to get you for a mother-in-law. Twice." She took a deep breath and backed away. "I think I'll go get us some coffee, okay?"

Mrs. Freed nodded, distracted by the heavy green satin that pooled around my ankles. "Go on," she said around a mouthful of pins. "I'll be finished by the time you get back."

Karen shot me a last warning glance and hurried down the stairs that led from the small apartment to the gift shop below.

True to her word, Mrs. Freed finished pinning the hem and I was comfortably back in my jeans and polo shirt by the time Karen returned.

She carried a cardboard tray of paper coffee cups and a white bakery bag from Lighthouse Coffee next door. Setting the coffee on the kitchen table, she held the bag out to Mrs. Freed. "I really appreciate what you're doing," she said. "And Pansy says to tell you hello."

Mrs. Freed opened the bag and sniffed appreciatively. "Lordy, that woman knows her way around a cruller, doesn't she?" She took a shiny glazed twist and passed me the bag.

Still warm, the pastry was irresistible.

"Careful," Karen commanded. "You still need to fit into that dress."

"Do we really need to do all this?" I knew I was whining, but Karen's wedding was still six weeks away. A lot could happen in that time.

"Glory!" Karen's impatience with me was evident in her voice. "We had to book the church a year ago, and the florist wanted more than six months.

"Weddings take time," she said, as though that was a real answer.

"They don't have to," I argued. "People get married without all this," I searched for a description, and came up with one of Memaw's favorites, "fuss and feathers."

I knew better than to continue, but I couldn't stop myself. "It's only Monday. You and Riley could go to the courthouse tomorrow, get your license, and get married on Friday. Or we could get on a plane tomorrow morning, fly to Las Vegas, and you'd be married before suppertime."

"And my mother would never forgive me." She shook her head. "I did the no-fuss thing the first time I married Riley, remember? Maid of honor and best man as witnesses, with a justice of the peace. I think my mom was still holding a grudge when we got divorced. So we better do it right this time."

I followed Karen and Mrs. Freed down the stairs to the shop. It was time for my assistant Julie to leave, and I had to relieve her.

We all hugged Mrs. Freed good-bye, then Julie dashed out to retrieve her toddler from Grandma. Anita Nelson doted on Rose Ann, and one of these days she hoped to retire and keep her only grandchild full-time. But that day wasn't today, or likely very soon.

"Besides," I continued once Karen and I were alone, "your mother is three thousand miles away."

"Not for long," she shot back. "She decided she's needed, and she's planning to come for a month before the wedding."

"What about the latest stepdad? Doesn't he have a say?"

"That's the worst of it," she moaned. "He's coming with her! Remember she said he was some high mucky-muck in the Navy? He was in charge of that base up in Washington state or something like that. I figured that would keep them there."

I just nodded. No sense trying to get a word in while Karen was on a roll.

"Well, he might be transferring to Pensacola." She groaned. "Can you believe it? She wouldn't just be in the same state, she'd be in the same *county*."

Karen paced through the store, dodging around the merchandise shelves and T-shirt racks. I cringed as she waved her arms in distress, imagining a display of mugs and shot glasses crashing to the floor. To my amazement she managed not to knock anything over.

"@!^$#%%$#!!" The string of curses startled Karen, stopping her mid-rant.

"Sorry, Bluebeard," she muttered.

Bluebeard ruffled his feathers and fixed one beady eye on her. He ruled the roost, and we all knew it.

The parrot had been here longer than any of us, after all. I'd inherited him with my 55 percent of Southern Treasures. Along with him, I'd inherited the ghost of Great-Uncle Louis Georges, the previous owner of my shop.

Uncle Louis had definite opinions about how things should be, and he sometimes used Bluebeard to express his disapproval. In fact, you could say Uncle Louis specialized in meddling in my life. A lot.

"Sorry," Karen repeated, offering him a shredded-wheat biscuit from the tin underneath his perch.

The treat bought her a temporary reprieve from Bluebeard's glare, and she turned back to me.

"I do want her to be happy," she said. "Really. But can't she be happy somewhere far away from me? Isn't Admiral What's-His-Name enough?"

"Is he really an admiral?" I asked. I didn't think she'd ever told me anything about Stepdad Number Three, except that he was in the Navy.

"I don't know," she admitted. "She met him a few months ago, and the next thing I knew she called me from Hawaii saying they got married on the beach."

"So why can't you do the same thing?"

Karen rolled her eyes. "Haven't you been listening? I never had a 'real' wedding, according to her. She's had two—three if you count the one on the cruise ship—and she didn't want this one to be a big deal.

"Besides, if anyone is going to run off and get married, it should be Felipe and Ernie."

She had me there. Our friends couldn't get married in the state of Florida, though I hoped that would change someday. I raised one hand in surrender. "Do what you have to. I'll do my part." I thought for a minute before I continued. "But if I ever get married, Vegas is looking pretty good."

Karen's eyes narrowed. "Is there something you aren't telling me? Something I ought to know?"

I shook my head. "No."

"You sure?"

I shook my head again. My relationship with Jake Robinson had become closer over the last year, but wedding plans were a long way off. I wanted to survive Karen's wedding before I even considered the possibility.

And I'd meant what I said about Las Vegas; an elopement might be more my style.

Chapter 2

BY THURSDAY MORNING, I HAD SHOVED KAREN'S question to a dark corner of my mind and slammed a heavy door on it. I didn't want to think about anything wedding-related. I was spending the day with Jake, and I just wanted to enjoy our time together.

Julie was watching the store, and Jake had a clerk who could run Beach Books on a quiet weekday. We didn't often get the same day off, but we'd planned this one several weeks ago.

We headed north in my pickup. The truck was old, a 1949 Ford with a complicated history. Lovingly restored, the truck had once belonged to Uncle Louis, and had come "home" when my old Civic got torched. Elegant gold script on the doors and tailgate made it a rolling advertisement for my shop.

Besides, it was just darned cool to ride around in.

We took the back roads between the fields of scattered farms, and past the crossroads gas stations and tiny stores.

Our pace was slow, but it felt right. Driving the vintage truck on the old farm roads felt like we'd gone back sixty years, as long as you ignored the occasional satellite dish and the signs that read "Speed Limit Enforced by Aircraft."

"Is the quilt supposed to be ready?" Jake asked as we neared the Alabama border.

"I'm not sure," I answered, watching for the brightly painted fence that marked the turnoff.

The fence stood out in an area of dusty split rails and sagging wire. I didn't know why the owner kept the posts and rails painted in rainbow hues, but I appreciated the landmark.

I turned off the two-lane highway onto a dusty road that wound through the trees. "Beth told me to check after the first of the month."

"You could have called her," he said.

"Yeah, but where's the fun in that?" I shot him a quick grin before turning my attention back to the winding dirt track. I tried not to think about what the dust was doing to my beautiful truck. I'd wash her just as soon as we were back in Keyhole Bay.

"Besides," I said, slowing for yet another curve, "this way I get to do some treasure hunting on the way back."

From the corner of my eye, I could see Jake's nod. "As long as I get lunch," he teased. He'd seen me stash a picnic hamper behind the seat before we left.

I laughed. "You had Pansy fill your thermos with coffee, and I know there were at least three muffins in that bag when you got in the truck." I gestured at the crumpled white pastry bag in the litter sack hanging from the radio knob. "I only ate one of them."

He quickly changed the subject. "Are you sure it's okay to just drop in?" He gestured out the windshield at the empty road. Trees closed in on either side, forming a shield for houses hidden down narrow dirt paths. The only evidence of human habitation was the occasional dilapidated mailbox at the side of the road. "Doesn't look like the kind of place where visitors show up unannounced."

"She's expecting me," I said, with more confidence than I felt. The truth was that we had settled on a date, but when I'd called Beth to remind her of my visit, I'd just gotten her voice mail.

She hadn't returned my call, or the two others I'd made in the last couple days. Which made me more determined to check up on her. I'd made a sizeable deposit on the wedding quilt Jake and I had commissioned for Karen and Riley, and the wedding date was fast approaching.

I slowed to a crawl, watching for Beth's mailbox on the right. I spotted it, a tin box painted like a log-cabin quilt on a carved wood post, and turned down the washboard driveway.

Around a sweeping curve about a quarter mile off the road, we spotted the weathered cottage. I didn't see Beth's car, but since they only had one, it was possible her husband had taken it somewhere.

"What do they *do* out here?" Jake asked, swiveling his head to take in our surroundings.

The cottage, little more than a clapboard shack, sat in a clearing surrounded by scrub pine, live oak, and several other species of trees I didn't immediately recognize. A few yards from the cottage stood a low shed, several times larger than the house. The wide doors of the shed were closed and locked with a heavy padlock. Next to the shed, an oil drum hinted at the presence of a generator, a common sight in the backwoods where power lines didn't reach.

"Whatever makes them happy." I shrugged. "She sews and quilts for cash, and he makes furniture. They have a garden around back, grow a lot of their own food. I think they even keep a few chickens for eggs. They told me they wanted to get 'off the grid' and live off the land. All very romantic and idealistic." I smiled and added, "Which is great when you're twenty."

Jake chuckled. "You mean you don't want to go back to the land? Get away from it all?"

"From what?" I shot back. "Indoor plumbing? Air-conditioning? The best coffee in the Panhandle right next door?" I shook my head. "I was born in the twentieth century for a reason."

I looked toward the cottage, wondering why no one had emerged to greet us. Beth must have heard us drive up.

I stuffed the keys in my pocket and opened the door. "Maybe we better go find Beth," I said. "So we can get back to civilization and find you some food before you starve."

Jake followed me up onto the front porch. I knocked on the door and waited, but no one answered. I knocked again, and called out, "Beth! It's Glory Martine. You around?"

Silence.

We waited a few minutes more, knocking and calling without any response. We left the porch and walked around the cabin. Maybe Beth and Everett were out in the garden, though I couldn't imagine why they hadn't heard us, or answered our calls.

Something moved in the woods beyond our view, and I jumped. It was faint, little more than the rustle of leaves, but there was no wind. Undoubtedly an animal, probably a deer startled by our intrusion, or a cat looking for a way into the henhouse.

Whatever it was, I was getting spooked over nothing.

Finally, I had to admit the place was deserted. I even checked the front door, but like the shed, it was firmly locked, and curtains were drawn closed over all the windows.

We climbed back in the truck and Jake looked at me. He raised his brows in question, but waited for me to speak.

"She knew I was coming. We set this up several weeks ago." I tried not to sound defensive. "Something must have come up."

Jake nodded, one corner of his mouth quirked up in the

hint of a grin. "Clearly," he said. "Looks like we aren't going to pick up a quilt today. So how about we find a place to eat and go gather some treasures?"

I was reluctant to leave without finding Beth, but I had to admit I had no idea where else to look. There weren't any close neighbors, and the couple had only been here a year or so, not long enough to make many friends in this isolated area. Besides, as Jake had pointed out, this wasn't a place to just go wandering onto someone's property.

Without a reason to stay, I started the truck, turned around in the hard-packed clearing, and headed back the way we'd come, along the dirt road. We hadn't seen another vehicle the entire time we were off the highway, which was probably just as well since the road was too narrow for two cars to pass each other.

We reached the county road and turned back toward the highway.

Once on the highway, we found a small park with just a few parking spaces and a couple picnic tables. Exactly what we needed. Jake hauled the hamper to a table near a stream and we unpacked our lunch.

The picnic hamper looked as old as the truck, but with the help of some very modern gel packs, it kept the potato salad and fried chicken properly cool.

Jake let out a low whistle as he took the chicken out of the hamper. "This is homemade, right?"

I bristled with fake indignation as I spread an oilcloth cover on the rough wood table. "Of course it is! Would I serve any other kind?"

He grinned and continued setting out our feast. In addition to the chicken and potato salad, I'd packed a small fruit salad, a jug of sweet tea, and fresh cookies.

"I have to admit," I said, putting the plate of cookies on the table between us, "these are Miss Pansy's cookies. I'm a good cook—"

"You're a great cook," Jake interrupted.

I shrugged. "Even so, my cookies don't come anywhere near hers. With something that good right next door, it seems foolish not to take advantage of her talents."

As we ate, we watched the sparse traffic speed by on the highway. "Where to from here?" Jake said, helping himself to another one of Miss Pansy's cookies. "I've never actually been treasure hunting with you before. I don't know how this works."

"There are a few places I usually stop," I explained as I collected the remains of lunch. "I've got a little network of folks who watch jumble sales and flea markets for me, and a couple quilters like Beth. I've spent years developing my contacts all over the Panhandle."

"And you're taking me to meet them?" Jake asked as he stowed the hamper back in the truck. "I'm honored."

"You should be," I answered, climbing back behind the wheel and starting the engine.

We wandered the back roads around the north end of the county, past tiny ponds and wide pastures, and along muddy creeks. Treasure hunting was one of my favorite pastimes, cruising slowly down an unmarked country road and stopping to visit with the suppliers who had become friends over the years.

There were stories of children and grandchildren, births and deaths, marriages and separations. We drank what felt like gallons of lemonade and sweet tea, and the pickup bed slowly filled with vintage kitchenware and knickknacks that would keep my shelves and my website stocked for several months.

The sun dipped low on the horizon as we headed south after a mostly successful trip. Jake took over driving once we were back on familiar roads, and I leaned back in the passenger seat, pleasantly tired from the day, glad I didn't have to cook dinner.

Thursday nights I took turns cooking with my three best friends: Karen, Felipe, and Ernie. For the past several months, we'd been including Jake and Riley, though we hadn't officially expanded our group. Tonight was Ernie's turn, and I was looking forward to good food and good friends.

All in all, a pretty great day. We'd be home in time to unload the truck and close up our shops before dinner. The only bad thing was that I still didn't have the quilt.

I'd tried to call Beth before we headed south, but once again it just went to voice mail. I told myself not to worry; cell service was notoriously spotty in the rural area around the border, and we still had a month or more before the wedding.

Everything would be fine.

Chapter 3

JAKE STOPPED ON THE SIDE STREET BEHIND SOUTH-
ern Treasures and backed the truck into the parking area,
carefully lining the bed up with the back doors. For a guy
who could back a forty-foot fire truck down an alley, it
wasn't even a challenge.

I unlocked the back door into the storage area. We carried in stacks of vintage spatterware and were headed back
for more when Julie called for me to come up front.

Jake waved me away, saying he'd finish unloading, so I
hurried up front to the retail area. Julie was waiting for me
with a worried expression. "Bradley Whittaker's been looking for you all day," she said. "He won't tell me what it's
about, just that he needs to talk to you right away."

Pansy Whittaker, the Miss Pansy who'd baked my picnic cookies, owned Lighthouse Coffee next door to my
shop. Bradley, her oldest son, visited his mother regularly.
I knew him well enough to say hello, but I couldn't imagine what was so important that he wouldn't tell Julie.

She was right to look worried.

"Tell Jake I'm next door," I said. "I assume that's where Bradley is?"

Julie nodded and I dashed out the front door.

Next door the shop was open, but there were no customers. The familiar smell of fresh-baked bread filled the small dining area. Bradley was behind the glass bakery case, deep in discussion with Chloe, the barista. He saw me come through the door and waved me over.

Chloe turned to look at who had come in. Her appearance sent a wave of shock through me. Her usual cheery expression was somber, and her red-rimmed eyes made it clear she'd been crying. She broke away and ran toward me.

"It's okay, Glory," she choked out between renewed sobs. "Everything's really okay."

I hugged her and patted her on the back, concern growing with every reassurance she sobbed out. Clearly everything was not okay, despite what she said.

"What? What's okay, hon?"

I looked over her head, buried in my shoulder, to Bradley. He was nodding, as though in agreement with Chloe, but I wasn't convinced.

He came a few steps closer, his expression serious. "Mom's in the hospital," he said. "The doctor is calling it a 'cardiac event,' whatever that is. Says he wants her to stay for a few days, have some tests."

Chloe pulled away and raised her tear-stained face. "We were making scones, like we do most mornings. She turned kind of gray and slumped over." She drew a deep, shuddering breath. "I thought she was—" She stopped, as though giving voice to her fears would make them too real.

"You did great, Chloe," Bradley said, smiling kindly at the distraught girl.

He looked back at me. "She called the paramedics and did exactly what they told her to. Wouldn't let Mom get up and go back to work, even though she tried."

I felt a smile lift the corners of my mouth. I could see Pansy doing exactly that. But a tiny eighty-something woman wouldn't have been much of a match for the sturdy young college student with a stubborn streak a mile wide.

Bradley apparently had the same thought, and a flash of amusement lit his eyes for a moment. "The doctors tell me they think she'll be fine, but she needs to slow down."

"I've been telling her that," Chloe sniffed. "But she won't listen to me. Thinks I can't manage without her."

"You can't, honey. Not as long as she carries all those recipes in her head," I reminded her.

Chloe gave me a look I couldn't fathom, but before I could ask her anything more, Bradley spoke again.

"I've spent most of the day with Mom," he said. "It took a lot of time and persuasion, but with the doctor's help, I have managed to convince her it's time to retire."

His announcement caught me by surprise. I'd begun to think Miss Pansy was going to work until the day she dropped over dead in her kitchen. Which she'd apparently come close to doing today.

"She had some reservations," he said without irony. "And she insisted I had to talk to you before anyone else.

"Miss Gloryanna, Mom would like to know if you're interested in buying Lighthouse Coffee."

Chapter 4

I KNEW THE ANSWER WITHOUT ANY THOUGHT. OF course I was interested. What I didn't know was how I could possibly pay for it. Even with the money I'd put aside to buy out my cousin Peter's 45 percent of Southern Treasures, I wouldn't have nearly enough.

"Uh, well. Wow!" I stalled, trying to figure out how to answer Bradley. "I, um, I hadn't really thought about it," I lied. I'd thought about it, all right. Just not in terms of it happening anytime in this decade.

"Can you, um, can I take a little time to think this over?"

He frowned, and I hurried on before he had a chance to say no. "This is pretty sudden. There's so much to think about, like how I could even run both places, and how much Miss Pansy wants me to pay, and if I even know enough to run a coffee shop.

"But I guess if all you're asking is if I'm interested, well, then the answer has to be yes. Yes, I would be interested."

Chloe grabbed my arm and held on like a drowning

woman clinging to a life ring. "I'll help, Glory! There's lots I can do, I promise! I can work for you and run the place and you won't have to do everything yourself. I'll even come in early and do the baking—"

"That's another thing," I interrupted her torrent of words to address Bradley again. "This place is worth a lot more if whoever buys it has Pansy's recipes."

Again the funny look from Chloe, but I dismissed it. The girl was still so shook up from the events of the day that there was no telling what was going on in her head.

"A few days," Bradley said. "But I'm afraid I can't wait much longer than that. Every day that goes by is a chance for Mom to change her mind and insist on coming back to work. And we are very much afraid that if she comes back, we will never get her out again."

His eyes misted up and he swallowed hard. "I know how much she loves this place, and how much she enjoys coming in here every day. I love my mom, and I hate like hell—pardon my language—to take that away from her. But if I don't, this place will kill her, sure as anything."

I nodded. "Give me the weekend," I said. "I should be able to give you an answer by Monday."

I put my hand over Chloe's, still clinging to my arm. "I'll talk to you tomorrow, okay? For now, you need to close up and go get some rest."

She shook her head. "I have to go see Miss Pansy first. She told me to mind the shop while she was gone today, and I need to let her know everything's being taken care of."

Bradley managed a weak smile. "She'll rest better knowing things are under control, even if she doesn't really believe us," he said.

"How about you?" I asked him. "Are you okay?"

"We all knew this day was coming," he answered. "Mom's nearly ninety, and the doctors say she'll see a hundred if she takes care of herself. We just have to convince her to do that."

His expression was still serious, but he looked calm and

a lot less worried than Chloe. Of course, he hadn't been there when his mother collapsed, either.

"We're going to close up here and head for the hospital," he continued. "My brother's there now, with the rest of the family. Mom insisted I come back here and wait for you."

I nodded. "Please keep me posted on her condition," I said. "And tell her I send my love." A thought occurred to me as I headed for the door. "Is she here?" I asked. "Or in Pensacola?"

"Bayside Hospital in Pensacola," he replied. "Her doctor said they have the best cardiac unit in the area."

My heart was racing as I walked back to Southern Treasures. I accepted Bradley's assurance that Miss Pansy would be okay, but the rest of his news had my head spinning. How could I possibly buy Lighthouse Coffee while Peter still owned 45 percent of Southern Treasures?

Having my meddlesome cousin as a partner had its drawbacks. Like his continual attempts to tell me how to run the store. Peter had a master's degree, which he thought made him an expert on absolutely everything, including retail, which he'd never worked in his life. His degree was in mechanical engineering, and he held an important position—according to him—with a firm in Montgomery, a hundred miles from Keyhole Bay.

Even so, he thought he should tell me how to run Southern Treasures.

I'd worked in the store since I was a teenager. I'd laid off my last hired manager many years ago and I ran the place by myself. Peter got a check every month for his share of the profits, which I considered a clear signal that I was doing all right without his interference.

But could I buy Lighthouse and run it as a separate business? And if I somehow managed to find the rest of the money I needed, how would I ever get rid of my not-so-silent partner?

Chapter 5

"I THOUGHT YOU WERE NEVER COMING—" JULIE stopped midsentence as she caught sight of me. The bantering tone in her voice disappeared, and she came around the counter to put her arm around me.

"Glory? Are you all right? You look like you've seen a ghost. What did Bradley want that has you so upset?"

I tried to ignore her choice of words. I hadn't told Julie about Uncle Louis. She still brought Rose Ann into the store from time to time, and I wasn't sure how happy she would be, knowing there was a ghost living here.

"I'm okay," I said, shrugging out from under her arm. "But Miss Pansy's in the hospital."

Her hand flew to her mouth, and her blue eyes opened wide. "Oh my goodness! What happened? Is she going to be okay?"

Jake came through the door from the storage area just in time to hear her last question. "Is who going to be okay?"

"Miss Pansy," I said.

I locked the door and turned the sign from "Open" to "Closed" before I explained what had happened. "She collapsed this morning while she and Chloe were baking," I said. "Chloe called 9-1-1 and the ambulance took her down to Pensacola. To Bayside. Bradley said they called it a 'cardiac event,' and they say she'll be fine."

"You didn't hear the sirens?" Julie asked.

I thought for a moment. "I hear the sirens every time," I said. "Nearly every emergency call goes right down the road outside my door." I gestured toward the highway that formed the main drag of Keyhole Bay. "After enough years, it just becomes part of the background noise."

I shook my head. "I might have heard them this morning, but I can't remember."

Julie glanced at the clock. "I hate to run off, but if you don't need me, I better get going. Mom's expecting me to pick up Rose Ann. You'll keep me posted if there's anything we can do?"

I shook my head. "No reason for you to stay. I'll call you if I hear anything." I waved her toward the door. "You need to get home."

Once Julie was gone, I shooed Jake out to go close up the bookstore. Julie's mention of the time had reminded me we had plans for the evening. "Don't forget, we still have to be at Ernie's for dinner at seven."

"I'll be right back," he said, kissing me quickly before heading out the door.

I locked the door behind him and began the routine of closing up for the night. As I tidied the shelves and checked the stock, I thought about Bradley's—well, Miss Pansy's—offer.

"What do you think, Bluebeard?" I said as I cleaned his cage and gave him fresh water. "Do you think we ought to buy the place next door? Even if it means we can't get rid of Peter as soon as I hoped?"

"Buy it." The voice wasn't Bluebeard's, but Uncle Louis's.

The first time I'd heard that voice as an adult, it had scared me silly; but I'd eventually become accustomed to Uncle Louis's habit of using Bluebeard as his spokesbird. Now it held a strange kind of comfort.

Especially when he validated my own choices.

In the storeroom, I opened the small refrigerator to retrieve some cut melons for Bluebeard. He loved fruit, and I always gave him an extra treat when I'd been away for the day.

In the fridge I found the leftovers from our picnic. Jake had unpacked the hamper and put the food away. I smiled to myself as I dished out the leftover fruit salad.

Jake was definitely a keeper.

I shoved the thought away. There were a lot of other things I had to worry about right now. My relationship with Jake Robinson belonged back in that far corner, locked away for the time being.

The man himself was waiting at the front door when I returned. I let him in before I put the fruit in Bluebeard's cage.

I was rewarded with a head butt before the parrot hopped over to the bowl. "Buy it," he repeated, then turned his back on me and concentrated on the food.

"Buy what?" Jake asked as we made our way through the storeroom. He had spent enough time in the store to recognize the voice, just as I had. "What was he talking about?"

"Lighthouse," I said. "I'll explain when we get to Felipe and Ernie's," I promised. "That way you won't have to listen to the story twice."

Jake's car was parked on the side street behind the store. "I thought I'd offer to drive tonight since you had to do most of the driving today."

"Thanks." I climbed in the passenger side without protest. Truth be told, I hadn't been looking forward to more time behind the wheel, even if it was only five minutes each way.

Everything in Keyhole Bay was only five minutes from

anywhere else in town. Except in summer, when the tourist traffic jammed the main drag and doubled or tripled drive time. Then the locals stayed off the highway, wound around back roads, and cut through residential neighborhoods that visitors didn't know existed.

As he pulled away from the curb, Jake teased, "How am I supposed to think I'm special, if you don't tell me first? How can I lord it over the rest that I already knew?"

"You think you're special?" I teased back.

"I do," he said. "Think about it. I know about Uncle Louis—who likes me, by the way. I helped you figure out how you could buy out Peter. I get invited to dinner with your secret club"—he pointed to the house as we pulled up in front of Felipe and Ernie's.

"It's not a secret club," I protested. "Just a bunch of friends who have dinner together once a week."

He parked the car and turned to look at me, his expression clearly skeptical. He leaned over and kissed me rather thoroughly. "And then there's that," he added.

I took a shaky breath. Yeah, there was that.

"Okay," I said. My voice quavered a little, and I laughed nervously, trying to lighten a suddenly serious moment.

"Bradley wanted to deliver a message from his mother. Miss Pansy wants to know if I'm interested in buying Lighthouse Coffee."

Jake gave a huge grin and started to say something. I held up my hand to stop him.

"He said I could have a few days to think about it, but only a few. I promised him an answer by Monday."

"Of course you'll buy it! Why wouldn't you? It's a wonderful opportunity." The grin returned. "Even Uncle Louis said so."

I shook my head. "I told Bradley I was interested, but there are a lot of things I need to consider."

I looked out in time to see Karen and Riley climb out of

Riley's truck. They stopped at the back of the truck, looking expectantly at us.

"We can talk about this over dinner," I promised.

Jake took my hand and gave it a squeeze. "We'll figure this out," he said.

"I hope so," I said cautiously. I wanted to believe him, but I knew there were a thousand ways it could go wrong.

Chapter 6

THE HEAVENLY FRAGRANCE OF ERNIE'S COOKING greeted us the minute Felipe opened the door.

Riley took a deep breath and sighed. "Oh, my! What's on the menu tonight? Smells wonderful, whatever it is."

Felipe welcomed each of us with a hug, collecting jackets, caps, and purses in the process. By the time he was done, the pile in his arms touched his chin.

Jake and Riley both offered to help, but he turned them down. "I'll just put these on the bed in the guest room," he said, disappearing down the hall.

The rest of us followed our noses to the kitchen. Ernie was the most committed cook in the group, and we always looked forward to his dinners.

"Whoa!" Karen stopped in the kitchen doorway. "What's that?" She pointed at a giant stainless steel range.

A grin split Ernie's face, his perfect teeth white against his dark skin. "Isn't she a beauty?"

He gestured toward the huge appliance like a spokesmodel

on a game show. Dressed in jeans that looked like they'd been made for him and a white oxford-cloth shirt with the sleeves rolled up to expose the chiseled ebony of his forearms, Ernie had managed to cook something redolent of tomato and garlic while keeping his clothes spotless. With his slender build and elegant posture, he probably *could* have been a model.

"It's really . . . big," Riley said.

"Yep." Ernie's grin grew wider, if that was possible. "Went to an estate sale last week—a retired chef from up north—looking for inventory." With his partner, Felipe, Ernie owned Carousel Antiques. They carried high-end furniture and collectibles, and Ernie was a savvy shopper when it came to estates and auctions.

"This is in your kitchen," I pointed out. "I don't think that qualifies as inventory."

"You furnish your place with inventory from your store," he reminded me.

He had me there. Most everything in my small apartment had come in through Southern Treasures, sure. But I had plates and bowls, and the occasional lamp or kitchen chair.

"Not a bazillion-dollar stove," I protested.

"That's what made this so great," Felipe said, coming back from depositing the coats. "Nobody wanted to move this sucker."

"I could see why," Riley said quietly.

"But we do this stuff all the time. Have a regular crew we hire for the big jobs. So we were able to buy it for about ten cents on the dollar, and Ernie has his Christmas present early."

Jake whistled. "You ever want to get rid of it, the guys at the fire hall will take it off your hands." As a member of the volunteer fire department, Jake was always on the lookout for ways to improve the station.

Ernie had gone back to stirring the pot that was giving off the spicy, tomatoey smell of something decidedly Cajun.

He gestured at the steaming pot. "Tonight I made gumbo, the way my granny made it."

Ernie paused, looking at the simmering concoction. "Well, the way Granny would have made it if she'd had more than just what Pop-Pop caught that morning."

He stopped himself, as though he had revealed more than he'd intended to. "Anyway, this is chicken, sausage, and seafood. It still needs to simmer for twenty minutes or so. But if you're hungry"—he opened one of the many oven doors on his new range with a flourish—"we have boudin balls and fried okra."

He deftly transferred the bite-size pieces to a platter and placed it on the elegant teak dining room table. Their shop might tend toward ornate antiques, but at home both Felipe and Ernie were definitely midcentury modern, and the expansive dining room set was one of their treasures.

The sizzling bits of boudin sausage and cornmeal-dusted okra were an instant hit. We scooped them onto colorful pottery plates and added dipping sauces from the array Ernie provided.

Just like every other Thursday, conversation centered around the food for the next hour as we settled at the table and tasted the night's offering. Ernie kept the meal simple: steamed long-grain rice as a base for his spicy gumbo, sweet tea, and French bread and butter.

"Now I know we've had the argument time and again about what is and isn't traditional Southern cooking," Ernie said. "But it's been a while, and I want all y'all to think about this: We've been doing traditional every week for a couple years. A hundred meals or more."

There was a murmur of assent around the table. It was getting harder with each passing week to find new dishes, or new ways of preparing old ones.

"I hadn't thought about it that way," Karen said, nodding. "That's a lot of meals."

"I agree with Ernie," I said. "It's almost impossible to find something we haven't done several times already."

"I don't know what we want to do instead," Ernie said.

"But Felipe and I have been talking this over, and we think it's time for a change."

"Maybe we can each try a different theme," Karen suggested. "Ernie likes to do Cajun and Creole—and judging by tonight's meal, I'd be happy to have him do more."

She glanced at Riley. "We could always do fish, depending on what Riley brings home from his latest trip." It was a safe bet; Riley owned a commercial fishing boat.

"We don't have to decide right now," Felipe said. "In fact, we don't have to make any decision. We can just do what we like for a while, and see what happens."

"Sure," I said. "As long as we don't let Freed go back to pizza." I grinned at my best friend. Her lack of kitchen prowess had been a running joke for years.

"You will notice," she said, "the quality of the food at Chez Freed has greatly improved over the years."

"I'll vouch for that," Riley said, drawing laughs from around the table. "You wouldn't believe what used to pass for dinner when we got married.

"The first time," he added hastily, in response to an elbow in the ribs.

"How *are* the wedding plans going?" Ernie asked.

Karen, always happy to talk about the wedding, launched into a story about her latest encounter with the caterer. But talk of the wedding reminded me of the missing quilt, and the missing quilter.

I couldn't very well tell the whole story in front of Karen and Riley—the quilt was a gift for them, after all— but I could tell my friends about the mystery that had dropped into my lap.

Again.

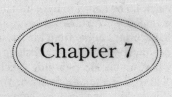

Chapter 7

KAREN WENT ON WITH HER STORY ABOUT THE caterer, and her problems with the wedding cake. "I wish," she said with a sigh, "Pansy still did wedding cakes. I'd have her do it in a heartbeat."

Next to me, Jake groaned at the choice of words.

"What?" Karen said.

"Just, well"—Jake looked at me. "You want to explain?"

I nodded and quickly filled my friends in on the developments at Lighthouse Coffee. Karen flinched when I told them Miss Pansy had a "cardiac event."

"So," I concluded, "Bradley says they have convinced Miss Pansy to sell, and she wanted me to have the first chance at the shop.

"I really, really want to," I went on, "if I can just figure out how to make it work. The biggest hurdle is going to be the money."

That shouldn't have been news to them; they all knew

that every penny I could pinch was going into my Buy-Out-Peter Fund.

Felipe and Ernie exchanged a glance, and I saw Ernie nod slightly. Felipe turned to me. "Southern Treasures and Carousel are two sides of the same coin," he said. "Ernie and I have been kicking around the idea of offering to buy out part of Peter's interest for a while now." He shrugged. "We already cooperate on buying inventory. You call me when something is too big for Southern Treasures, and we send people to you when their items don't fit our shop.

"Maybe it's time we talked about some kind of partnership."

Stunned didn't being to describe how I felt. Felipe and Ernie were among the best businessmen in town, and two of only a handful that I trusted completely.

"Maybe it is," I said slowly. "But I wouldn't want the business to interfere with our friendship."

Felipe nodded. "Agreed."

"I don't have much time," I reminded him. "Bradley wants an answer on Monday."

Jake chuckled. "You have your answer, Glory, and you know it. You want Lighthouse. The only question is how we do that and buy out Peter." He put his arm around me and gave me a reassuring hug. "All that's left is the arithmetic."

His use of the word "we" was still reverberating in my head when Karen spoke up. "So," she said, "do you want to do a wedding cake?"

The group erupted in laughter, the serious moment past.

I shook my head. "Isn't it more than enough that I am going to be your maid of honor? Again."

More laughter.

I glanced around the table at the friends who had become my family. As an only child, orphaned before I finished high school, I'd had to create my own family, and I was grateful for the warmth and support of the one they'd helped me make.

Our conversation spun on for another hour, sharing local news, gossip, and rumors. We talked about the Merchants' Association lobbying for more tax money to promote tourism while we cleared the table and loaded the dishwasher.

The question of whether Coach Bradley would retire when the football season was over was debated over dessert—an amazing bread pudding with warm caramel sauce that nearly put me in a food coma.

Ernie provided us all with copies of his recipes, a habit we'd developed when we started sharing dinners. Over the years I'd amassed a lot of recipes, and I'd used many of them.

"I'll definitely be trying this one," I told him. "Maybe it ought to go on the Lighthouse menu," I said, as though I owned the coffee shop already.

Ernie beamed. "I'd be honored," he said.

In between topics, I kept thinking of my missing quilter—but I couldn't find a way to bring up the subject without saying why I was looking for her; there just wasn't a graceful opening.

At last Riley yawned widely and reached over to rest a hand on Karen's back. "As much I am enjoying this," he said, "I was up early, and I'm running out of gas."

Karen nodded and rose from her chair. "I'm afraid I have to agree," she said. "I promised Riley we'd make an early night of it, since he was out of the house before daylight."

Ernie excused himself and returned a moment later with their coats and Karen's shoulder bag.

Ten minutes and many hugs later, they were out the door and headed for Riley's truck.

As soon as they were gone, Ernie turned to me, his brows drawn together in concern. "What's bothering you, darlin'?" he drawled.

"Who said anything was bothering me?"

"Um, you've been sitting there for the last hour looking like there was something you wanted to say. But every time you looked at Karen, you bit your lip. Like you didn't want her to hear whatever is on your mind."

"Is it that obvious?" I asked.

The three men nodded. I sighed.

"I, well, *we* had a strange experience today," I said, motioning to Jake to indicate he'd been with me. "I was supposed to see Beth. You remember the quilter, up north of Century?" Ernie waved for me to go on, though his expression told me he didn't remember Beth.

"We drove all the way up—it's practically to the state line—and she wasn't there. Her husband was gone, too. No sign of anybody around. Place all locked up tight."

"Of course it was locked up. It's out in the middle of nowhere," Jake said.

"That's not the point. The point is that she was supposed to be expecting me, and nobody was home."

Felipe shrugged. "I don't get it. You went to see someone and they weren't home. Why is that something you couldn't talk about in front of Karen?"

"Because of the reason we went up there. I commissioned a quilt for a wedding present for Karen and Riley. I couldn't very well say why it was so important."

Ernie shook his head. "You're overthinking this, Glory. I think you've caught some of Karen's wedding jitters." He gave me a reassuring hug. "I'll bet that gal just forgot you were coming. She'll probably call you tomorrow or the next day with some lame excuse, and expect you to go all the way back up there to see her."

"Happened to me just last week," Felipe said. "Ernie almost didn't get his range. The woman running the estate sale missed two different appointments with our delivery crew.

"I don't know what she was thinking," he continued.

"Wasn't like anyone else was lining up to throw money at her. But she just 'forgot' twice."

The conversation turned toward difficult suppliers and troublesome customers, and I tried to put aside my worries about Beth and her husband, Everett.

And my missing quilt.

Chapter 8

ON THE WAY HOME, I ASKED JAKE, "DO YOU THINK I'm overreacting? Maybe Beth and Everett just flaked out?"

He shrugged. "I don't know. You said they weren't the type to do that, but how well do you know them, really?"

I thought about it. I had met the young couple several times, but our conversations had never gone much beyond merchandise costs and delivery dates. I might not know as much about them as I thought I did.

Jake took his eyes off the empty road long enough to give me a worried look. "Glory, you've managed to stay out of trouble for more than a year. I like that; so do the rest of your friends." He chuckled briefly. "Boomer *really* likes that."

"That's Sheriff Hardy to you Yankees," I said with a touch of irritation.

He shook his head. "We got to know each other pretty well, bailing you out of that last jam. He told me to call him Boomer," Jake said lightly, ignoring my jibe about being a Yankee.

I bristled at the implication I had needed rescuing. "I didn't need to be bailed out."

"Maybe not," Jake conceded. "But either way, why borrow trouble? Beth and her husband weren't home. There's nothing sinister in that. Is there?"

I stared out the side window at the darkened storefronts as we drove down the highway toward my shop. Jake had a point, darn it. "Still," I said, "something about the place didn't feel right." I couldn't explain what was wrong, but something didn't quite fit.

"How do you feel about Felipe and Ernie's offer?" Jake said, deliberately changing the subject. "Are you okay with just changing partners instead of being on your own?"

"It worries me," I admitted, following his lead. "I want to be rid of Peter, but it just seems like a huge risk. What if something goes wrong?" I thought about how I'd felt earlier. "This group is my family," I said. "Peter, his mom and dad and wife and kids, they're relatives. Karen and Riley, Felipe and Ernie . . . " I hesitated, drawing a deep breath. ". . . and you—you're my real family."

I stole a sideways look at Jake. His face was hard to see in the low illumination of the streetlights, but it was clear he was smiling.

"Getting rid of Peter isn't worth risking that."

"Okay."

Butterflies danced in my stomach and made my heart race. I'd known from the moment Bradley had made the offer that I was going to take it. As Jake had said earlier, now it was just arithmetic.

Jake parked at the curb and walked me to the front door of Southern Treasures. He followed me while I checked the alarms and the back door locks. Jake knew the ritual well; I'd installed the security system after Julie's drug-addled ex had broken into the shop, and I had maintained it faithfully ever since.

Okay. Maybe Jake had a point about me getting into

trouble. But it wasn't like I went looking for it. Things just happened.

Strategically placed night-lights showed the way between the displays as we walked back to the door. Jake put his arms around me and pulled me into a warm hug. "I just want you to stay safe," he said, his chin resting against my head. He loosened his embrace and held me at arm's length. "Okay?"

I sighed. "I know."

Jake kissed me good-night and waited on the sidewalk until I locked the door behind him.

A wolf whistle came from Bluebeard's darkened cage. He only stayed in the cage at night, with the door open and a blanket over the wire mesh to block the glow from the streetlights outside the big front windows.

"Bluebeard!" There were some things about having a permanent companion that weren't always perfect. A constant chaperone at the end of every date was one of them.

"Pretty boy," he said.

I made my way through the dimly lit shop and gave him a scritch. "Yes, you're a pretty boy."

"Not me," Uncle Louis's voice came clearly. "Your young man."

"He's not 'my' young man," I protested. It sounded weak, even to me.

"He should be."

Bluebeard turned and hopped back into his cage.

"Trying to $*&*%^#$%^ sleep here."

I took the hint and climbed the stairs to bed.

I CALLED BETH SEVERAL TIMES ON FRIDAY, IN between deliveries, occasional customers, and enough math to make my head swim. I tried to guess how much it would take to run Lighthouse Coffee, and what additional expenses I could handle.

I soon realized I needed real information, not guesses. A

quick call to Bradley elicited a promise of recent financial statements, as long as I promised to keep them confidential.

Finally, with numbers buzzing in my head like a swarm of angry bees, I decided to go next door and have a little talk with Chloe. I didn't think I could make it work if she wasn't willing to stay.

I hung the "Back in 15 Minutes" sign on the door and stuck my phone in my pocket. Beth hadn't called me back yet, and I didn't want to risk missing her.

Chloe spotted me while I was still on the sidewalk and started a vanilla latte before I was through the door. She looked haggard, as though she hadn't slept the night before, which I realized was a real possibility.

"Do you have a minute?" I asked as I took the cup from her and handed over my punch card.

She glanced around the empty shop. "Sure. It's not like there's a rush this morning."

She poured herself a cup of coffee and joined me at a table in front of the window facing the street. From my vantage point, I could see if anyone approached the door of Southern Treasures.

Good manners, and genuine concern, dictated that I ask about Miss Pansy before I talked any business.

"She's sitting up and taking nourishment," Chloe said.

"I haven't heard anyone say that in years," I said. "It's something Memaw used to say."

Chloe studied her coffee cup as though the wisdom of the world was contained in the inky brew. "Miss Pansy says it a lot."

"Do they know when they'll let her come home?"

"Bradley called a little bit ago. Said she had a good night, but they want to keep her another night, just to be sure." She smiled briefly. "It sounds like he wanted them to make her stay, just so she'd rest for another day."

"I can believe that. I don't know what he'll do with her

if she retires. That woman doesn't know the meaning of taking a day off."

I took another sip of my drink. It reminded me of Chloe's barista skills, and the real reason for my visit.

"Chloe," I said, "I need to talk to you about this place." I waved vaguely, taking in the entire operation. "If I'm going to buy—"

"Would you?" she interrupted with the first glimpse of her normal bubbly personality. "Would you really buy it? I really hoped you would, and that you'd let me stay." She paused to take a breath, but started again before I could stop her. "I love working here, Miss Glory. I'll come in and do the morning baking. I'll work whenever you need me—"

I held up a hand to deflect the torrent of words.

"That's what I came to talk to you about, Chloe," I said. "If I'm going to buy this place—and I'm trying to figure out how to do just that—I'm going to need someone I can count on to manage the bakery and coffee shop for me."

I remembered her promises from the day before, but I didn't want to count on that to make a business decision. I needed a commitment, not an emotional outburst.

"I know how to run a retail business, but I don't know how to bake, or make coffee, or a million other things. I need you for that, if you're interested." I smiled at her. "And I'd guess from your reaction that you are."

"I am very interested," she said. "Staying at Lighthouse, working for you, it would be really great, Miss Glory."

I offered her my hand. "Okay. If I buy Lighthouse, you've got the job. On one condition."

Chloe hesitated, her fingers just inches from mine. "What?" she asked warily.

"It's just Glory. Or Miss Martine, if you're talking to a customer. When you call me Miss Glory, it makes me feel about a million years old."

She ducked her head for a second. "My mama would

pitch a fit if she heard me talk to one of my elders that way," she said. "But if you're my boss, I guess it's all right."

We shook hands, and the giddy smile returned to her face. "You really mean it? Really?"

"I need a baker," I said. "And you've been watching Miss Pansy for a long time. You're going to be my secret weapon in the bakery."

Her smile shifted, and I thought she was going to say something more, but she just nodded.

The door opened and a well-dressed couple in their sixties came in. Chloe hastily excused herself and rushed behind the counter, greeting the new arrivals. She spoke to them cordially and I left them chatting like old friends while she deftly made their drinks.

I checked my shop as I walked past. It was quiet. The only people I'd seen on the sidewalk were the couple that had just gone into Lighthouse Coffee.

I glanced at my phone, as though checking it every ten minutes was going to make it ring.

No joy.

Chapter 9

I HESITATED AT THE DOOR TO SOUTHERN TREAsures, but there was someone else I wanted to talk to, so I kept going. The Grog Shop, on the other side of my shop, belonged to Guy and Linda Miller.

Linda was like the older sister I never had. A young friend of my mother's, she'd been my babysitter when I was little, and my foster mother for the months following my parents' deaths. I trusted her advice, and Guy's, and I wanted to share my news with them.

The bell over the door announced my entrance, and Linda looked up from her book. Apparently her business was quiet too, and Linda was in her favorite place, a tall stool behind the counter with a cold drink and a fat novel.

She slipped a bookmark into the paperback before setting it down, then hopped out of her chair and came around the counter to greet me with a warm hug. Linda was good at hugs.

"Hey, stranger," Linda chided. "I haven't seen you in days. Where have you been?"

I thought for a minute. I hadn't been over to check in with Guy and Linda since Monday; a long time for us.

"Sorry," I said, returning her hug. "Been busy with wedding stuff for Karen, and then a buying trip yesterday with Jake."

I looked around for her husband. "Is Guy here? I have some news I want to talk to y'all about."

Linda's eyes lit up and I realized too late that the juxtaposition of my thoughts had her speculating in ways I hadn't intended.

"No, not that," I said hastily.

Her shoulders dropped and she sighed dramatically. "I can only hope," she said with exaggerated disappointment. "You know it's up to me, since your mom isn't around to ask when you're going to settle down."

I laughed. "Linda, I've been settled down for years. Running a business settles you down real fast."

She shook her head. "That isn't what I meant, and you know it." She turned her head and hollered toward the back. "Guy, Glory's here!"

A moment later Guy emerged from the storeroom, pushing a hand truck full of beer cases. I held the door of the walk-in cooler open for him, and the two of us quickly stacked the cases in the chilly interior.

Helping Guy stock the shelves had always been a favorite activity. I'd started helping in the store when I was a young teenager, far too young to actually sell beer or wine, but old enough to move cases and feel important. Guy's appreciation and encouragement meant a lot then, and helping him now reminded me of those times.

We emerged a few minutes later to find Linda waiting with a fresh pot of coffee. She held a mug out in my direction, but didn't fill it.

"News?" she said, keeping the pot just out of reach.

"Did you hear about Pansy?"

Linda nodded, but still didn't pour. "Of course we did.

But I'm pretty sure that wasn't what you wanted to talk about."

"Ha! It is, too." I savored a brief moment of triumph before I continued. "At least it's related."

Linda relented and filled my mug. "Go on."

I cupped my hands around the mug, warming them from the chill of the walk-in. "Her son offered me the chance to buy Lighthouse."

Linda broke into a grin, and Guy nodded. "You are going to do it, aren't you?" he asked.

I exhaled, letting out a breath I hadn't realized I was holding.

"Yes." The giddy feeling that you get just before jumping off the high dive made me light-headed. "I'm not sure exactly how I can manage the finances, but if I can, then, well, yes."

"If you need help, you know you can always ask me," Guy said. He was a whiz with math. I'd always done my own books, and I was no slouch, but Guy could make numbers dance in ways I could barely follow.

"I will," I said. "Jake said the same thing."

Linda gave me a raised-eyebrow look that said as clearly as words that she was thinking about her initial assumption.

"Yeah, I told him. And Karen and Riley, and Ernie and Felipe. Last night was Thursday," I defended myself, "and we all had dinner.

"Besides, Bradley—you know Miss Pansy's son—made the offer just before I left for Ernie's house. I didn't have time to talk to anyone else."

"I'm sure that's the only reason," Linda said in a tone that clearly said otherwise.

"It is," I insisted.

Linda just smiled.

Guy looked from Linda to me and back again, then shrugged. He'd learned long ago to simply accept that Linda would eventually fill him in.

I drank down the coffee and handed the mug back to Linda. "Thanks," I said. "I better get back to the store."

She pulled me into another hug. "You'll tell us if there's anything you need?"

"Promise." I hugged her back and gave Guy a hug before heading to Southern Treasures.

The phone still hadn't rung.

Where was Beth? Where was my quilt? And why wasn't she returning my calls?

Chapter 10

KAREN CALLED JUST AS I WAS UNLOCKING SOUTH-
ern Treasures.

"Want to nag some more?" I asked.

Her laugh came through the phone. "Just wanted to see
how you're getting along. You seemed pretty distracted
last night." Her voice rose at the end, turning her explanation into a question.

"It's just this thing with Lighthouse," I said, hoping she
would accept my reassurance. It was the truth; I was pre-
occupied with the Lighthouse offer. Even if it wasn't the
only thing on my mind.

"It's a big deal," she admitted, "but you know you want
it. You've wanted it for a long time. Don't try to tell me you
haven't."

"I have," I said. "I decided years ago that if Pansy or
Guy and Linda, either one, wanted to sell, I'd be at the front
of the line."

"So, what are you up to tonight?" she asked in typical

Karen fashion. Her conversations swooped from one subject to another without warning, and I had learned long ago to go along for the ride.

"No plans," I said. "Why?"

"Riley's heading out before dawn again, so I'm batching it tonight. Thought you might want to grab some dinner if you didn't have plans."

"Sure." I checked the time. "I'm not supposed to close up for another hour. Want me to meet you somewhere?"

"I'm out running errands; I might as well swing by for you." I heard her rustling in her bag, a cavernous satchel she carried everywhere she went, followed by the crinkling of paper. "I still have to see the printer," she said, as though reading from a list. "And talk to the organist at the church." She sighed dramatically. "I should be able to make it there in an hour."

In the meantime, I started updating the website with new merchandise from our treasure hunt. I had only done about half the items when the phone rang.

I picked it up without looking, although I knew better.

It was Peter.

With a new scheme.

"Hi, Glory. How are you?" Peter tried to observe the niceties of social interaction, but I didn't really believe he cared a whit for how I was.

"Fine, Peter. And you?" Two could play this game.

"Doing fine. Job's great! Peggy and the kids are fantastic, getting ready for Thanksgiving with the family. You coming up this year?"

Every year he invited me to join his family at my aunt and uncle's home, and every year I declined. I would much rather spend the holiday with my friends in Keyhole Bay who were my family of the heart.

For an instant I entertained the wicked thought that I ought to accept his insincere invitation, just to see his reaction. But I didn't want to go to Uncle Andrew and Aunt

Missy's for Thanksgiving, and I didn't want to deal with the fallout from accepting and then canceling.

But it was amusing to think about.

"I don't think so, Peter," I said with as much regret as I could muster. "It's a long drive, and I can't close the shop for more than a day or so."

"That's what you have employees for, isn't it?"

"But I don't feel it's right to ask her to give up her holidays, either." As far as Peter knew, I only had Julie; and I wasn't going to tell him anything different, at least for now. "Your boss doesn't expect you to give up your holidays so he can spend time with his family, does he?"

His indulgent chuckle told me what was coming. "Oh, Glory. You really don't understand corporate life, do you? We plan ahead for every holiday, so everyone gets their time off."

I told you he didn't understand retail.

My patience with his version of small talk was wearing thin. "So what did you call for, Peter?"

"Do I have to have a reason to call my only cousin? Can't it just be for a visit?"

"But you don't call just to visit, Peter. We aren't those kinds of cousins. So what did you call for?"

"Well . . ." he hesitated, and I knew we were getting to the real reason. "I saw something in the news this morning that I wanted to talk to you about."

I rolled my eyes. One advantage of talking to Peter on the phone instead of in person: he couldn't see my expression.

"Yes?"

"It was about this store somewhere up north. I didn't catch where, but you know how these things are, it happens one place and then everybody jumps on the bandwagon and then it's happening everywhere."

"Go on."

"There was this store, and they had a cat in the store. Not just wandered in, you know, but it lived there and the store owners kept it as a pet and fed it and all."

I bit my tongue, mentally urging him to get on with it.

"Anyway, the cat scratched a kid and the parents sued the store for keeping a dangerous animal on the premises. The insurance company had to give the family a big settlement to keep it out of the courts."

Like all my conversations with Peter, this one had reached the count-to-ten stage.

One.

Two.

"The owners were ordered to keep the cat out of the store, and had to pay a bunch of fines . . ."

Three.

Four.

". . . for violating some law or other about animals in a public space."

Five.

I took a deep breath.

Six.

Seven.

Eight.

"I'm concerned about that parrot, Glory."

Nine.

"What if he hurts someone? What if he attacks a kid? We could lose everything, Glory. Everything."

Ten.

I remained calm. I told myself that Peter wasn't in the store, he didn't know how Bluebeard behaved, and he certainly didn't know about Uncle Louis. Nor was I ever going to share that with him.

If and when Uncle Louis decided to make himself known to Peter, it would be his choice. But I wasn't going to tell him.

"Peter, that bird has been in this store longer than I have. He is more than a pet, he's the symbol of Southern Treasures, and customers expect to see him when they come in.

"There is no way, *no way*, Peter, that I am taking him out of the store. This is his home, and it will be his home as long as he lives. And he has a name, Peter. His name is Bluebeard, not 'that parrot.'

"It that very clear?"

I wasn't actually shouting, but I had adopted a forceful tone. It got my point across.

"Y-y-yes," he stammered. "But Glory," he whined, "we could lose everything if someone got hurt."

"First, there is no law in Keyhole Bay against animals in public places. Second, Southern Treasures is private property, so that doesn't even apply. Third, Bluebeard is well behaved, and he has safe places to go if anyone is bothering him. Fourth, we are well insured, and my agent added a rider for Bluebeard many years ago."

I took another deep breath. "And last, *we* wouldn't lose everything. *I* would lose everything. *You* would still have your fabulous job and your beautiful home, and your retirement account. You would lose a small part of your investments. I would lose my home and my job.

"So if I am not worried about 'that parrot,' as you call him, then you shouldn't be either."

I bit back the rest of my rant. "I have to go now, Peter. The store needs my attention.

"Good-bye."

I hung up, my hand shaking as I put the cordless back in its cradle.

Peter had to go.

Now.

IT WAS CLOSER TO TWO HOURS THAN ONE WHEN Karen finally showed up. I had recovered from the anger Peter triggered, but I was more determined than ever that I had to buy him out.

"Sorry," Karen said when I unlocked the front door for her. "The organist took forever to find the right music, even though I'd told her several times exactly what we want."

I could only imagine what the poor woman had been through in the last hour. I had seen for myself how Bridezilla Karen told someone exactly what she wanted.

I grabbed my purse from behind the counter and followed Karen out to her car, locking the door behind us.

"How about Jake?" Karen asked, starting the engine. She glanced across the street at Beach Books.

"Some Merchants' Association thing," I answered. "Even for Jake, I won't go to one of those things."

"I know," Karen said. "'Not a boy, and not nearly old enough,'" she quoted my stock answer for why I didn't belong to the good ol' boys club.

"Someday that may change," I said. "But for now, I just can't spend time with a bunch of men who call me sweetheart because they can't remember my name."

"Hey," Karen said. "This is me, remember? I'm on your side."

I shook my head. "It's not about sides."

"Okay. I agree with you then."

"Better."

After a moment's silence, I asked, "Where are we going?"

"How about Neil's? Pizza sounds good to me."

I agreed, and a few minutes later we were seated in a high-backed wooden booth, sipping sweet tea and waiting for our pie.

"I've been thinking," she began. That always scared me. When Karen started thinking, it usually meant complications.

"Yes?" I said warily.

"It's the wedding. Sort of. I know it's kind of odd to be re-marrying your ex. But I think I'm really lucky; Riley and I figured it out while there was still time to do something about it."

I waited, wondering where this was going.

"But it makes me feel bad for the people who miss their

chance. We were talking about Felipe and Ernie the other day, about how they couldn't get married."

"They could in several states, just not here. Yet. But things are changing."

"True," she said. "But this is their home. Anyway, that started me thinking about what happened to Sly. Did he ever tell you anything more?"

I shook my head.

Our friend Sly was nearing seventy. Last year he had told us the story of his lost love, a romance doomed by 1950s Florida laws forbidding interracial marriage.

But he hadn't given us details, and I didn't feel it was my right to ask. "He mentioned her name—Anna—but that's about it. It's so hard for him to talk about it. I just figured he'd tell me when he's ready."

"I know things were different when Sly met Anna," Karen said. "But just imagine if he'd met her now, though. Those laws are long gone. There wouldn't even be a question."

I still wasn't sure where she was going with all this, but I let her talk.

"So we know a first name, her approximate age, that she went to school in Keyhole Bay." Karen ticked off the items on her fingers. "We know she was white, and that she was still in town when Sly enlisted."

She stopped and thought for a minute. "Do you know when that was, exactly?"

"I think he graduated high school in 1962, give or take a year," I said. "But really, what does it matter? She moved away a long time ago. Sly said she was gone when he came back from the service."

"But what if we could find her?" Karen asked, leaning forward. "What if we could let Sly know what happened to her? I mean, not if it was horrible or anything. But if we could tell him where she went, what she did?"

"That's a terrible idea," I said without hesitation. "The

few times he's mentioned her, it was clear he'd been badly hurt. Why bring all that up again? What's the point?"

Karen looked stunned. "I thought you were the one who loved solving mysteries," she said. "I figured you'd like the idea. Besides, if we find out something awful, we don't have to tell him anything."

"And if we find out she fell in love with someone else and got married and is living happily in some fabulous place? Is that supposed to make him feel better?"

"It might," Karen argued. "If he truly loved her, it would make him happy to know that her life turned out well, and that she was happy."

"Anyway"—I abandoned the argument for a minute—"why would you want to do this? Don't you have enough on your plate right now, with the wedding and your mother coming?"

"That's exactly why I need this."

I was about to ask her how another project would help when I heard our number called. I got up from the table, glad of the interruption, and retrieved our pizza.

I carried the box to the table. Neil's was primarily take-out and they expected leftovers, so even in the store, pizzas were served in a takeout box.

When I got back to the table, Karen was on the phone. She put her finger to her lips as she listened intently.

I sat down quietly and waited. Over the years, I'd grown accustomed to Karen's "news face," the rapt expression that meant a hot story was in the offing.

"Be right there," she said.

She tossed her phone in her purse and reached to close the pizza box. "Take it home with you," she said. "I've got to go up to north county.

"Boomer's got two dead bodies."

Chapter 11

"WANT SOME COMPANY?" I TOLD MYSELF THE OFFER was just to keep Karen company on the late-night drive home. I didn't really think the bodies were related to Beth and Everett's disappearance. North county covered a lot of territory.

I didn't believe a word of it.

Karen shook her head, then reconsidered. "Are you sure?"

"Well, I could go home and obsess over my finances and not sleep, or I could ride along with you and maybe not obsess about my finances. What do you think?"

"Ride along it is, then. I'll stop and let you put the pizza away at your place since it's on the way."

Ten minutes later, the pizza was stashed in my refrigerator and we were on the highway heading north. Was it really only yesterday morning I'd driven this way? Of course, I'd been taking it easy on the back roads in my vintage truck. Karen was lead-footing it up the highway in a late-model SUV. Only the direction was the same.

We made the trip in a mostly silent forty minutes. I

didn't want to tell Karen about Beth and Everett, and I couldn't think of a single other thing to talk about.

Karen was focused on the road and on the chatter coming from the police scanner she kept in her car. A local sheriff's patrol was at the scene, thanks to a call from a hunter who had found the bodies. Boomer was on his way, as was the coroner and a medical transport.

"I'll be there soon," Boomer said on the radio. "No sense creating a disturbance with the sirens and all. They ain't going anywhere."

Dr. Frazier, the coroner, acknowledged the instructions, as did the ambulance drivers. It sounded like we were only a few minutes behind them.

Karen's GPS chimed. "Turn left in one-quarter mile."

I strained to see the road ahead. We were close to the road I'd taken yesterday, but in the dark, it was hard to be sure.

"Turn left in five hundred feet."

Karen slowed for the turn. I saw a familiar fence, brightly colored posts and rails caught for an instant in Karen's headlights.

I told myself there were lots of places out in these woods, lots of people who lived out here away from big cities and small towns. It meant nothing.

My heart raced. I tried to speak, but my mouth was so dry I couldn't form words. I swallowed and licked my lips, but still nothing came out.

Karen dropped her speed on the winding, unlit dirt road. Out here, away from any city lights, darkness crowded in on us. Somewhere ahead we could see the faint pulsing of colored lights, signaling the presence of emergency vehicles.

My internal argument continued, but reasonable doubt had given way to unreasonable hope. Even that was soon dashed as we came around another curve and spotted the first of a string of emergency vehicles blocking the narrow road.

Karen stopped and shut off the engine. "I'll walk in from here. You can wait in the car."

I climbed out after her. I had no intention of sitting alone in the car in the dark, not knowing what was lurking in the woods.

"I'm coming with you." I was surprised the words came out as steady as they did. I felt like my entire insides were shaking.

"Suit yourself. But Boomer isn't going to be happy to see either one of us." She was already several steps ahead of me, following the beam of a heavy-duty flashlight she'd taken from the SUV and digging in her bag for her pocket recorder.

This was Karen at work: one of the most organized, focused, and determined individuals on the planet. Hard to believe she still lived and worked in the same small town where she'd grown up.

I trotted to catch up with her and her flashlight. I didn't relish the idea of stumbling around out here in the dark.

The first thing I noticed was the complete absence of onlookers. In town, the presence of a police car or an ambulance meant neighbors and passersby stopping to gape, trying to catch a glimpse of whatever was going on.

Not out here. There wasn't a single person eager for gossip or trying to snap a picture they could post, tweet, or sell to the highest bidder. The police hadn't even set a guard to prevent civilians from walking into their crime scene.

And yet, I felt like I was being watched. Like there was someone or something hiding just beyond the reach of the floodlights, watching everyone.

Animals, I was sure. Just like the day before. There was plenty of wildlife in the sparsely populated north county. I tried to guess what creatures might be around, distracting myself from the real reason we were here.

It could be a deer, or raccoons or possums, maybe even a fox or coyote, curious about the disturbance but careful to stay in the shadows.

We were nearly to the shed, a vague outline in the glare of the floodlights, when a sheriff's deputy stopped us. "Pardon me, ladies. This is a crime scene. I'm going to have to ask you to leave."

"Karen Freed. WBBY." Karen flashed a laminated card at the deputy. "Can I ask you a few questions?"

"Ma'am, I cannot answer any questions. And I will have to ask you to leave." He reached for Karen's arm, but she pulled away and tried to push past him.

"Stop!" His voice had gone from polite and deferential to commanding in an instant. "Don't move!"

"Freed!" Boomer's unmistakable growl came from somewhere in the glare. "I should have known."

Sheriff Barclay "Boomer" Hardy appeared, silhouetted against the floodlights, casting a long shadow in our direction. His imposing bulk was exaggerated by the lighting, his features obscured in the glare.

"Sheriff Hardy," Karen said.

Her words were formal and polite, but her tone was casual. We'd both known Boomer since we were teenagers and he was a rookie, and Karen crossed his path regularly in the course of her job.

"I know what you're doing here," he said. "But what are you doing with her, Miss Glory? I thought you'd decided to stay out of trouble?"

That final question sounded less like a question and more like a warning. Just because I'd been caught up in a couple bad situations. Now Boomer treated me like a troublemaker, even though I hadn't been the one making trouble.

"I just came along for the ride."

I crossed my arms across my chest, partially as a defiant gesture, but mostly to hide the fact that I was shaking. I was sure I knew who the two bodies were.

I was going to have to tell Boomer. Or I was going to have to withhold the information.

Either way, I was way up the creek and there wasn't a paddle in sight.

Chapter 12

I BRACED MYSELF FOR THE BARRAGE OF QUESTIONS that would follow my revelation. I didn't want to talk about Beth and Everett—the truth was, I didn't know that much about them—but I knew I would have to speak up.

"Do you know the identities of the victims?" Karen asked. She hit record and pointed the digital recorder at Boomer.

"You know I can't tell you anything until we notify next of kin," Boomer answered wearily. He'd had similar conversations with Karen many times over the years, but it didn't stop her from asking.

"And turn that damned thing off!" He glanced over at me. "Begging your pardon, ma'am."

I waved away his apology. He'd be saying worse in a few minutes, when I told him what little I knew.

"What can you tell us?" Karen forged ahead, the record light still blinking.

"We have two victims. Both male. Likely mid-thirties.

That's all we have for now." He glared at Karen. "You didn't need to drive all the way up here and tromp around my crime scene for that. It'll all be in the record within the hour."

"My station manager says go, I go. He says ask, I ask. Just doing my job."

"And I'm trying to do mine." Boomer turned his back, clearly dismissing us.

"B-both male?" I stammered, finally able to corral my jumbled thoughts and form actual words.

"Yes." Boomer turned back and gave me a hard look. "What makes you ask?"

"I just, well, um." I stopped and took a moment to gather what little calm I could muster. "I know the people who live here."

There. I'd said it.

Karen whipped around and stared at me.

Boomer rolled his eyes and groaned. "Here we go again."

"No, nothing like that," I protested. "She's a quilter. Her husband makes furniture. I buy stuff from them for the shop. That's all."

"Do these people have names?" Boomer's sarcasm annoyed me, but annoyed was better than scared. Lots better.

"Beth and Everett." I dug through my memory for a last name. "Last name is Young, I think."

"You think? If you bought from them, what name did you put on the check?" More sarcasm.

"Paid cash. Always do. I get better deals if the money folds and they don't have to go to the bank, Sheriff. In any case, it's a man and a woman who live here, not two men."

"Could you identify the man?"

A chill ran down my spine. Did Boomer really want me to look at Everett's dead body? I didn't know the man very well, and it seemed somehow wrong for me to identify him.

But it might help catch his killer, and it definitely would make Boomer happier with me.

"I can try," I said. "I've only met him a few times, but I'll look if you want me to."

Instead of taking me to look at the two men, however, Boomer pulled a small electronic tablet from an inside pocket of his jacket.

"Don't look at me like that," he said to Karen. "You aren't the only one who knows how to run one of these things."

To me he said, "I have some photos on here—just faces, mind you. Nothing gruesome. They look like they're sleeping."

His voice was soft, his manner deferential. Far different from the man who'd been ordering us to leave a few minutes earlier. It was a side of Boomer I had rarely seen.

"Could you take a look and tell me if you recognize either man? You don't have to; I can't make you do this. But I would appreciate your help."

I swallowed hard and held out my hand for the tablet. Rather than hand it over, Boomer moved close to my side and held the display where we could both see. He kept the controls out of my reach.

"There are only two pictures you need to look at," he explained as he displayed the first photo. I could guess that there were many more pictures, none of which he wanted me to look at, and none of which I wanted to see.

Karen had crept up on my other side, silently moving to a vantage point where she could also see the display. Boomer ignored her and continued talking to me in a soft voice, asking if I knew the man in the photo.

The man was not familiar. Shaggy brown hair surrounded his thin face. His eyes were closed, but his mouth was open slightly. Sunken cheeks hinted at missing teeth, and the ones I could see were crowded into his narrow jaw.

I shook my head. "I don't know him," I said.

Boomer nodded and changed the display.

I didn't know this man either. His round face and blond

pompadour were in sharp contrast to his companion, but there was nothing familiar about him.

I shook my head. "I'm sorry, Sheriff," I said. "I don't know him either. Neither one of them is Everett Young."

Boomer switched off the tablet and glared at me, the moment of deference gone. "And I'm supposed to believe you're just along for the ride?"

He shook his head. "I should have known better. I've got two dead bodies, your friends Everett and Beth are nowhere to be found, and you just happened to come along with Freed here"—he pointed a thumb at Karen without taking his eyes off me—"to what? Keep her company?"

"I am very sorry, Sheriff Hardy," I bit back a "sir" that would have laid it on too thick, even for Boomer. "Karen got the call while we were at dinner, and I offered to ride with her so she wasn't driving alone late at night.

"I didn't know we were coming here, and I didn't know that Beth and Everett aren't around." I looked at the house. If someone was in there, they would certainly have come out to see what all the commotion was about.

If they could.

The thought sent another chill through me, and I shivered.

Boomer saw my reaction and guessed what I was thinking.

"We looked in the house first thing," he assured me. "Nobody inside, and it looks like they've been gone a while."

The glare returned. "When was the last time you saw the Youngs?"

"Several weeks," I answered truthfully. The last time I had actually seen Beth was the day I paid the deposit on Karen's wedding quilt, right after Labor Day.

"How many is several?"

"It was just after Labor Day. I made a buying trip up this direction. Stopped in, had a glass of sweet tea, and picked up a couple little pieces. So probably nine or ten weeks."

A deputy approached us and signaled to Boomer. He stepped away and the two men held a whispered conversation intended to exclude us. When Boomer returned, it was clear he had something else on his mind.

"I still have some questions for you, Miss Martine. But right now there are other, more important things I need to do. I'll expect you in my office at ten tomorrow morning."

He nodded at us in dismissal. "The deputy here will see you back to your car."

"No need," Karen said. "I've got my flashlight."

The deputy, taking his cue from Boomer, led the way back to the road, his own five-cell flashlight casting a powerful beam into the darkness.

"No problem, ma'am. I'm glad to help you out."

I could feel Karen's retort building, and I dug an elbow into her side. "Thank you, Deputy," I said before she could make matters worse with a smart remark. "We're fine from here." I pointed in the direction of Karen's SUV. "We can see the car."

Karen managed to hold her tongue until we were in the car, safely out of earshot. But just barely.

She was on me before she even started the engine. "What didn't you want Boomer to know?" she demanded.

"Who says there was anything for him to know?" I countered. I was hoping the old saying was true, that the best defense was a good offense. "I just wanted to get us out of there before you managed to tick him off and get us invited to the station."

"Me? I wasn't the one who was all buddy-buddy with his prime suspects."

"I am not buddy-buddy with them. I know them, that's all. And what makes you think they're suspects? Just because they're not here doesn't make them suspects."

Karen started the engine. Emergency vehicles blocked the road ahead, and with no other choices she had to spend the next few minutes carefully going back and forth until she had managed to turn around in the single lane of gravel that passed for a road.

The tight maneuvers took all her attention, and I hoped the question of my relationship with Beth and Everett had been forgotten. But the second she was clear and headed back along the rough road to the highway, the interrogation started up again.

"You were holding something back, Glory. Something you didn't want Boomer to ask you about." When I didn't answer, she continued her speculation. "He asked you when the last time you saw them was."

"And I told him the truth. I haven't seen either one of them in several weeks."

Our headlights cut through the dark ahead of us, but they didn't penetrate into the woods alongside the road. I shivered, imagining what might be hiding just beyond the reach of our headlights.

Darkness crowded in on all sides, making the road feel even more remote. The woods seemed to close in on us as we bumped along the rough surface.

"That may be true," Karen said, her voice tight. She could feel the same isolation and vague threat I did. "But that isn't all of it."

She braked, moving even slower as she rounded a tight curve. I knew it was all in my imagination, but I half expected something—or someone—to step out in front of the slow-moving car, like the serial killer in a bad movie.

"You might not have seen them," Karen said, breaking into my cheap-horror-film fantasy, "but I'd be willing to bet you've talked to them since then."

We reached the highway at last, but instead of turning onto the pavement, Karen stopped dead and turned to look at me. "In fact, you were just up here. Yesterday. You and Jake came up on a buying trip. And if you were in the neighborhood visiting suppliers, what are the odds you went by your pals' place?"

I couldn't lie, not directly, and Karen knew it.

"You were out here. But you didn't see your pals. You wouldn't have told Boomer a direct lie."

"They aren't my 'pals,'" I insisted. "But yes, I was by here. They weren't home. Nothing to tell. But you saw how Boomer was, just because I know the people that live there. Imagine if I'd said I was out there yesterday."

"Yeah," she agreed as she finally turned onto the highway. "And I'm getting tired of posting bail."

Chapter 13

KAREN TURNED UP THE VOLUME ON THE SCANNER, and we listened to the chatter as we drove back to Keyhole Bay. I didn't volunteer any more about Beth and Everett, which wasn't difficult since I really didn't know much more.

"You want me to drive?" It was one reason I'd offered to come along. Sometimes I'd drive while Karen would call or text the station.

But not tonight. "No," she said, staring at the dark road ahead. "There isn't anywhere convenient along here to pull over and swap, anyway."

I didn't argue. Although there were several turnouts on the highway, none of them was well lit, and I didn't think either one of us was particularly interested in getting out of the car on the deserted highway.

"You wouldn't have had to post bail. Boomer could have insisted I talk to him, but there wasn't anything for him to charge me with."

"That wouldn't have stopped him," she said darkly. Karen had never really forgiven Boomer for arresting Riley's brother, even though we'd eventually proven Bobby was innocent.

"Maybe." When it came to me, Boomer seemed to run hot and cold. We'd found an amiable truce after Lacey Simon had drugged and nearly killed me over a year ago, but I'd also managed to stay off his radar since then.

Now I was involved in his business again, and if he thought I was interfering in any way, he wouldn't hesitate to break the truce. It wasn't a comforting thought.

I forced my thoughts away from Boomer.

"So, Freed," I said, reaching back to our earlier conversation, "what makes you want to track down Sly's old girlfriend? Why add that to all the things you've got on your plate right now?"

She sighed dramatically. "Because I have to have *something* to take my mind off this wedding and off my mother. Do you have any idea how stressful this all is?"

I bit back the truthful answer, that we were all very well aware how stressed she was because she was sharing it with everyone around her. "I can only imagine," I said instead. "But wouldn't another project just add to the stress?"

"I don't think so." She paused, as though searching for a way to explain it to herself. "See, the wedding and my mother and Stepdad Number Three, that's all stuff I *have* to do. It's not my choice, it's my mother's."

She held up her hand, palm out. "I *know!* I am a grown-ass woman—pardon my French—and I should be able to stand up to my mother and do things the way I want. But you know her, Glory. She doesn't hear what she doesn't want to."

That much was true. I'd seen her mother in action since we were in elementary school. Until two years ago, her Christmas cards had still been addressed to Mr. & Mrs. Riley Freed, even though they'd been divorced more than a

decade. She didn't believe Karen and Riley should have
ended their first marriage.

"I haven't even told you the worst of it," she continued.
"The station manager told me today that he's giving me the
month of December off as a wedding present. He heard my
mother was coming, and he thinks he's doing me a big
favor, giving me time for my family and all the last-minute
wedding stuff."

She slammed her palm against the steering wheel in
frustration. "I can't take a month off. I'll lose my mind;
especially if I have to spend that month with my mother
dictating wedding instructions the whole time.

"I *need* a distraction."

I sighed in resignation. "What do you want me to do?"

"I don't know. We need to do some research, see if we
can find out more about her. There couldn't have been that
many kids in Sly's graduating class, could there?"

"Keyhole Bay was pretty small back then," I said. "But
who says they even went to the same school? The schools
were still segregated back then, and if her family had a
little money, she might even have gone to a girls' school
somewhere out of town. I don't think that was all that
unusual back then."

"It's a place to start," she said. "There are copies of the
Keyhole Bay yearbooks in the library, and the *News and
Times* publishes a list of the graduates every year. We can
start with those, see how many Annas we find."

"I'll do what I can, but my boss didn't give me the
month off. In fact, she's reminding me I have to get up for
work in the morning."

Karen chuckled as we approached the streetlights at the
edge of town. "You do work for a slave driver, Glory. And I
bet she's only going to get worse when she buys Lighthouse."

"Undoubtedly," I agreed.

Karen pulled up to the curb in front of Southern Treasures. I reminded her of our pizza in my refrigerator, but

she waved me off. "Riley's leaving for a couple days, and I won't eat it all by myself."

"And I will?"

"No. But I'm certain you'll have help." She looked pointedly at the closed bookshop across the street. "Tell Jake to enjoy the pizza."

"I will."

She waited at the curb until I was safely inside the shop, then pulled away.

For once Bluebeard didn't swear at me for interrupting his sleep. I was kind of disappointed.

BOOMER'S OFFICE CALLED THE NEXT MORNING AND rescheduled my meeting with the sheriff. He'd been at the crime scene until after daylight and was out of the office for the rest of the weekend, giving me a reprieve until first thing Monday morning. It felt more like a stay of execution.

Late in the morning, Bradley stopped in the shop and dropped off a fat envelope of financial statements. We talked for a minute, but it was clear he was anxious to get going.

"Mom's still in the hospital," he told me. "But she's raising the devil with the doctors about going home. The doctor told her a couple days observation, and she's insisting it's been two days and she's leaving.

"I have to get back over there and try to keep her from breaking out."

Foot traffic was light, so I spent most of the afternoon staring at the numbers until I could close up and take them upstairs to do a more careful analysis.

SPREADSHEETS COVERED THE TABLE IN MY APART-ment, relegating the box of takeout pizza to the kitchen counter.

Jake rang the bell downstairs and I ran down to let him in.

Back upstairs, he grabbed a piece of pizza and sat next to me, listening intently as I pointed to the columns of numbers that I'd arranged and rearranged several times before he arrived.

"Southern Treasures is doing fine," I concluded. "Another six months—a year tops—and I'll have enough to get rid of Peter. Of course there's no guarantee he'll sell, but I think he will.

"Lord knows, I hope he will. If not, there may be bloodshed." I filled him in on the phone call from my dear cousin and his concerns about Bluebeard. "Of course I could tell him that Uncle Louis wouldn't let any harm come to any visitor to the store. But Peter's a perfect engineer—just the facts, ma'am—and he wouldn't believe me.

"Besides, it's up to Uncle Louis to choose who knows he's here. And he hasn't chosen Peter. At least not yet."

I pointed to another column. "These are the figures Bradley gave me for the last two years of operation at Lighthouse. The shop is turning a profit. He said the family could keep it, hire a manager, and still at least break even. But all of Pansy's kids have lives and jobs of their own, and even with a hired manager, there's a lot of work that *someone* will have to do."

I glanced up at Jake. "I know that all too well. I had someone else running Southern Treasures for several years before I took over. In some ways it's actually less work to do it all myself."

"So the shop can support itself," Jake said.

I nodded and continued. "If Chloe stays—and she says she will—I can promote her to manage daily stuff. A raise, sure, but nowhere near as expensive as adding a full-time employee. She'll do the baking that Pansy was doing, and I'll handle the administrative side."

"So the operation is covered, and it won't impact your cash flow from Southern Treasures."

I nodded. "There's still the question of the purchase price." I showed Jake the number Bradley had given me.

He gave a low whistle. "Yeah, that gets your attention."

"Yep, it does." I tossed my pencil on the table and grabbed a piece of pizza. Even leftover and reheated, Neil's was the best pizza I'd ever eaten.

"So what do I do?" I asked after I swallowed.

"Welllll," Jake said slowly, drawing the word out. "You have had a couple people offer their help."

I shook my head. "I've thought a lot about it, Jake. Felipe and Ernie are wonderful friends. I'd trust them to the ends of the earth, and I love them for offering.

"But like I said, I've thought about this a lot—*a lot*—over the last couple days. I don't want more partners, not even people as remarkable as those two. I won't risk losing any of my friends over business. You should know that better than anyone."

He nodded. He'd put some of his own money in the Buy-Out-Peter Fund. An investment, he'd said. But I had insisted that he keep it in a separate account. I guess technically there were two Buy-Out-Peter Funds, but neither one was enough to cover what I was considering.

Jake turned back to the spreadsheets, as though something new might have emerged in the two minutes we'd looked away.

"Can you buy it on a contract?"

"I already talked to Bradley," I said, joining Jake's staring party. "He said Miss Pansy was willing to carry a note on the place, but her family doesn't want her to. They're afraid she won't let go."

I sighed. "So we're back to the same question we started with. How do I—"

I was interrupted by the ringing of my cell phone. Out of habit, I glanced up at the cat-shaped novelty clock on my kitchen wall. It was after nine P.M. on a Saturday, and

my mother would have been scandalized that someone
would call so late.

I checked the phone display. When I saw Beth's number, it dawned on me that I hadn't filled Jake in on last
night's excitement.

"I've got news," I said to him. "But I have to take this
first." I quickly accepted the call, before she could change
her mind.

"Beth!" I said, making sure Jake knew who was calling.
"Are you okay? We came up on Thursday, but you weren't
home. Is everything all right?"

"I'm fine, Glory. We just needed to come up and see my
granny. We should be back soon."

I hesitated, not knowing whether to tell her what had happened. It really wasn't my place, and I didn't think Boomer
would appreciate my interference.

"How about the quilt?" I asked as I carried on my internal debate. "Is it ready?"

"Not quite," she said apologetically. "I thought I'd have
time to finish it before we left, but we ended up leaving in
a rush, earlier than we'd planned.

"I should be back in plenty of time to have it ready
before the wedding," she promised. "It's put away in my
cedar chest, safe and sound. Just needs a little finishing
work when I get home."

Someone spoke to her in the background, and she relayed
the message to me. "Everett says he'll drive it down to you
once we're home, if you don't have time to come up and get
it. Says since this trip was his idea, he'll take care of it."

"Then you'll be back soon," I said. That would be a
relief; Boomer could deal with telling them what had happened while they were gone.

"I think so," she said. She sounded far less confident
than I would have liked. If she didn't come home right
away, I knew Boomer would somehow blame me, but I
couldn't tell her why she needed to come back.

"Beth, can I call you right back? Will you be there? I need to check my schedule."

"No need, Glory. I can call you when I know we're headed back, and we can set it up then."

"I'd rather take care if it now," I said. It was a lame excuse, but I needed to talk to Jake.

"I'm kind of busy here," she said. "I just had a minute to call you about the quilt so you wouldn't worry."

"Well, can you just hang on a couple seconds then? I promise I won't be long."

"I guess so." She didn't sound happy about it, but she agreed to wait.

The instant I set the phone to mute, I told Jake about what had happened with Karen the night before and about our encounter with Boomer. "He had me look at pictures of both men," I said, feeling the same cold shiver up my spine that I'd felt when I looked at the pictures. "I didn't know either of them, but it was creepy to think they might have been out there when we were there on Thursday."

"Did you tell Boomer we'd been out there?" he asked.

I shook my head. "He asked when the last time was I'd seen Beth and Everett, and I told him. It was the day I went up and paid the deposit for the quilt. Which," I added, "I couldn't explain in front of Karen."

"Keeping Karen's wedding present a surprise may be the least of your worries. He didn't ask if you'd talked to them?"

"He didn't have time. He got called away, and told me to come to his office this morning."

"And?"

"And nothing. His office called, said he was back out at the crime scene this morning, and would I please come in first thing Monday morning."

"I think you better call him."

"Of course." I had no intention of getting in any more trouble with Boomer. Not for someone I hardly knew. "But

I have to finish talking to Beth first, in case I can find out anything to tell Boomer."

Jake looked skeptical, but he didn't argue.

I took the phone off mute, fingers crossed that Beth would still be there, not sure what I'd do if she wasn't.

"Hello."

The single word let me breathe again.

"Hi, Beth. Thanks for waiting."

"It's okay," she said. "But I still don't know what else we needed to talk about."

"Well, do you have any idea when you'll be back?" I didn't want to tell her why. "I'm anxious to get that quilt. The wedding is only a month away." That much was a slight exaggeration, but it was basically the truth. It just wasn't the whole truth.

She hesitated, whispering urgently to someone in the background. I couldn't make out the words, but it sounded like she was asking someone else how to answer my question. Although she kept her voice low, it was clear she was disagreeing with whoever she was talking to.

I paced across the kitchen and stared out the window toward the tiny harbor that gave Keyhole Bay its name. Riley's slip would be empty, his boat *Ocean Breeze* still out fishing. Not that I could see anything but the occasional streetlight in the dark. I tried not to think about how long Beth was taking to answer my question.

Finally Beth finished her hushed conversation and spoke to me. "We aren't completely sure, Glory. We'll be here a few more days is all I know."

"Where did you go?" I asked in what I hoped was a casual tone. "You said you were visiting your granny?"

"Up north," she answered in a deliberately vague manner. She hesitated. "Um, Granny sounded sick when I talked to her the first of the week." The words came out in a rush, as though she might forget her story if she didn't hurry through it. "So we came up to check on her."

I didn't believe her, but there was nothing to gain by telling her so. "So you've only been up there a couple days," I said, fishing for more information.

"I think we left Tuesday." She laughed nervously. "You know how it is when you work for yourself, the days all run together. I should have called you earlier, but it kept slipping my mind—I've just been so busy with Granny."

"Is she okay?" I just wanted to keep her talking in the hope that she'd say something useful.

"She's fine. She said she was just tired when I called and I was overreacting. But after we drove all this way . . ." Her voice trailed off into an apologetic little laugh that didn't sound natural.

"Anyway, it should just be a few days. I'll call you when I get back and we can make arrangements about the quilt."

"Long drive, huh?" It was the best I could come up with, and it sounded silly, even to me.

"Yeah. Kind of. Anyway, I, uh, I have to go. I'll talk to you soon, okay? Bye!"

The connection went dead. I wasn't getting anything more out of Beth. Worse, I still had to call Boomer and I didn't have anything more to tell him, except that Beth was alive and somewhere supposedly visiting family.

I told myself that was his problem, not mine.

I wasn't convinced.

Trying to ignore what I knew Boomer's reaction would be, I dialed the sheriff's office. A female deputy answered the phone and informed me that Sheriff Hardy wasn't available. Did I want to talk to someone else?

No, I didn't. What I knew, or more precisely what I *didn't* know, was something for Boomer alone. I declined the offer and asked to leave a message for the sheriff.

The deputy tried to convince me I should talk to one of the other officers, but she finally accepted that I wanted to talk directly to Boomer.

She put me through to his office, where a recording told

me Sheriff Hardy was unavailable and to please leave a detailed message.

I left my name and number. I told him I'd had a call from Beth Young, I'd see him on Monday morning, and I didn't have any other details.

Not that that would keep Boomer from harassing me.

Chapter 14

MONDAY MORNING STARTED OUT GREAT, BUT MY upcoming meeting with Boomer cast a shadow over the day.

With Jake's help, I had worked out a plan for financing Lighthouse. I called Back Bay Bank—well, it wasn't Back Bay anymore, but everyone still called it that—and made an appointment to meet Buddy McKenna right away. Buddy swore I'd saved his life when Lacey Simon had tried to kill him, and maybe I had. With luck, he'd repay the favor.

I ducked next door to check on Miss Pansy. The aroma of fresh scones, sweetness and faint hints of citrus, cinnamon, and vanilla, tickled my nose and made my stomach growl. Behind the tall glass counter, Chloe was stocking the pastry case with freshly baked goodies—cookies, donuts, and cupcakes, as well as the scones—smiling like she knew a particularly good secret.

She looked up as I came in and the smile disappeared, replaced with an expression that looked to me like guilt.

What did Chloe have to look guilty about?

I instantly decided it didn't have anything to do with Lighthouse; she'd been an exemplary employee from her first day in the shop, according to Miss Pansy, and I didn't see any reason for that to have changed.

I didn't pry. Chloe wasn't usually secretive, and eventually she'd tell me what was on her mind.

"You made scones?" I asked, examining the display case.

She nodded. "Want to taste one? Tell me if they're okay?" She took one from the case and handed it to me without waiting for an answer.

"Is Bradley going to be in?" I asked before taking a nibble of the still-warm pastry.

She shrugged. "He doesn't have a schedule or anything, but he's been stopping in several times a day. Just checking in, he says, but I think Miss Pansy insists.

"I'm not sure what time he'll come in, though. Miss Pansy's supposed to be going home today. Is there something I can do?"

"Just tell him I came by." I took another taste of the scone, nodding my approval as I chewed.

She looked at me, her unasked question clear on her face.

"Very good," I told her when I finished my bite.

She thanked me, but I knew that wasn't the question she wanted to ask. I took pity on her. "Please don't tell Bradley—I want to do that myself—but I am going to accept his offer.

"In fact," I continued before she could interrupt, "I'm on my way to the bank to work out the financing.

"Just tell him I came by and I want to talk to him."

I left her to finish her stocking and headed back to Southern Treasures. I think I heard her whistling cheerily as I closed the door behind me.

Julie arrived early. She had Rose Ann with her, and an active toddler could be a handful in the shop, but she assured me her mother would be by within the hour to pick up her granddaughter. "She has a doctor's appointment," she explained, "but she'll pick up Rosie as soon as she's done. Until then, she has her playpen in the back."

"That's fine," I assured her. "It's been quiet. One thing I need you to do is check stock on the Bluebeard T-shirts and call Mandy with an order. There were several online orders for them this morning, so take care of those before you do the stock count."

"Will do."

The website sales had surprised me. When I finally got the website running at SouthernTreasuresShop.com, one of the instant hits was T-shirts with Bluebeard's picture on them. They were a steady seller in the shop, too, but the online sales had proven more popular than I could have imagined. They were my secret weapon in the Buy-Out-Peter plan.

Buddy was busy with another customer when I got to the bank, but he quickly excused himself. "Ms. Martine." He shook my hand warmly. "It's so good to see you."

"Please, Buddy, everyone calls me Glory. Or Miss Glory when they want to make me feel old."

Buddy chuckled. "You know I haven't got the hang of calling people Miss This or Mister That. The Yankee in me, I suppose."

As I followed him back to his desk, I asked after his wife and children back in Minneapolis.

"Doing fine," he said. "Wishing I came home more than one week a month. They spent the summer here, you know."

"I heard something about that," I said, taking the chair he indicated across the broad maple desk. "I'm just sorry I didn't get the chance to meet them."

"They came by the store a couple times, but you were out. Fell in love with the parrot, I can tell you."

"I have some kid-size Bluebeard shirts. You ought to take them each one." I thought about offering to give him the shirts, but with the reason for my visit, the gesture might well be misconstrued, or put Buddy on the spot.

"Great idea! I'll stop in before my next trip home."

"Be sure you do."

We chatted for another couple minutes, as required by good Southern manners, before we got down to business.

"So what brings you in today, Gloryanna?"

"I need a loan."

"You came to the right place. This is where the money is." He chuckled at his own joke before turning serious. "Sorry. Banking humor. What do you need it for?"

I gave him the condensed version of the offer from Pansy, and hauled out the sheaf of papers I'd put together for him.

"I have current statements for both businesses," I said, laying out the paperwork. "Cash projections. Business plans."

I shuffled a couple sheets to the top of the stack. "I think everything is here."

"Can you give me a minute?" Buddy asked as he pulled the pile toward him. "There's coffee, if you'd like a cup." He looked sheepish. "I should have offered earlier."

I declined the offer. I'd had most of a pot before I left home, and my nerves didn't need any more stimulants. I already felt like a piano wire stretched tight.

I waited, trying to contain my impatience, as Buddy leafed through the stack of paper. He stopped several times to jot a note on a pad, and twice he reached for his calculator.

After several minutes of silence, he looked up. "How long did you spend on this?"

"Most of the weekend," I admitted. "I'd have taken more time with it, but the Whittakers are anxious to move ahead before Miss Pansy has the chance to change her mind."

I grinned at him. "You've met her. You can understand why they want to move quickly."

"Yes, I can. But what I meant was that this is very well put together. Usually I'd have dozens of questions, but all the information I need seems to be here.

"There are just a couple things I want to go over before I take this to the loan committee."

My disappointment must have shown on my face, because he immediately began to reassure me. "Honestly, Gloryanna, this is a solid proposal. I can't promise anything, but as the interim manager and the leader of the transition team, I do have some influence, shall we say."

He took a couple pages off the top of the stack. "I think this should pass with flying colors, but let me show you the things I think will make it even stronger."

An hour later, I walked out of the bank with Buddy's reassurances still echoing in my head. He'd gone over the numbers that had had my head spinning all weekend, and given my business plan a thumbs-up.

I didn't have a loan approval, and I wouldn't for several days, but it didn't matter. I knew this was my future.

Even if the bank turned me down, I would find a way.

My next stop was the sheriff's station, and my interview with Boomer.

I was pretty sure my day was about to go to hell.

Chapter 15

BOOMER DIDN'T LOOK HAPPY. "YOU DIDN'T THINK I needed to know about that phone call?" he demanded.

"I called you as soon as I got off the phone," I replied. "You were out."

"And you didn't think it was important enough to talk to someone else in the office? You just left me a message and said 'See you Monday'?"

I lowered my head and avoided looking directly at the sheriff. I knew I'd been ducking him when I chose to leave that message, and he was making it quite clear he knew it, too.

"I just didn't have anything I could tell you." It sounded weak, even to me. And Boomer wasn't buying my explanation.

He let the silence build. I was sure he was staring at me, but I didn't look up. I knew if I did, he'd be able to see the real answer written all over my face.

At last he sighed with exasperation. "You didn't think the fact the Youngs were alive and well wasn't vital to this investigation? That knowing we were looking for live suspects, not additional victims, might be useful?"

"I told you Beth had called. You knew she wasn't a victim. But I don't think she's a suspect, either.

"She didn't tell me much else, and I'll bet you anything what she did tell me was a lie."

"When you find two homicide victims on the property and the people who live there are missing, chances are they're either victims or suspects. That's just the way it is.

"And how, pray tell, did you determine that she was lying?"

"It just didn't make sense." I paused, trying to remember her exact words. "She said her granny sounded sick on the phone, so they decided to go check on her.

"Who does that? You call a friend, or a family member who lives nearby, or even 9-1-1 if you think it's really bad. But who packs up and *drives* hundreds of miles because someone sounded sick on the phone?"

Boomer nodded in agreement. "No one," he said, his tone somewhat mollified. "But if you know where she went, you should have told me."

"I didn't. Don't. She just said it was a long drive is all. I guess I just assumed her idea of a long drive would be a day or more. But all she told me was that they went 'up north.' "

"And you hadn't seen her since right after Labor Day?" he circled back around to the questions I'd answered on Friday night.

"No, sir. I ordered a quilt from her for Karen and Riley's wedding gift, and paid the deposit. That's why I didn't explain on Friday, because Karen was there and I was trying to keep the gift a secret. But that's how I know for sure what day it was."

"And you haven't seen her or her husband since."

I shook my head.

"Have you talked to them?"

I'd been expecting that question since I arrived in his

office. "Yes," I said. "I usually talk to her every couple or three weeks. Either I call her or she calls me. Usually about stock for the store, or occasional special orders. Like Karen's quilt. I do that with most of my suppliers."

"And they hadn't mentioned taking a trip?"

I shook my head. "We talked about business. It's not like we're best friends or anything. We're on a first-name basis, but I don't know much about her or her family." I thought for a minute. "In fact, now that I think about it, I don't know anything about her, except that she and her husband decided to come down here a year or two ago to get 'off the grid.'" I made finger quotes in the air.

We'd seen many people like the Youngs over the years, mostly in the northern part of the county. Young and not-so-young folks who thought they could get away from it all and live cheaply in the rural areas of the Panhandle. They wanted to grow their own food and live off the land.

Most of them lasted a few weeks, or months, before they went running back to whatever city they'd come from. Back to water that came from a tap instead of a pump, food from a supermarket, and a steady flow of electricity to feed their appliances and electronic gadgets.

Not that I blamed them. I was pretty attached to my version of civilization.

Boomer understood what kind of people I meant. I might have let him believe I didn't think much of Beth and Everett, which wasn't quite true. But it put me and Boomer on the same side, at least a little.

And I needed him to believe that, since I still hadn't told him about being out there on Thursday. And now was as good a time as any.

"There's something else I think you better know," I said.

His face clouded up and he gave me a curt nod. "Yes?"

"I was out to their place on Thursday."

Boomer opened his mouth, but I rushed ahead. There

was an explosion coming, and I wanted to divert as much as I could.

"I was supposed to pick up Karen's quilt, so I couldn't really tell you in front of her, could I? There wasn't anybody home, which makes sense if they left on Tuesday. I did tell you she said she thought it was Tuesday, right? She didn't sound like she was really sure, but she said Tuesday.

"Anyway, I had an appointment with Beth on Thursday. Jake and I drove up, but nobody was there. We knocked, and looked around the cabin. Everything was locked up tight and the car was gone. We didn't see anyone, and there weren't any neighbors we could talk to, so we left."

Boomer made a face like he'd bit into a lemon, but he didn't yell. Which was better than I had expected. Instead he just looked at me and shook his head. "And is there anything *else* you think I should know about?"

"No."

"All right. You do have the same cell phone number we do, correct?"

I opened my cell phone and read the number I had for Beth.

"Same number," Boomer said. "Just wanted to be sure, since you seem to have a lot of information you didn't share with us."

"Have you been able to reach her?" I asked.

He hesitated. I think he wanted to tell me it was none of my business, but he didn't. Instead he sighed and shook his head. "She hasn't returned any of our calls."

"Maybe you can track down who her granny is, and find out where they went?"

"We're working on that. And on the identities of the two bodies we found." He looked back at the sheet of notes on his desk. "You sure you've never seen either of them before?"

"Not that I remember. They didn't look familiar. I don't know a lot of people in north county though, except the ones I do business with. And I don't know any of Beth's neighbors."

We'd been going around and around for more than an hour. My throat was dry, and I had answered the same questions with the same answers several times. I needed a drink of water and the restroom, not necessarily in that order.

All this fuss, and I wasn't even a suspect. I could only imagine how a real suspect would feel. I was beginning to think I should just confess to some random thing, so that we could get this over with.

Boomer asked a few more questions, but it was clear he didn't expect to get anything useful from me. He finally turned me loose with a final warning, reminding me for about the millionth time that I was to call him immediately if I heard from Beth again.

Or if I remembered anything.

"And Miss Martine," he said as I reached the office door, "please do not interfere with my investigation. I have a staff of trained officers. I think we can handle this."

I didn't necessarily agree with him; he'd been willing to believe Bridget McKenna's death was a self-inflicted drug overdose. But he'd also stood up to the feds when Bobby Freed was suspected in the murder of an undercover agent.

I went with the smart choice and didn't argue.

Back in my truck, I headed home. I needed to relieve Julie for lunch, I still hadn't talked to Bradley Whittaker, and I'd promised to call Jake as soon as I got back from the bank.

When I walked in the back door, I could hear voices up front. I hurried through the storeroom past Rose Ann's empty playpen, feeling guilty about leaving Julie alone well past her normal lunch break.

I needn't have worried.

Julie sat at the counter and Chloe stood across from her. On the counter between them was a white pastry bag from Lighthouse and two coffee cups.

"Glory!" Chloe spotted me and broke into a grin. "Bradley's back. I came over to get you, but Julie told me you were gone all morning, so since it was getting late I brought her a sandwich and coffee."

I wondered if there was more to this little visit, but even if there was, I didn't really have time for any more drama in my life. It made a strange kind of sense that Julie and Chloe would become friends.

Outwardly they seemed opposites: the classic pretty-blonde-former-cheerleader and the goth-chick-student-barista. But they shared amazing ambition, business sense, maturity, and the aura that they were determined to succeed on their own terms.

That final quality reminded me of me at their age. It could be why I thought Julie was my perfect employee, and I expected Chloe to be the same.

"Can you hang on a few more minutes?" I asked Julie. "Go ahead and eat if you want." Normally food wasn't allowed up front, but this wasn't a normal day.

"I can wait," she said, but I saw her eyeing the bag on the counter.

"If Chloe doesn't mind, maybe she can stay while I run next door and talk to Bradley. Chloe, could you stay a few minutes?"

Chloe grinned. "Sure, boss!"

"Not your boss. Yet." I smiled back, feeling giddy at the thought of what I was about to do.

Giddy, and terrified.

Chapter 16

BRADLEY LOOKED UP AT THE SOUND OF THE BUZZER when I opened the door to Lighthouse. A shadow passed over his face, and I realized he had been expecting Chloe.

"Chloe's covering for me," I said. "I hope that isn't a problem, but I wanted to come see you as soon as I got back."

"Not at all," he answered.

I glanced around the shop, verifying for myself that Chloe's absence wasn't causing an issue. A white-haired man lounged next to the front window, sipping a steaming cup, his attention focused on the newspaper spread across the table. The only other patrons, a young couple, sat at a table against the far wall, their coffee cups next to an empty paper plate. The woman daintily licked crumbs from her fingertips. I'd seen that same gesture from thousands of Pansy's customers over the years.

Was I crazy to think I could do as well?

I drew a deep breath and reminded myself that Pansy's recipes were part of this deal. Without them, Lighthouse was just another coffee shop. With them, the place was legendary.

I wanted to keep that legendary reputation.

Bradley waited patiently behind the register for me.

Moment of truth.

I felt like my head was a balloon, floating several feet above my body. My heart raced, and sweat ran down my back even though the weather was cool.

Bradley looked at me expectantly.

I stuck out my hand. "You've got yourself a deal."

He shook my hand with genuine warmth, and a relieved smile spread across his features. "I, *we*, are all delighted. Mom was starting to waver, but she said she'd made you a promise and she would keep it."

He continued to pump my hand, as though he was afraid I'd change my mind if he let go. "We've been so worried she'd insist on coming back to work if you decided not to buy the shop."

"I still haven't lined up all the financing," I reminded him. "But I did call my lawyer this morning and gave him the outline of your terms. He said he could have a contract drawn up and ready for signatures later this week."

Clifford Wilson had been our family lawyer for several decades before I was born. He'd drawn up Uncle Louis's will that left Peter and me Southern Treasures. Approaching ninety, I worried every time I called that I'd find him retired, and some stranger taking his place.

Fortunately for me, he was still in the office three days a week, and with the courtly manners of an earlier generation, had insisted he would have the papers drawn up overnight.

I protested, but he was insistent. His actual words were, "If Miss Pansy Whittaker is ready to sell, you best strike while the iron is hot. That little gal is stubborn as a mule, and if she takes it into her head to back out, you're going to need an ironclad contract."

Mr. Wilson had known Miss Pansy her entire life, so he

had a lot of evidence to back his opinion, and he brooked no argument. He said he would e-mail a draft the next day, I could send back any changes, and the contract would be ready on Wednesday or Thursday. He might have been born in another century, but he was up-to-the-minute when it came to his practice.

"I will look forward to that," Bradley said.

"I better get back to work," I said. "I'll send Chloe back over. Thanks again for letting me borrow her."

"She'll be working for you soon enough," Bradley said as I left.

I walked into Southern Treasures and found Chloe and Julie huddled at the counter, their attention focused on something Chloe was writing.

Julie glanced up at the sound of the bell, startled. She poked Chloe, who looked up and saw me. They both looked guilty, as though I'd caught them doing something they shouldn't be doing.

As I approached, Chloe hastily folded the paper she'd been writing on and laid her hand oh-so-casually on top of it.

"Glory," Chloe said, "we were wondering, are you going to invite us to Karen's bridal shower? I mean, we feel like we're her friends, but you hadn't said anything to either of us, and we just wanted to know."

I furrowed my brow. "What bridal shower?"

Julie spoke up. "You're the maid of honor, right? One of the things you're supposed to do is host a bridal shower. At least that's the way my mama taught me." She stopped and a blush crept up her fair skin as she remembered I hadn't had a mama to teach me any of these things.

"No. I think I knew that," I admitted. "But since this is a second wedding with the same bride and groom, I guess I just didn't think about it."

Great, one more thing to add to my growing to-do list. I didn't know where I would find the time for party planning, but I supposed I would have to.

Chloe, however, was several steps ahead of me.

"I thought that might be it," she said. "And when Julie said she hadn't heard anything either, well, we were just talking about what we could do. That is, if you'll let us?"

"Julie and I can handle the planning. I can take care of the food, and Julie says she knows all the games and stuff, and I think I can get Shiloh to help with the decorations. She left Fowler's, you know, and went to work at Flower Power, and she's really good at that kind of thing."

"Whoa! It sounds like you've got this all figured out, but I promised Bradley you'd be back to work. Can we talk about this later?"

"Sure! Just let me know when, okay?" She was out the door in a flash, and the shop was suddenly silent.

"So, you two were plotting while I was gone?"

Julie looked sheepish. "We were trying not to think about you talking to Mr. Whittaker, and we got to talking about the wedding and, well, it just kind of went from there."

"Seriously though, would you two actually be willing to do that for me?" The sense of relief at Chloe's offer was overwhelming, but I didn't want to overload my employee and my soon-to-be employee.

"Truth?" Julie said. "You've been so busy with the business stuff we figured you really didn't have time for this. And we'd love the chance to be part of it. I think Karen is amazing. I'd love to do this for her, and for you.

"And it was Chloe's idea, so I think she's good with it."

"Well," I felt like a huge weight had been dropped on me and then just as suddenly lifted off my shoulders. "If you're sure, I would be delighted to have your help.

"Now what do I have to do?"

"Nothing," Julie said. "Well, except we'll have you approve whatever we do, of course. And we will need your help to make sure we don't miss inviting someone."

I laughed. "This is Karen. Maybe we should just post a notice in the *News and Times* and invite the whole town."

Julie giggled, a lighthearted sound that I'd realized had been missing for a long time when we first met. It was good to hear her happy and relaxed, and I marveled at her resilience. She'd been through a horrible time with her ex, but she'd come out the other side stronger and more mature, with a beautiful daughter. She didn't just survive, she thrived.

"I'm sure anything you two come up with will be fabulous. And I'll be glad to look at the guest list when you have it ready."

"Thanks, Glory."

"No, thank you—you and Chloe—for thinking of this for me." I flashed on the impending arrival of Karen's mom and Stepdad Number Three. I could only imagine the dustup that would have ensued if there wasn't a bridal shower, and my gratitude grew even more.

"Did I tell you Karen's mom and stepdad are coming down for the wedding?"

Julie shook her head.

"Yeah, she thinks Karen needs her help, so she's going to be here for the month before." I lowered my voice to a whisper, even though we were alone in the store. "If you really want to help Karen, you'll distract her mom with shower plans."

"We can try," she promised.

With the bank, the sheriff, Bradley Whittaker, and the bridal shower all taken care of for the moment, I settled down to take care of some store business.

But as soon as I logged into the bookkeeping program, the bell rang over the door and I heard Jake's voice.

I'd promised to update him as soon as I got back, and I'd completely forgotten. I quickly shut down the computer, promising myself I'd work late to catch up on all the things I'd left undone while I worked on the proposal for the bank.

Chapter 17

"SORRY," I SAID, GIVING JAKE A QUICK KISS ON THE cheek.

A wolf whistle came from the front corner of the shop, followed by a cackling laugh.

"Bluebeard!" It did me no good to admonish him, but I still tried.

"He only does that because he knows it bugs you," Julie laughed. "He's like a two-year-old with feathers."

"I guess you'd know about two-year-olds," I said.

I turned my attention back to Jake. "I meant to call you, but Chloe was here looking for me for Bradley, and then we got caught up in some wedding stuff before I sent her back to work."

I glanced at the clock and decided I wasn't getting back to my paperwork before the end of the day, and there were some things I wasn't ready to talk about in front of Julie.

"Julie, if you want to take off, I can handle the rest of

the afternoon. Doesn't look like we're going to be overrun with business."

She gave me a grateful smile. "Thanks. I'm sure my mom would appreciate my picking up Rose Ann a little early."

"Is she all right?" I asked. "You mentioned her having a doctor's appointment."

"Cellulitis," she answered. "She's doing okay, but I hate to leave her with Rose Ann when she's hurting. You sure it's okay for me to go?"

I assured her it was just fine, and she left quickly, as though she was afraid I might change my mind.

Alone with Jake, I filled him in on the visit to the bank.

"So Buddy's going back to Minnesota?" he asked.

"That was what he said. They'll be getting a permanent manager soon, and his transition team will be able to go home. At least until the next assignment."

I couldn't imagine a job that took me to a new city every few weeks or months. I'd been born in Keyhole Bay, lived here my whole life, and had no reason to ever leave. I liked knowing my neighbors and having lifelong friends like Karen and Riley.

"He said his family would like him to be home more, but they're getting used to the schedule. And I think he enjoys the work."

"But he'll be here long enough to get this application through, won't he?"

I nodded. "I sure hope so. Two years ago, I would have said I knew everyone on the loan committee and they knew me. But now that Back Bay's been sold, the new owners have brought in a lot of their own people."

Jake put his arm around my shoulders and gave me a reassuring hug. "Either way, Buddy thought it was a solid plan, right? It's going to be just fine."

"Just fine," Bluebeard echoed.

"You really think so?" I wasn't sure which one I was

asking, but both Jake and Bluebeard answered "Yes" in unison.

"Now that we have that settled," Jake said, "what about your visit with the sheriff? I gather you didn't want to talk about it until Julie left."

"I didn't." I leaned against Jake, comforting myself with his presence. "It wasn't awful," I told him. "But it wasn't good, either. Boomer acts like he's halfway convinced I know more than I'm telling him. Even when I told him everything I knew and everything I *thought* I knew.

"And he keeps giving me the speech about not interfering with his investigation. Like I'd ever do that!" I pulled away, my voice rising as I released the indignation I'd held in check since I left Boomer's office.

I made the mistake of looking at Jake as I spoke that last sentence. He was biting his lip, trying not to laugh.

"No," he said hastily. "You wouldn't. At least not on purpose. But Glory"—he struggled to keep his voice serious—"you have gotten involved in several investigations in the past. You really can't blame Boomer for being concerned."

My anger vanished as quickly as it had come. "I hate it when you're right."

"No you don't," he said, pulling me close once again. "You already knew why Boomer was worried. You just needed to vent."

"Yeah. Still, I *did* tell him everything I knew. I even gave him Beth's cell number, which it turned out he already had."

Jake let me go and walked over to Bluebeard. He offered him a biscuit and scratched his head, and was rewarded with a head butt. "What do you think, old man? You think Boomer has reason to be concerned?"

The parrot bobbed his head as though agreeing with Jake. Then Uncle Louis's voice said clearly, "She can be a handful."

I sputtered. There wasn't really much of anything I could do when the two of them ganged up on me. "Just remember who gets you treats," I said darkly.

"You love me," Bluebeard replied and cackled again. That laugh was a new addition to his repertoire, a warped imitation of Rose Ann's high-pitched little-girl giggle.

"Yes, I do." I joined Jake in front of Bluebeard's perch. "But you can be a handful, too."

"You still love me." He cocked his head, staring at me with one dark eye. "I love you, too." Uncle Louis again.

It still unnerved me occasionally when Bluebeard slipped between his own voice and Uncle Louis's. I had accepted the fact that my great-uncle had never left the store he'd owned for many years. I had accepted his use of Bluebeard as his spokesbird. I had accepted, and even sort of appreciated, his interference with my personal life.

But it was still weird.

Jake suggested dinner when we closed up, and I agreed. "My place or yours?" I asked.

"Mine. I've got chili verde in the slow cooker, if that works for you?"

"Sounds good. Can I bring anything?"

"Just your appetite," he said.

After Jake left, I tried to settle back down to bookkeeping and inventory, but I kept coming back to my interview with Boomer. Had I told him everything? I couldn't think of anything I'd left out, but the feeling of guilt, the need to confess to *something*, persisted.

I wandered around the shop, straightening shelves that didn't need attention and restocking the few items that had sold during the day. Behind the counter, I found a neat stack of papers Julie had left, including a copy of the order she'd given Mandy for the Bluebeard T-shirts and copies of the packing lists for the shirts she'd shipped.

It was the reassurance I needed. In spite of my misgivings about Boomer, the rest of my life was moving in the right direction. Julie's competence once again validated my decision to hire her, and Buddy's confidence in my business plan reinforced my gut feeling that this was the right thing to do.

My spirits lifted, and I went back to work. Knowing dinner, and Jake, were waiting at the end of the day didn't hurt either.

As I worked, the thought of Beth and Everett kept tickling at the back of my brain. If I could just convince them to come back, Boomer would have to see that they were innocents whose only crime was being in the wrong place at the wrong time.

Beth had trusted me enough to call back, although she hadn't told me where she was or when she'd return. I just needed to come up with a reason for her to come back to Keyhole Bay and talk to Boomer.

Yeah, I thought as I forced my attention to the stack of invoices. *And maybe I should figure out world peace while I'm at it.*

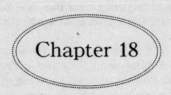

Chapter 18

"YOU COOKED," I SAID, GETTING UP FROM MY CHAIR. "My turn to clean up."

Jake agreed, but he could only sit still for a couple minutes. Soon he was up from the wooden table in his kitchen and putting away leftovers while I ran water for the dishes.

I washed and he dried; a comfortable routine we'd developed over the course of many shared meals. I liked sharing the tidy kitchen with Jake, "accidentally" bumping into each other as we worked, and he seemed to feel the same; we'd discovered a lot of things we enjoyed doing together.

"Are you staying?" Jake asked, hanging his dish towel on the rack over the sink once the kitchen was tidy enough to meet his standard. He called it "squared away," a remnant of his years in the firehouse.

For several months I'd had an overnight bag stowed in the truck, but a few weeks ago Jake had casually suggested I just put my things in a spare cupboard. Now the question of spending the night didn't require planning and preparation. We just did what seemed right for the moment.

"Is that an invitation?" I teased.

"I guess it might be."

He gave me a kiss that left me a little breathless. An invitation, yes, but there wasn't any question whether I'd accept.

IN THE MORNING I SLIPPED IN THE BACK DOOR OF Southern Treasures before the late autumn sun was over the horizon. I hastily reset the alarms and started up the stairs, walking softly at the edge of the treads, trying to avoid the squeaky steps.

It didn't matter.

I'd only gone up three steps when a loud squawk came from the shop. "Awk! Naughty girl, out all night!"

I sighed and continued up the stairs without worrying about making noise. "I'll be down to take care of you in a few minutes," I called out.

It was worse than breaking curfew as a teenager.

Fifteen minutes later, coffee made and a load of clothes in the washer, I came back downstairs to deal with Bluebeard.

"Coffee?" he asked.

Maybe he thought my guilty conscience would make me weak, but if so he was sadly mistaken. "No coffee for you. You know better."

He did—we had this conversation several times a week—but it didn't stop him from asking. Coffee was toxic for parrots, and no matter how much Uncle Louis missed his coffee, his host couldn't tolerate it.

Besides, I didn't feel particularly guilty. As Karen would say (and then apologize for her language), I was a grown-ass woman.

As though called by my thoughts, Karen appeared at my door a few minutes later.

"I stopped at Lighthouse for coffee," she said when I opened the door, "and I saw your lights were on."

I took the cup she handed me, abandoning my own mug of French press from upstairs. I was careful to put the mug where Bluebeard couldn't get to it. Not that I didn't trust him, but I didn't. Not where coffee was concerned.

I brought her up to date on my meeting at the bank, told her about my interview with Boomer, and moved on to Bradley Whittaker without giving her the chance to ask about Beth and Everett.

"So what are you doing out so early?" I asked as I finished the rundown of my Monday without mentioning Jake. "Early morning at the station?"

"No." She groaned. "I'm on my way to the airport. Stepdad Number Three had an appointment at the naval station. So, for my sins, I have to pick up my mother and bring her up here while his driver takes him out to the base."

She looked at me, a glimmer of hope in her eyes. "You wouldn't want to go for a little ride, would you? We won't be long, I promise."

"I wish I could help you out," I said. "But I've got a lot to do here before I open up."

"Naughty girl, out all night!" Bluebeard squawked.

I felt a blush creep up my face as Karen's eyebrows shot up. "Really?" she said. She gave me a knowing smile. "So maybe there *is* something I should know?"

I shook my head. "You know I spend time at Jake's, and he spends time here. And sometimes, well, you know.

"And when there's something to tell, you'll be the first to know."

"Me first," Bluebeard squawked.

"Well, you'll be the first to know after Bluebeard. I have no secrets from him, even if I try to."

I remembered there was something I needed to tell Karen, and it just might make her happier about her mother's arrival.

"I do have something that might be good news for you," I told her. "Chloe and Julie want to throw you a shower. Actually, they said as maid of honor it was my job, but they knew I was busy and they volunteered." I stopped and sipped my cooling latte.

The milky concoction reminded me of Chloe's barista skills. I was glad she wanted to stay.

"I don't need a shower," Karen said impatiently. "I still have the house we bought when we were married, and I think we have everything we need already, times two."

"But that's not the good part," I said. "They said they'd try to get your mom involved in planning the shower, and maybe keep her off your back a bit."

Karen looked like she wanted to cry with relief.

"It's not a done deal," I reminded her. "And there's no guarantee they'll be able to keep her distracted. But it might give you a break now and then."

"Right now, even a little break sounds wonderful. I don't know what I'm going to do with Mom here for the next month. I'm actually wishing Stepdad Number Three—do you think I should actually, like, learn his name?—has some huge emergency and they have to go back to Washington right away."

She threw her shoulders back and put her chin up, her chestnut curls tossing defiantly. "Okay, here I go. I can do this."

But as she went out the door, the defiant posture slumped and she looked so miserable, I reconsidered my answer.

Grabbing my wallet and keys, I stuffed them in my pockets and ran out the door after her.

Chapter 19

"JUST THIS ONCE," I SAID, AS I SLID INTO THE FRONT seat and fastened my seat belt. "And I'm already regretting it."

I glanced at the dashboard clock. "There's time, just barely."

We pulled onto the empty early morning highway and headed for Pensacola, the ever-present police scanner blinking silently in its cradle under the dash.

Karen was as silent as the radio, and I looked over at her. Her hands were white-knuckle tight on the steering wheel, her mouth drawn into a flat line of concentration. Or stress.

I searched for something to say, something to distract her from the family reunion that awaited her in Pensacola. I envied her that; I wished I had a mother to fuss over me. On the other hand, I'd seen firsthand how the relationship made them both crazy.

Karen was the only child of a single mom with enough maternal instinct for a dozen kids, and she'd suffered from the overabundance of attention throughout her childhood.

Her mom was Mrs. French when we were kids, and in my teens I'd heard her say that the name and the kid were the only things she got from her ex-husband. The ex-husband himself had taken on a legendary quality, having disappeared before Karen was a year old. He was one of the very few taboo subjects in Karen's life.

Now we were heading down the highway toward the only person guaranteed to make Karen even crazier than she'd been for the last few weeks.

Why was I in this car? Deliberately putting myself in the middle of this encounter went well beyond friendship. And I needed to stop obsessing about it and try to enjoy our last few minutes of freedom.

"Any luck tracking down Sly's friend?" I asked.

Karen shook her head. "A lot of the records from that time are only available on paper, and I couldn't get access over the weekend. I thought I'd spend some time this afternoon—until mother called and said they were coming in earlier than planned."

And there we had circled right back around to the subject I was trying to avoid.

"They aren't staying with you, are they?" I couldn't imagine Karen and her mother surviving thirty hours in the same house, much less thirty days, or more.

"No, there's some kind of visiting bigwig quarters at the naval base. They're expected to stay there. But instead of going there and getting settled in, Mom insists she has to come up here and—I don't know—start meddling, I guess."

Traffic was light and we made good time, arriving at the airport before the plane. Pensacola International was a small airport: a single terminal with twelve gates. We parked in the garage and walked across to the terminal.

Karen fidgeted, retrieving her e-mail and voice mail every couple minutes. She had an app for the airline on her phone, and she checked the progress of her mother's flight constantly. I wasn't sure whether she was hoping they'd arrive soon, or not at all.

"Are you expecting something?" I asked when she hit refresh on her messages for the fifth or sixth time.

"Boomer was supposed to have some preliminary information on Friday night's victims," she replied. "There was a rumor yesterday that there might be an identification coming. And he hasn't released the autopsy results, either. I know Dr. Frazier was called out Friday, so he should have something by now."

"They still haven't identified them?"

"You saw that place," Karen said. "Some of those neighbors aren't exactly neighborly, and some of 'em don't care much for any kind of law enforcement."

"Nobody likes to talk to the cops," I said. "That seems pretty normal to me."

"Are you really that innocent, Martine? Really?" She shook her head. "Did you look around when you were up there? Some of the locals have been out there for generations, and their means of support is the kind that doesn't exactly meet with official approval.

"There's a reason some of those guys stay deep in the woods."

"Oh!" I tapped my forehead. "Duh! You mean the 'shiners? I didn't think the sheriff paid them much mind."

"He might not, normally. But he's got two dead bodies. That changes things. He wants to talk to everybody that was out there, including you."

"He already talked to me," I reminded her.

"Yeah." She looked at her phone again, tapping the screen. Every movement screamed impatience. "They should be on the ground," she said, taking a conversational left turn. "Just a few more minutes."

I checked the time and mentally counted the hours to the West Coast. "How did they get a flight this early?" I asked, realizing it was still the middle of the night on the other side of the country.

"Flew to Houston yesterday," Karen said. "He has a brother or something there, and they were supposed to spend a few days with him. But there was some change in plans and the Navy wanted the Admiral—and no, I don't know if he's really an admiral, but I have to call him something, don't I?—they wanted him here first thing this morning.

"So here we are at this ridiculous hour." She glanced at her phone again and tapped irritably at the display. "I'm texting her to meet us at the luggage carousel. The app says it's number two."

Without waiting for my response, she took off for the baggage claim. I trotted to keep up with her as she moved through the near-empty terminal. Everything she did was rapid-fire this morning, and I wondered just how much coffee she'd had before she stopped at Lighthouse.

We arrived before the first bags came off the plane. We stood a few paces back from the conveyor, leaving room for the passengers, who soon began arriving. They mobbed the conveyor, snatching near-identical bags from the belt.

Where were all these people going at this hour of the morning? Some were vacationers, eager to get an early start on their trip, and the young men in Navy and Air Force uniforms made sense.

A group of men in pastel slacks and polo shirts bearing the name of a Houston country club claimed the golf bags a baggage handler brought out on a cart, and were whisked away by a uniformed driver who had been waiting with a card that read "Golf Trail Tours."

I was trying to figure out the rest of the passengers when I heard Karen's sharp intake of breath. "There they are." I think she meant to whisper, but nerves made her voice so loud that several people turned to look.

I looked in the direction she was facing. Sure enough,

there was her mother, with her arm linked with the arm of a man in uniform. His dark uniform jacket sported enough ribbons and medals that he might really be an admiral.

Karen's mother looked older, but her carefully applied makeup, the expert streak job on her honey blond hair, and a figure that caused other women to look daggers at her, disguised just how many years she carried on her slender shoulders.

She still knew how to dress, something Karen and I had never learned from her. Simple oatmeal-colored capris and a bright turquoise camp shirt emphasized her tiny stature next to the imposing military man beside her.

I squeezed Karen's arm in what I hoped was a reassuring way and guided her toward her mother and her new stepfather, talking softly to her as we walked.

They caught sight of us when we were still several yards away, Karen's mom breaking into a broad smile at the sight of her daughter. Karen flinched, then pasted a big smile on her face and hurried forward to greet her mother with a hug.

When I caught up with them, Karen had already managed to extract herself from her mother's embrace.

"Gloryanna!" her mother exclaimed. She was the sort of woman who actually did exclaim. "It's so good to see you! Karen didn't tell me you were coming with her."

"A full-service maid of honor," I said lightly. I accepted a quick hug. "It's wonderful to see you, Mrs. . . ."

My voice trailed off as I realized I had no idea what to call her. She hadn't been Mrs. French since Karen and I were in our teens, and I didn't know her new married name. For that matter, I didn't know if she'd taken her new husband's name, though I suspected military protocols would dictate that she should.

"Please, call me Catherine. You're not a child anymore, and I'm certainly not as old as that makes me feel." She gave me another quick hug and linked her arms with mine and Karen's before turning to her new husband.

I took a look past the medals and ribbons to the man who was now Karen's stepfather. Ramrod-straight posture would have identified him as a career military officer, even without the uniform. Dark hair, just past crew-cut length with hints of gray at the temples, and brown eyes with fine lines at the corners that gave him the look of having a perpetual squint. His deep tan spoke of years on the water, reminding me of the veteran fishermen in Keyhole Bay.

"Karen, Glory, this is my husband, Captain Clinton Fontaine. Clint, this is my daughter Karen and her best friend, Gloryanna Martine."

"Ladies," he nodded, a slight tip of his head. He waited politely for Karen to offer her hand, then took it in both of his. "I've heard so much about you, I'm honored to finally meet you. If even half of what your mother tells me is true, you're pretty remarkable." There was a twinkle in his eyes, a hint that he understood his wife's exaggerations well.

He released Karen's hand and turned to me. "Catherine mentions you fondly, Miss Martine. She seems quite impressed with your accomplishments."

I shook his hand and tried to accept the compliment gracefully, always a challenge.

"It's Glory to my friends," I told him.

"Glory, then." He flashed a warm smile and excused himself to collect their luggage. "Stay here with the girls, Cat," he told Karen's mom. "I know you have a lot of catching up to do."

He walked over to the baggage carousel, where three bags circled the otherwise-empty belt. The two larger bags, in matching black-and-white houndstooth-check pattern, sported bright red bandannas tied to the handles. I could guess that those were Catherine's. The third bag was well-worn leather, smaller than the other two. Captain

Fontaine deftly stacked the bags atop each other and wheeled them back to where we waited.

"Do you need your bags, Cat, or should I take them directly to our quarters?"

Catherine shook her head, gesturing to the hefty carry-on sitting at her feet. "I think I have what I need for today," she said. "You'll pick me up later?"

"Yes ma'am." He bent and gave her a kiss that had Karen and me both looking away. "The driver should be here," he said. "I'll call you when I'm through for the day."

He took the stack of luggage and strode toward the exit.

"My car's across the way," Karen said, grabbing her mother's bag. She staggered slightly as she added the heavy bag to the load of the carryall she toted everywhere.

I took pity on her. I took her mother's bag from her and slung it over my shoulder. I think Catherine must have been planning to go bowling later, judging by the weight of the thing.

We left the terminal just as Captain Fontaine was climbing into a dark sedan, a young sailor standing at attention, holding his door.

"I could carry my own bag," Catherine protested as we made our way across the street and into the parking garage.

"Mother," Karen said, "that bag would challenge an Olympic weight lifter. The only reason Glory can manage it is that she's used to heavy lifting."

"It's not that bad," I said, without much conviction. "And I'm not sure the comparison to an Olympic weight lifter is any kind of compliment."

The ride back to Keyhole Bay was almost as tense as the trip to Pensacola. Catherine immediately started quizzing Karen about plans for the wedding, and Karen's answers grew shorter and sharper with each question.

"Mom, for heaven's sake! Can we talk about something else, *anything* else, for just a few minutes? Tell me about

Clint, or your new place in Seattle, or what you had for breakfast. Just don't talk about the wedding. Please."

"I just wanted to know what I could do to help," Catherine snapped. "And we don't live in Seattle. It's Oak Harbor, and it's a hundred miles from Seattle."

"Really?" Karen latched onto the subject like a drowning man grabbing a life ring. "I didn't realize it was so far out of town. Tell me what it's like."

Temporarily distracted, Catherine launched into a description of an island paradise that sounded too good to be true. She loved her new home, she said, and was glad to be out of the big city and back in a small town.

"And speaking of small towns," she continued, "what's going on in Keyhole Bay? It's been so long since I've been back here, and I've lost track of all the news."

"Well," Karen said, "the big news is actually about Glory. It seems that Pansy Whittaker is finally going to retire and Glory's buying Lighthouse Coffee."

"Glory! How wonderful for you. I told Clint you were a successful businesswoman, but I had no idea you were getting ready to expand. You must be so excited!"

"I'm not sure if excited is the right word," I said. "Terrified, maybe. It's a big undertaking and we're just in the preliminary stages. There's still a lot that could go wrong before it's a done deal.

"I don't want to jinx it by speaking too soon."

We were nearly back to Keyhole Bay when Karen's phone rang. She tapped the control on the dash, activating the speaker, and answered.

"Karen Freed. I'm driving and you're on the speaker with my passengers," she cautioned the caller.

"Freed." I recognized the station manager's voice. "Sorry to interrupt, but Sheriff Hardy will have a press release in twenty minutes. Can you get there, or should I send someone else?"

"I'll be there. I'm about ten minutes away. I just need to drop off my mom and Glory." She broke the connection and glanced over at her mother.

"You're going to have to entertain yourself for a little bit, I'm afraid. I wasn't planning on being off work until late next week."

"I understand," Catherine said. "But are you going to leave me at your house while you're gone, or what?"

Karen blanched at the thought of leaving her mother alone in her house. She'd come home to find the laundry done, the floors cleaned, and the entire kitchen rearranged. Not to mention whatever her mom might choose to snoop around in while she was gone.

Once again, the maid of honor rode to the rescue.

"Why don't you stay at my place?" I offered. "There are several breakfast spots within walking distance, or you can take a nap upstairs if you're tired. You must have had to be up at an unholy hour for that early flight."

I mentally reviewed the state of my apartment. I hadn't eaten at home last night, or slept in my bed, so it shouldn't be too bad. I hadn't even had time to change my clothes before Bluebeard and Karen started interfering with my plans.

"That's very generous of you, Glory, but I couldn't impose," Catherine's voice rose at the end of her sentence, inviting my reply.

Social convention dictated that she give me the opportunity to rescind the hasty invitation, but we both knew it was a ritual and I quickly repeated the offer.

"Not at all," I said.

"If you're sure?"

"It'll be fine, Mom," Karen cut in.

I'd run out of the shop so fast I hadn't brought my phone. "Karen, can I borrow your phone? I left mine in the shop."

She handed it to me, reaching for the control pad on the dash. "I assume you don't want us all to join in your conversation," she said.

"Thanks." Whether for the phone or the privacy, I wasn't sure.

I dialed Julie's number. It was still early, but Rose Ann usually had her up with the chickens, and today was no exception.

"Hi, Julie. It's Glory. I know it's your day off, but I wondered if you could come in this morning?"

"I don't have a babysitter," she said. "So I don't know how long Rose Ann will last in the store.

"And why are you calling from Karen's phone?"

"Don't worry about Rose Ann. I just wanted you to meet Karen's mother. They had a change in plans, and we just picked her up at the airport, which is why I'm using Karen's phone; I forgot mine. Anyway, I thought maybe you and Chloe would like to talk to her about the shower."

"I suppose I could do that, even with Rose Ann along. Give me time to get her fed and changed, and we'll be in."

"Thanks, Julie."

I hung up and handed the phone back to Karen. "I think that will keep us busy for a while."

Catherine turned around, an expectant look on her face. "A bridal shower?" she asked.

"Yes." I hoped I sounded more enthusiastic than I felt. "Julie and Chloe offered to host, and they would love to have your help. Chloe works at Lighthouse, so we can go over and get a cup of coffee"—I hoped she hadn't noticed the discarded cups that revealed we'd already been there once this morning—"and I can introduce you to the girls."

"That sounds fine," she said. "But who's Rose Ann?"

"Julie's daughter. She's two."

"A baby!" Catherine was exclaiming again. "How wonderful! I can't wait to meet her."

I couldn't see Karen's expression, but I didn't need to. Grandchildren were one of the many contentious subjects between Karen and her mom. Catherine had made it abundantly clear that she was willing and eager to be a grandmother, but her only child wasn't sure she wanted to be a mother. Now, or ever.

A few minutes later, Karen dropped us off in front of Southern Treasures.

I made her promise to call me as soon as she could, to fill me in on whatever information the sheriff released. Beth and Everett hadn't been far from my thoughts ever since the station manager's call, and I was anxious to know what was going on.

I showed Catherine upstairs to freshen up and went back down to get the store ready to open.

Chapter 20

CATHERINE WAS STILL UPSTAIRS WHEN JULIE AND Rose Ann arrived. "Thank you for coming in." I got a hug from Rose Ann, who trotted over to talk to Bluebeard. "Could you run next door and let Chloe know that Karen's mom, Mrs. Fontaine, is here, please? Ask her if she'd be available at some point to talk about the shower."

I had already heated my leftover coffee in the microwave, finished it, and was craving a mocha, but I forced myself to wait until Catherine joined us. Memaw would have been scandalized if I hadn't waited for my guest, no matter the circumstances of her visit.

"Leave Rose Ann," I told her. "I'll let her feed Bluebeard a treat. You know how much she loves that."

Bluebeard loved it, too. He had been charmed by Julie's daughter from the first day she'd come into the shop, and over the months, as she grew from infant to toddler, they had formed a mutual admiration society.

I helped Rose Ann get some grapes from the small

refrigerator in back, and she carefully pulled them from the stems, putting some in a bowl for Bluebeard and popping a few directly into her own mouth.

"Hello, sweetheart," Bluebeard greeted her when she returned to his perch with the bowl of grapes. Normally he would greedily devour any treat, but with Rose Ann, he waited patiently as she held out each grape. He took the grape from her fingers carefully and gently, and thanked her for each one.

Still, I always supervised.

Catherine came down while we were feeding Bluebeard. She made a beeline for Rose Ann, every latent grandmother gene surfacing.

Rose Ann took the attention in stride. Having spent time in the store since she was a baby, she'd gotten used to strange women cooing over her.

"Chloe has a break in about twenty minutes," Julie said when she returned. "She said she'd be over then."

"Catherine." The name still felt strange on my tongue. She'd always been Mrs. French in my mind, and it seemed wrong somehow to address her by her given name. "This is Julie Nelson. She works for me, and she's Rose Ann's mom.

"Julie, this is Mrs. Fontaine, Karen's mom."

"Call me Catherine," she said immediately. "I'm so glad to meet you."

I asked Catherine what kind of coffee she'd like, and excused myself to call Chloe with our order. I told her to put the coffee and cookies on my tab, and she laughed and said, "Sure, boss!"

When I rejoined Julie and Catherine, they were having the kind of conversation you have after being away from a small town for a long time: who got divorced, who got married, what business closed or grew, who moved away, who passed away. It was a distillation of the last six years of the *News and Times*.

As I walked up, I heard Catherine's, "Matthew Fowler

is still married? I thought she would have tossed him out years ago!"

"You should see the rock she's wearing," I said. "Oh, and the new Cadillac she got last year. You can't say Mr. Fowler doesn't pay for his mistakes."

"That hasn't changed," Catherine said. "He's been that way as long as I've known him."

"You worked for him, didn't you? I'd forgotten all about that until just this instant." I blurted it out before I thought about the implications of what I was saying.

Fortunately for me, Catherine didn't take offense. "Yes, I did," she said. "For about a day and a half."

I filed that away. As a struggling single mother, she wouldn't have quit a job on a whim. I wondered what the story was, but she didn't volunteer anything more, and I didn't ask.

A few minutes later, Chloe appeared with a tray of coffee drinks and a white pastry bag. She passed drinks around, including cocoa for Rose Ann, as I made introductions. "I cooled it down," she told Julie as she handed her the child's treat.

She handed Catherine a cup. "Nice to meet you, Mrs. Fontaine. Chai latte, right?"

The three of them spent the next half hour chattering about the plans for Karen's shower. I mostly stayed out of the discussion, watching the clock and wondering when Karen would call with whatever news the sheriff would release.

Chloe went back to work, leaving Julie and Catherine happily planning games and menus and color schemes.

Rose Ann started to fuss, and Julie put her down in her playpen. In a rare moment of two-year-old cooperation, Rose Ann promptly fell asleep.

She was still asleep as lunchtime approached, and showed no sign of waking. Julie suggested I take Catherine to get some food. "I can mind the store while you go," she said. "Besides, if Rose is sleeping, I hate to wake her. She's getting to the point where she doesn't want to nap, no matter how much she needs it."

I called Karen, and she agreed to meet us at a small cafe near the police station and courthouse. "Boomer's press conference has been delayed about six times so far this morning," she said. "I'd love some lunch, but I can't go far, in case he finally gets around to talking to us."

The cafe catered primarily to municipal employees and people with business in the courthouse. Most of the dozen or so tables were packed with local men, the steady hum of conversation a deep bass rumble beneath the clatter of plates and silverware in the kitchen. The smells of fried chicken and slow-baked beans made my mouth water. My stomach gurgled, reminding me I'd had nothing but coffee and one of Chloe's cookies all morning.

Karen fidgeted through lunch, checking her phone for messages every couple minutes. It made the conversation choppy, and it raised my anxiety level with the constant reminder that I still hadn't heard anything more from Beth and Everett.

When Karen's phone finally did ring, it startled all three of us. I jumped about a foot, and knocked over my water glass. Fortunately, it wasn't full, but I was busy cleaning it up while Karen was on the phone and I didn't hear what she said.

When she finished, she tossed the phone into her bag, put some bills on the table, and slung her bag over her shoulder. "I have five minutes to get back to Boomer's office," she said. "I'll call you as soon as I can."

She dashed out the door and down the sidewalk at a pace that would have left me breathless.

Catherine and I tried to relax and finish our tea, but between Karen's abrupt departure and my spill, we were both ready to leave. We added to Karen's stack of cash and went back out on the sidewalk.

I checked in with Julie and she assured me Rose Ann

was still sleeping, so I took the scenic route back to Southern Treasures, letting Catherine rubberneck at all the
things that had changed since her last visit.

When we drove past Fowler Auto Sales, she let out a
low whistle. "He's done all right for himself, hasn't he?"
She craned her neck to take in the expansive used-car lot
and the repair bays. "Does he own all that?"

"Not as much as it looks like," I told her. "See that
chain-link fence behind the service area? That's the salvage yard. Friend of mine owns the place and he flat
refuses to sell, especially to Fowler. There's several acres
back there that Sly says Fowler will never get his hands on."

"Sly?"

"His name's Sylvester, but I've never heard anyone call
him that." That wasn't exactly true; Uncle Louis had called
him Sylvester the first time he'd come in the shop. But I
wasn't about to mention Bluebeard's job as spokesbird for
my great-uncle.

"I think I remember him," she said slowly. "Had some
kind of car repair. A fair man, as I recall."

"That's him. He's the one who sold me this truck." I told
her a sanitized version of how I got my truck, leaving out
the part about the arson of my old Civic behind the store.

My phone rang while I was parking the truck, and by
the time I picked it up it had gone to voice mail. Karen's
number showed on the call log. Finally, some news.

I didn't stop to listen to her message, just dialed her
back, anxious to know what Boomer had to say. Catherine
continued on toward the front of the shop as I stopped in
the storage area to talk.

"I have some information," she said when she answered
my call, "but you aren't going to like it."

"No surprise there. What did you hear?"

"The two victims have been identified. They were familiar to the police a couple counties over. Moonshiners.
Killed by gunshots, and the sheriff is calling it homicide."

"We already knew, or guessed, most of that. What's the part I won't like?"

"According to Boomer, there are two 'persons of interest' who fled the area just before the bodies were found and are wanted for questioning. He didn't name names, but it sure sounds like your pals from north county. He didn't call them suspects, but he might as well have.

"Your friends are in trouble, Glory, and it's going to get worse real fast."

Chapter 21

"BUT DID THEY SAY WHEN THESE GUYS WERE killed? I mean, I think 'my pals,' as you call them, left early in the week. If they weren't even here, how could they be suspects?"

"All they said about the autopsy was that they died of gunshot wounds. Nothing else. As press releases go, it wasn't much, and Boomer wouldn't answer any questions. In fact, he seemed unhappy about the whole thing."

I would have to call Beth again. She needed to realize that Boomer wouldn't just give up if she stayed away, not if he was calling her and Everett "persons of interest" and saying they "fled" the area. He'd already started looking for them, and after this announcement, I could expect the hunt to intensify.

I put aside the question of Beth and Everett for a minute, and asked Karen when she was going to come for her mother. "It's not that she's a problem or anything," I said. "But I just need to know what the plan is."

Karen always had a plan.

"Since I'm already here, I'd like to spend a little time going through the courthouse records. See if I can find anything about Sly's Anna. I expect I'll have better luck with the high school and the newspaper archives, but it's at least worth a look."

I couldn't imagine what she might find with the paltry information we had available, but there wasn't any harm in looking. Except that it meant I would be entertaining Catherine for a little longer.

Karen said she'd be by in about an hour, unless she hit pay dirt in her search. Then she'd call and let me know.

I finished my call and went up front to let Catherine know when Karen would be back. I found her deep in conversation with Julie and bouncing Rose Ann on her knee. She was clearly throwing herself into the surrogate grandmother role with enthusiasm. I probably should warn Karen, though I doubted Catherine's yen for grandchildren would be any surprise to her.

"Look who woke up all smiles," Catherine cooed as I walked in. Rose Ann rewarded her with a big grin. The kid was a charmer, no doubt about it, and she had never met a stranger. To her, everyone was just a friend she didn't know yet.

"I thought we'd go over and talk to Chloe," Julie said. "That is, if you don't mind?"

"Of course," I answered quickly. "You came in on your day off, and you covered the store half the day. Thanks again for doing that."

I assured Catherine that I had work to do, and I didn't mind her "deserting" me to go with Julie. The truth was, I hoped for a few minutes of privacy to call Beth and try to talk her into returning to the Panhandle.

I pulled out my phone, then set it aside as an older couple came in the store. Hand in hand, they wandered through, looking at the shot glasses, postcards, and T-shirts before stopping in front of the rack of vintage newspapers.

I had discovered a stash of newspapers buried in a far corner of the storeroom a few years back, mostly from the '40s through the '60s. On a whim I had put some samples in plastic sleeves and put them on display. They turned out to be wildly popular with the middle-aged-and-older snowbirds that flocked to the Panhandle in the late fall and winter.

The couple flipped through the display, occasionally pointing out articles to each other. They looked as though they could have been newlyweds, their mutual affection evident in the attentive way they spoke to each other and the glances they exchanged.

They finally came to the counter with a couple child-size Bluebeard T-shirts and one of the old newspapers. "From the year we were married," the woman said as I rang up the purchase.

I glanced at the date. Nineteen sixty-six. "Congratulations," I said. My newlyweds had been married almost fifty years.

"Congratulations," Bluebeard echoed, getting a laugh from both of them.

They left, chattering about how they would have to bring the grandkids next time, and how those grandkids would love the parrot.

Sometimes I had the best job in the world.

Other times, not so much. I picked up the phone and dialed Beth's number. I didn't really expect her to answer, but I had to keep trying.

As I expected, the call went to voice mail. "Beth, you need to call me back. Right away. It's really, really important. I need to talk to you."

I figured she was getting calls from Boomer, and possibly from others. I could only hope that she would trust me enough to return the call. If not, after today's announcement,

I was likely in for another session with Boomer, and I wasn't looking forward to it.

Karen showed up a few minutes later to collect Catherine. "They're next door," I told her.

"They?"

"Julie was here, remember? She covered the store while I met you for lunch. And she took your mom next door to talk to Chloe some more." I glanced up at the clock. "They've been over there almost an hour," I said. "What could be taking them that long?"

I tried not to worry about what they might be cooking up.

"And you should know that she's quite taken with Rose Ann," I added. "Just fair warning."

Karen groaned.

I quickly changed the subject. "Did you find out anything at the courthouse?"

She shook her head. "I didn't have much to go on. But you already knew that. I did find the birth records for the mid-forties, but that was the beginning of the baby boom. Do you have any idea how *many* kids were born in those years?"

"Lots?" I guessed.

"Lots," she agreed. "And without pinning it down to a single year, it's nearly impossible to sift through all those records and find the one we want."

Bluebeard had made his way across the room, hopping from one display rack to another. There wasn't really enough room for him to fly easily in the confined space, though he did occasionally take a spin around the warehouse. Now he sat near the counter where we were talking, his head cocked as though he was listening to our conversation.

"Baby?" he asked.

"Not Rose Ann," I told him. "Another Ann. Anna. From a long time ago."

"I know her?"

The question caught me by surprise. I supposed it was possible he did know her, but how do you question a parrot?

I could ask Uncle Louis about Sly. He'd befriended the couple, had even offered to help them elope. But even if he did know, I couldn't be sure he would actually tell me.

I was trying to frame a question when Catherine, Rose Ann, and Julie returned. In the hubbub that followed their entrance, any chance to ask Uncle Louis about Anna was lost.

Catherine was still entranced with Rose Ann. In her view, clearly, the child could do no wrong. Or maybe Rose Ann was on her good-behavior today.

Whatever the reason, Karen could see her mother was taken with the little girl. She leaned over and whispered, "I should have thought this through; letting Mom around a baby probably wasn't the best idea. But it's too late now."

Bluebeard stared at us, one dark eye sharply focused on Karen. He hopped closer, cocked his head, and said clearly, "It's never too late," before returning to his perch.

I knew from experience that it would be impossible to get him to explain what he meant. But I also knew he often wasn't referring to the current conversation.

I wondered, never too late for what?

Chapter 22

IT TOOK A WHILE, BUT EVENTUALLY I GOT KAREN, Catherine, Julie, and Rose Ann out of the shop. There were delays as Catherine and Julie exchanged numbers so they could continue planning the bridal shower, and as Catherine said good-bye to Rose Ann.

Finally I had the shop to myself. I tried Beth's number again, and left another pleading message. I was beginning to wonder if she thought she could ignore me, too.

I left a final message as I was closing up for the day. "Beth, this isn't going to go away. The sheriff wants to talk to you, and he knows you went to visit your granny. If you don't come back, he *will* track down your granny, and someone *will* show up at her door looking for you. Is that what you want?

"I know Boomer, Beth. He doesn't just give up because you want him to. One way or another, you're going to have to come back and talk to him."

I hung up. I didn't know if anything I said would make

a difference, but I had to try. I wasn't even sure why I felt it was my responsibility; Beth and Everett were adults and they were responsible for their own lives. But somehow I felt that I had played a part in whatever had happened.

Or it might just be the Boomer-made-me-feel-guilty thing.

My computer beeped, reminding me I had plans for the evening. I'd forgotten in the rush of Catherine's unexpected arrival, but Jake and I had promised to have dinner with my friend Sly. And if I didn't get moving, I was going to be late.

If it had been anyone else, I would have canceled. I was exhausted, and I hadn't even been upstairs since the previous morning. But Sly was special, and we hadn't seen him in a while. I went upstairs, changed, and was waiting when Jake arrived to pick me up.

"Sly said he wanted a steak," Jake told me once we were in the car. "He suggested Buccaneer Bay House."

I whistled softly. Bay House, as the locals called it, was the nicest place in town. "I may be underdressed."

Jake took a moment to glance over at my gray wool slacks and black sweater, accented with a vintage rhinestone brooch that would eventually find its way into the shop. "You look fine."

I tried to laugh, but all that came out was a nervous titter. Bay House was nice, but so were the prices. A dinner there could put a dent in my wallet, which I couldn't afford right now.

"He said he knows that place isn't in your budget. He's had a good week, he wants to celebrate, and dinner is on him. And, no, he wouldn't tell me exactly why there is cause for celebration. Insisted he'd tell us when we were both there."

A few minutes later, we pulled into the parking lot. Sly arrived at the same time, driving one of the dozens of cars he kept in the garages that dotted his junkyard.

Those garages were one of his best kept secrets. Most

folks seeing a fenced-off junkyard assumed it was full of, well, junk. But Sly had been on that piece of land since he was a kid—his dad had owned it before him—and over the years he had collected and restored scores of vehicles.

Today's car was something from the mid-fifties, as near as I could tell. Sharp fins, hooded headlights, lots of chrome, and a slick two-tone paint job that looked like it just rolled off the showroom floor.

I couldn't identify the make and model, I just knew it was gorgeous; flawlessly restored, or kept in a museum for the last half century. Knowing Sly, I voted for restoration.

We walked closer and I could read the chrome script on the left side of the trunk. *Studebaker.*

"She's a real beaut," Jake said to Sly as we approached. "You do the work?"

"Yep." A wide grin split Sly's dark face. "Took me years to find that last piece of chrome." He gestured to the script on the right that read *President.* "Been hunting that one for a long time."

"Is that what you wanted to celebrate?" I asked, skeptical that a small piece of chrome was worth a dinner at Bay House.

"Partly," Sly answered with a twinkle in his eyes that told me there was a lot more to the story. "Let's go on in, and I'll tell you about it once I wrap myself around a rare rib eye."

Seated across from Sly, I had to fight the temptation to quiz him about Anna, the girl he had almost married. Karen had planted the notion in my brain, and now the idea of reuniting the sweethearts more than fifty years later seemed like the right thing to do.

Instead I pushed the thought away, reminding myself that there were a million ways this could go terribly wrong. A million ways I could make Sly's heartache infinitely worse.

Times had changed, certainly. A lot had happened in that fifty years, and interracial couples were much more common than they had been in the early 1960s. But a lot could happen to *people* in fifty years, too. How could we know if Anna would even want to see Sly after all this time?

And if she didn't, wouldn't that break his heart all over again? In the last couple years, I'd learned of his connection to Uncle Louis and I'd come to think of him as family. I wouldn't do anything to hurt him, and I wouldn't let anyone else hurt him, either.

We chattered through our salads, with Jake and me taking turns filling him in on my offer to buy Lighthouse.

"There's still the question of Peter," I said. "I can't get him out of there fast enough, but I have to be careful I don't overextend myself."

"But if the bank financing comes through for Lighthouse, you should be fine." Jake winked at me and squeezed my hand.

"That boy at the bank purely owes you, girl," Sly said. "Just 'cause he's a Yankee don't mean he shouldn't honor his obligations."

"But the bank doesn't owe me," I said.

"Oh yes they do," Sly said. "You found out who killed that purty little gal came down here to check on Back Bay for 'em. And you saved Buddy's life. I'd say they owe you plenty."

"Even if they do," I said, "that doesn't mean they'll give me the loan."

"If they won't," Sly said, his voice dropping to a confidential whisper, "tell 'em I'll guarantee the loan. Put up the yard if I have to, but my word should be good enough."

His offer, the offer of his home and his livelihood, brought tears to my eyes. I wanted to tell him I couldn't possibly let him do that, but I couldn't speak around the lump in my throat.

At that moment the waiter appeared with a heavily loaded tray. He deftly slid the plates off the tray and onto the table, serving my tenderloin first, then putting platters with monstrous rib eyes in front of both men. The steaks were so large that the accompanying mashed potatoes and creamed spinach were served on a second plate.

Sly dug in with gusto. The first bite went in his mouth, and an appreciative sigh followed. "Somebody back there"— he gestured to the kitchen—"knows his way around a good steak."

"It might be *her* way," I said with a grin. It was a running joke. Sly had always acted as though a woman could do anything she put her mind to.

"Well, whoever it is," he said after another bite, "they surely know how to do right by a piece of beef."

Conversation slowed to a crawl as we worked our way through the perfectly cooked meals, savoring the prime cuts served by Bay House. Their reputation as the best steakhouse in town was more than justified.

Finally Sly pushed his empty plate away and leaned back with a contented sigh. I had no idea where he found room for so much food, but I'd seen how hard he worked, and I knew he'd use up every calorie tomorrow.

"So what's the occasion?" I asked, pushing my plate away also. Unlike Sly, I'd have enough leftovers for another complete dinner.

"Couple things," he said. "First, like you said, was finding that little piece of chrome. It was the only thing left to make that car like new, and I been waiting a long time for that." He smiled and nodded in a self-satisfied way.

He stopped, drawing out the moment.

"And the other?" I prodded.

"I got a buyer for her. Wasn't sure, it had been a long time. But I called him today, told him I had that bitty piece of chrome, and he 'bout jumped through the phone." A grin flitted across his face, then he sobered. "So this is my last trip with her, one last night out on the town before she leaves for good."

The comment made me think of Anna again. But I couldn't ask about her, so I shoved the thought away.

I looked up to find both men watching me expectantly. "What?"

"I think Sly has something more," Jake said.

I'd seen that expression on Sly's face once before. The day he'd sold me the truck that had belonged to Uncle Louis.

"Oh no," I said, shaking my head. "You aren't going to do this again. Uh-uh."

"Do what?" he answered with feigned innocence. "Whatever do you mean, girl?"

"You know," I said accusingly. "Try to rope me into some deal to do with that car." Sly had sold me the truck, but he'd insisted that I pay him what he'd put into it, which was a small fraction of what the beautifully restored vehicle was worth.

"Me and Mr. Louis were partners in the President," Sly said. "He bought her from one of his customers, and I gave her a home while I worked on her. Put her in my name when he took sick, and made me promise to fix her up right.

"She's been in that garage near thirty years while I searched for parts."

"Which means she's yours, Sly. Uncle Louis gave her to you and you took care of her like he asked."

He shook his head. "That may be, but I'm a man as pays his debts, and I owe Mr. Louis more than I can say." He reached in his wallet and took out a piece of paper; a check. "I got a fair profit for my work, but it's only right that you get a little bit, too."

Though I tried to refuse, he gave me the check, taking my hand in his and placing it against my palm.

Curiosity got the better of me, and I unfolded it to look at the amount.

Five figures.

"No." I set it back on the table. "That's way too much."

"No it ain't," he said, shaking his head. "It's just a taste of what I got for her.

"Your uncle knew what he was doing when he bought that car. She's a rare model—one reason it took so long to find parts—and I got a fair price."

"But you stored her for almost thirty years," I protested.

"And I got a fair price for that. I'm telling you, that money's yours fair and square. You don't believe me, you check with Mr. Louis hisself."

It was the one argument I couldn't refute, and he knew it. If I went to Uncle Louis, he might or might not answer a direct question, and he might or might not make sense.

Sly knew he had me. With a triumphant flourish he opened the dessert menu. "I think I am ready for coffee and something sweet," he said, his tone clearly indicating the subject of the check was closed.

I picked at a small scoop of gelato while Sly devoured a slice of cherry pie and Jake had cheesecake. Jake offered me a bite and I took a nibble of the creamy cake, savoring the tang of the sour cream topping, but I was too full to do more than taste.

True to his word, Sly picked up the check. "It's my celebration," he said. "Only fair."

How could I even *consider* doing anything that might hurt this man?

Chapter 23

IN THE MORNING I TOOK ANOTHER LOOK AT THE check. I thought about simply putting it away, not taking it to the bank. But that would only mean another argument with Sly down the road, when he realized the check hadn't been cashed.

The only remaining question was whether I owed Peter a percentage of the money.

When Jake stopped in before he opened Beach Books for the day, I posed the question to him.

"What do you think I should do? Technically, if this is for the car, it should be split between us, right?"

Jake looked at the check. "It's made out to you, not Southern Treasures," he pointed out. "And Louis split the store between the two of you, not his entire estate, correct? So who inherited the rest?"

I had to confess I didn't know. "I suppose I could check with Clifford Wilson. I'll be talking to him later today anyway, since he's supposed to have the final contract for Lighthouse ready this morning."

"You could probably just check the probate records at the courthouse, too," Jake suggested. "All that kind of thing is a matter of public record."

"If I have the time to go down there and dig through the records."

"True," Jake said. "Wilson might know, or be able to look it up more easily. Depends on what he keeps and what's in storage. Or destroyed."

I must have looked puzzled by his last suggestion. "Why would he destroy his records?"

"Glory, those files were closed more than twenty-five years ago. Everything was placed on the public record. Why would he keep them?"

"I don't know. I hadn't thought about it, just assumed that lawyers kept their records forever, I guess."

"They could be in storage," Jake said. "And he could even remember. From the way you talk about him, anything's possible."

"So you think the money should go to whoever inherited the rest of Uncle Louis's estate?" I went back to my original dilemma. "Whoever that is?"

Jake shook his head. "I think the money should go to you. That's obviously what Sly wants, or he'd have made the check to Southern Treasures. But if you're concerned about it, then I'd say follow the terms of Louis's will."

There was one other person who knew what those terms were, and he chose that moment to join the discussion.

"For you," Bluebeard said in Louis's voice. "For your mom, now for you."

"But what about Peter?" I blurted out. I knew better than to try and quiz Louis, but I still tried. "Doesn't he have a share of this?"

"Ask Wilson," the parrot said. He retreated across the room and into his cage, his way of telling me he was through.

I sighed and made a note to ask Mr. Wilson when I talked to him later in the day.

Jake had only been gone a couple minutes when the phone rang. I checked the display to make sure it wasn't Peter, and saw Beth's number.

I grabbed the phone. "Beth?"

"Glory, why are you hounding me?" Stress pulled her voice into a high-pitched whine. She sounded like she might burst into tears at any second.

"Beth, I'm so sorry. I didn't mean for you to feel like you're being hounded, but I know the sheriff is trying to reach you and he's getting pretty agitated. I was trying to warn you, to give you a chance to fix this before it gets any worse."

"Worse? I come up to see my granny, and you call and tell me the police are going to come track us down? How does it get worse than that?"

"Beth, listen to me." I stopped and let the silence stretch for several seconds. I had to be sure she was listening, not just waiting for the next opportunity to screech at me again.

I continued slowly and deliberately, trying to keep my voice low and forceful without sounding threatening. "Right now they just want to ask you some questions. But if you don't talk to them, if you continue to hide from them, the sheriff will get tired of playing games. He will decide that you have something to hide, and he doesn't like people who hide things from him."

On that score I had plenty of personal experience. Keeping anything from Boomer was a seriously bad idea.

"When he loses his patience, you will stop being someone he wants to talk to. Instead you will become someone he finds suspicious.

"And when he thinks you're suspicious, Beth, he will send officers with arrest warrants for you and Everett."

I stopped and let that sink in for a minute. Beth was stunned into silence, though I could hear her rapid breathing.

She had good reason to be afraid. She obviously knew

way more than she had admitted to me. She and Everett had left abruptly, making up the story of a sick grand-mother to cover their sudden departure, and it was obvious the sheriff wasn't buying it.

"There's only one way out of this for you. Come back here on your own and answer Sheriff Hardy's questions. If you do anything else, *anything* else, you will be sorry.

"That isn't a threat, Beth. I'm not hounding you. I am warning you. I know the sheriff, I know how he thinks, and I know how he runs his department.

"I'm trying to help you, whether you believe me or not."

I didn't have any other argument, so I shut up and let Beth think about what I had said. I clutched the phone so tightly my fingers started to cramp as I waited her out.

At last she let out a deep sigh. "Okay," she said quietly. "Let me talk to Everett. When we figure this out, I'll call you back. Just give me a little time to work things through."

Chapter 24

I PACED THROUGH THE SHOP, TOO AGITATED AND nervous to sit still. I checked my e-mail and tried to review the new contract draft from Clifford Wilson, but I couldn't concentrate enough to read it.

I'd never been good at waiting, and this morning was worse than usual. I told myself it would be better once Beth called me back, once I knew they were coming home. But I knew it wouldn't be, not until they were back in Florida and safely in Boomer's office. Until then I would continue to worry.

Normally I would call Karen while I waited, or visit with Jake. But I was afraid to even use the phone for fear I would miss Beth's call.

I made a pot of coffee and drank two cups while I puttered about, fussing with displays and straightening shelves.

I kept up a running dialogue in my head, arguing that this wasn't a decision they could make instantly. Beth was convinced, but what if she had to persuade Everett? I hadn't told her why the sheriff wanted to talk to them, and judging by her reaction, I didn't think the sheriff had either.

None of my arguments did anything to diminish the growing tension that knotted my shoulders. I realized I was gritting my teeth so hard my jaw ached. If I kept this up, I'd be a complete basket case by noon.

Fortunately for me, Beth called back before I completely fell apart.

"Glory, we're leaving in a couple hours. We need to pack and get the car ready to go, and Everett needs a little nap before we hit the road."

"Okay," I said. "And?"

"It's usually a two-day trip. No matter how we figure it, we're going to have to stop for a few hours and sleep."

I waited, biting my lip to contain the questions that threatened to spill out.

"We should be back to Florida by about noon tomorrow. But there's one condition, Glory. One thing you have to do for us."

I waited, unwilling to agree to anything until I knew exactly what it was she wanted me to do.

"You have to come get us, Glory. We don't know this sheriff of yours, and according to the people we've met, he doesn't much like people from north county.

"We've got no reason to trust him, Glory. So if you really want us to come back and turn ourselves in, or whatever, you have to be the one. We'll turn ourselves in to you, and you can take us to the sheriff.

"Those are our terms. We will trust you to do right by us, and we'll come back. But only if you promise to come and get us when we get home tomorrow."

I struggled with my answer. Part of me wanted to tell her she was in no position to be setting terms. She was just lucky the sheriff hadn't caught up with her yet, and she ought to be grateful for the opportunity to come in on her own.

But another part of me understood her precarious position.

She didn't know the sheriff, hadn't been around the area since she was a kid and the sheriff was a brand-new deputy, like Karen and I had. And she lived in a part of the county where most of the scattered residents preferred to keep their distance from any kind of law enforcement.

Add to that the stereotypical bad image of a small-town Southern sheriff, and it was no wonder she felt like she needed an escort to the sheriff's office.

I bit back my annoyance and accepted the proposed arrangement. I would meet her and her husband at their cabin no later than noon tomorrow.

I hung up and breathed a sigh of relief. In a little over twenty-four hours, I would escort Beth and Everett to Boomer's office and turn them over to answer his questions.

My part in all this would be over and I could go back to taking care of my business and buying a bakery. That would be plenty to keep me busy for the foreseeable future.

That, and getting rid of Peter.

Then it hit me. I had just agreed to drive to north county and pick up the Youngs tomorrow. On Thursday. When it was my turn to cook dinner.

I had a problem, and I cast about for a solution. I had planned to cook black-eyed peas and ham hocks with fried cornbread. The weather had turned cool, and it was the kind of warm, filling comfort food that fit the shorter days and chilly evenings.

But I couldn't cook an all-day meal if I was gone for several hours to get Beth and Everett. Sure, I could leave a pot simmering, but it would still need tending, and what if something went wrong and I didn't get back in time?

I kept coming back to the question of dinner as I read over the contract draft from Mr. Wilson. I still felt like I'd been punched in the gut every time I looked at the amount of money I was offering, but I was starting to feel a little less terrified each time I read the number. Eventually I would be desensitized.

Mr. Wilson hadn't missed a thing, as far as I could see. He had covered all the questions I'd brought up and several I hadn't thought of, and still kept it in language I understood.

I loaded legal paper into my printer and started printing the documents. The click as each page fed into the tray was like a countdown to the starter's gun at the beginning of a race; in just a few minutes, I was going to change my life forever.

With the contract printed, I signed the purchase offer and folded it into a large envelope. I wrote Miss Pansy's name on the outside and sealed it up.

"Well, Bluebeard," I said, tucking the envelope under my arm, "here we go."

"Go!" he repeated, and whistled shrilly. "Go!"

With his endorsement ringing in my ears, I walked next door and presented the envelope to Chloe. "Will you give this to Bradley when he comes in?"

"You bet, boss," she said with an excited grin, guessing at the contents of the envelope as she hefted it in her hands.

"Not yet," I cautioned. "There's still a zillion ways this can go wrong. I am not counting on anything until it's all done."

"Gotcha."

The smell of sweet apples and cinnamon tickled my nose and made my stomach growl. Chloe shook her head. "Don't you ever eat breakfast?" she asked.

I shrugged. "If I get busy in the morning, I forget," I said. "I've got so much on my mind right now . . ." My voice trailed off, and I eyed the array of pastries displayed behind the glass front of the bakery case.

"Let me fix you something," Chloe offered. "Any idea what you'd like?"

"The apple turnovers smell delicious," I said. "But I really don't need anything sweet right now. What would you suggest?"

She quickly ran through several options, and I settled on a slice of ham-and-Swiss quiche with a fruit cup to take back to Southern Treasures with me.

I e-mailed Mr. Wilson while I ate, to let him know the contract met with my approval and had been sent to Miss Pansy for her signature. I also asked him if he could tell me who inherited Uncle Louis's estate, aside from Southern Treasures. I didn't go into detail, just asked if he remembered.

While I was thinking about it, I also called Buddy Mc-Kenna to tell him I had made an offer, contingent on financing.

"That's great, Glory," Buddy said. "The full loan committee meets on Friday, so I might have an answer for you that afternoon. But don't count on hearing before Monday. Sorry it can't be sooner."

I thanked him and hung up. More waiting. You would think with all the practice it would get easier, but it didn't.

And there was still the question of tomorrow's dinner.

Jake called to check in, and I told him about Beth's call. "She says she'll be home tomorrow, but she insists that I have to come and carry them to Boomer, that they won't come otherwise."

"Are you sure you want to do that?" Jake asked.

"I have to. The only way to get Boomer off my back is to make sure Beth and Everett get back here and talk to him."

"I don't like the idea of you going up there alone," he said. "Would you like me to come with you?"

I wanted to say yes, but it wouldn't be right to ask him to do that. It would mean closing up Beach Books and losing a day's sales. "No," I said. "I'll be fine."

"I'd still feel better if you didn't go alone." Jake kept his tone conversational. He knew better than to try and tell me what to do, but he still wanted to voice his objections.

"Really, I'll be okay. I just wish I didn't have to do it tomorrow."

"Tomorrow?" Jake thought for a minute. "It's Thursday. You'll have to miss dinner?"

"No. If they're home by noon, I should be able to make the drive and be back in plenty of time for dinner. But it's my turn to cook." I sighed. "I'm going to have to come up with something I can do quick, in case I get held up along the way."

"Let me cook."

I started to protest that it wasn't his responsibility, but he kept talking. "You've included me in a lot of your dinners over the last year or so, and I haven't returned the favor.

"Let me take care of dinner for tomorrow night. It won't be Southern—maybe Southwestern—but that way you won't have to worry about it on top of everything else you have to do."

"You sure?"

"Absolutely. And we can eat at my place, so you don't have to worry about what time you get back."

The offer was too tempting to pass up, and I agreed to let him host my week. Another step in our relationship dance.

Chapter 25

IT WAS NEARLY CLOSING TIME WHEN BRADLEY Whittaker appeared at my door with a fat envelope in his hand. He made a ceremony of handing me the envelope and shaking my hand.

"Congratulations, Miss Glory. Mom's signed the papers. Soon you'll be the new owner of Lighthouse Coffee."

He shook my hand again. "And thank you, from all of us, for helping us get Mom to slow down."

Then he handed me another envelope, this one just as bulky, but sealed tightly with Miss Pansy's rather shaky signature across the flap.

I looked at him quizzically. "What's this?"

"That's her recipe file. She told me not to open it and to give it directly to you."

I thanked him and he left.

I immediately went to the safe, an old iron monster that lived under the stairs, and locked both envelopes inside. Whatever Chloe was doing in Miss Pansy's absence seemed to be working, and I didn't feel right about even opening the recipe file until the deal was complete. To do otherwise felt like cheating.

As I climbed the stairs, looking forward to a quiet evening alone, I ran through the mental checklist of my various projects. The immediate problem of tomorrow's dinner was in Jake's capable hands; if he could feed a ravenous firehouse crew, dinner for a few close friends wouldn't be an issue.

The purchase of Lighthouse was settled; all that was left was to wait for the bank to approve my loan. I could worry about what to do if they didn't, but there was, as Memaw would say, no sense in borrowing trouble. Besides, there wasn't anything I could do until I knew their decision.

The wedding still loomed ahead of me, but at least Chloe and Julie had taken over planning the bridal shower. All I would have to do for that was show up, bring a present, and foot the bills. I said a fervent prayer that they didn't get carried away with their plans. Or worse, let Catherine get carried away.

Even the question of Beth and Everett would be settled by early tomorrow afternoon, the plan already in place to take care of my part of the problem.

I hadn't paid much mind to the victims of the shooting; that was the sheriff's mystery to solve and I was determined to keep out of his way. I was sure he preferred it that way, too.

Still, it seemed curious that we had heard so little about what had happened out at Beth's place. The lack of information bothered me, and by the time I'd heated some leftover soup and eaten it with a few crackers, I decided to call Karen and see if she had heard anything.

Karen's phone rang several times without an answer. About the time I expected it to go to voice mail, Karen picked up, sounding harried and out of breath.

"Yes?" It wasn't so much a greeting as it was a challenge.

"Is this a bad time?" I asked. "I could call back later."

"No, no, no. Just hang on a second." She spoke to someone, and then I heard footsteps and the sound of a door closing, followed by a deep sigh.

"Okay, I've locked myself in the bathroom. I should be safe for a few minutes."

"What in the name of heaven is going on, Freed?" Karen wasn't the type to hide in the bathroom. From anything.

"My mother," she said, as though that explained everything. Which maybe it did. At the very least, it explained Karen's bizarre behavior.

"What is she up to now?" I tucked the phone between my ear and shoulder and started sorting laundry. I could tell I was in for a long-winded explanation.

"We're having a 'family' dinner." I could hear the quotes around the word family, even through the phone. "Just the four of us: Mom and Clint, Riley and me. I cooked, which naturally gave her an opening to suggest ways I could learn to be more domestic.

"Then, if that wasn't enough, she started quizzing Riley about his plans for the honeymoon. You *know* he wanted to keep it a surprise for me, and she won't stop asking him about it. He keeps telling her he's working on it, but she doesn't stop."

"I'm sorry, Karen." There wasn't much else to say. Catherine was unrelenting once she got an idea in her head, and she would pester Riley until she was satisfied with his answers.

Karen sighed. "I know she's just excited, but I wish she would calm down and let us take care of things our own way." Her breathing slowed, and I could picture her forcing her shoulders to relax as she tried to calm herself.

"Sorry to dump on you," she said. "But I feel better having got that off my chest." She laughed, embarrassed by her tirade. "But I'm sure that's not why you called.

"What can I do for you?"

"I was actually just calling to find out if you'd heard anything more about the men out at Beth's place. Boomer didn't tell you much yesterday, and I figured you'd be on his case until he gave you something more."

"I would be, if I didn't have my mother trailing along behind me. But she's been here since the crack of dawn; showed up before I left for work and said she'd just tag along and visit with me when I wasn't on the air. Like I didn't have anything else to do between broadcasts.

"I would have refused, but Clinton dropped her and took off for some terribly important meeting and I was stuck."

"So, no news?" I asked.

"Not a word. I called Boomer several times today, but all I ever got was that simpering idiot who calls herself his 'public information officer.'"

I knew the one she meant. Twenty years ago she would have been called a switchboard operator, before switchboards were replaced with phone consoles. Basically she answered the phones and routed calls around the office. Occasionally she answered basic questions. But lately she'd been "putting on airs" (to use one of Memaw's favorite phrases) and revising her title.

"Karen, what are you doing tomorrow? Is your mom coming back up again?"

She groaned. "Probably. Almost certainly, if I can't come up with a solid reason to keep her away."

"What if you weren't in town? If something work related took you out of town for the day, and you couldn't take her along? Would that work?"

"It might," she conceded. "But I don't have anything like that coming up. Unless you have something?" she said hopefully.

I told her about Beth's phone call, and her insistence that I come to get them. "I'm going to have to drive up there early, and be gone all morning. If you went along, we might be able to talk to Beth and Everett before they see Boomer."

"Your truck wouldn't be comfortable for three," she said, suddenly much cheerier. "You must need me to drive, since the SUV has room for everyone."

"You have a point," I said, as though the whole thing had been her idea. And it would be, by the time she told her mother the story.

"I can pick you up. We better leave early, just to be sure we're there when they get home. Wouldn't want to miss them and then have them change their minds or something, and back out."

I agreed, and we made a date for early in the morning.

I checked one more thing off my mental list, started the washer, and set to work on dessert for tomorrow night. Whatever Jake decided to cook for dinner, I had planned on pecan pie for dessert. I could still do at least that much.

Chapter 26

THE DRIVE TO NORTH COUNTY WAS UNEVENTFUL, A welcome break after the commotion of the last few days. Karen was uncharacteristically quiet, the result, I guessed, of having spent the last couple days arguing constantly with her mother.

I hadn't called Boomer. I'd thought about it and even discussed it with Jake, but in the end I couldn't trust that things would go right. And if they went wrong, I didn't want to antagonize Boomer in the process.

Karen didn't ask for directions. She had driven this way just once, a week ago when the bodies were found, but she always seemed to remember a route once she drove it.

She slowed, and I caught sight of the colorful fence that was my signpost for Beth's turn. Karen seemed to hesitate, and I realized she had only been here in the dark.

"That's the corner," I said, answering the question she hadn't asked.

We bounced slowly along the narrow dirt road leading

to Beth's cabin. As we neared Beth's driveway, a grungy pickup approached from the opposite direction. There wasn't room for the two vehicles to pass each other, but we managed to reach the driveway and pull off before the pickup went past.

We pulled up in front of the cabin. No car, and no sign of anyone else around. Karen sighed, and I started to apologize but she just shook her head. "It's quiet here," she said. "If we have to wait a little while, so what? I could learn to like this."

"No you couldn't," I said. "You'd go crazy with this much quiet. You barely manage as it is."

She started to protest, but stopped as we heard another car coming down the driveway.

I climbed out of the car, anxious that Beth and Everett see me since they wouldn't recognize Karen's SUV. I didn't want them to get scared off, now that we had come this far.

But instead of their tiny hybrid, what rounded the curve into the packed dirt of the parking area was the dilapidated pickup that we'd seen on the road.

It roared up to me and stopped abruptly, sending a cloud of dust swirling around my ankles. I instinctively stepped back, putting more distance between me and the unknown passenger and driver. The truck rose above my head, its big tires and jacked-up suspension hinting at off-road adventures that I imagined involved poaching and other unsavory activities.

The truck idled loudly in the surrounding silence, an unmuffled rumble with an uneven rhythm Sly could have cured in two minutes, though I suspected these were not the kind of guys who took their vehicles to an actual mechanic.

The passenger opened his door, the hinges squealing in protest. He jumped down, scuffed motorcycle boots sending up another puff of dust.

Dirty jeans, a T-shirt with the sleeves ripped off, and an oil-stained denim vest made his outfit a match for the heavy-set victim Boomer had shown me. His face and hair were more like the other victim: hollow cheeks, long hair hanging in dark wisps, a bandana tied around his head.

I backed up another step.

The driver left the engine running and came around the truck to stand next to his buddy. Taller and wider, he was dressed in the same dirty jeans and denim vest, minus the T-shirt. His white belly reminded me of the underside of a fish.

The truck's rough idle made me wonder if he didn't dare shut it off, but I didn't figure it was a good idea to ask about it. In fact, I thought it was probably a bad idea to talk to these guys at all.

Not that they gave me any choice.

"What you doin' out here, city girl?"

"Just waiting for my friends. They're supposed to be home here in a few minutes." I didn't bother to protest him calling me a city girl. By the standards of north county, I *was* a city girl.

"Seems a strange place for somebody with a fancy car to be waiting for a 'friend.'"

"I just buy quilts from the woman who lives here," I answered. Not the whole truth, but mentioning the sheriff seemed like a really bad idea.

"Calvin," the thin man poked his friend in the arm. "There's another gal in that car. Looks like she's messing with her phone or something."

Calvin looked over at the SUV, now covered with a fine layer of dust kicked up by the truck's arrival. Anger flashed across his face, quickly replaced by a bland smile that I was sure some girl had told him was cute. It reminded me of a shark.

He walked toward the SUV and I followed, with Skinny Guy bringing up the rear. I slowed to let him pass, not wanting either man where I couldn't see him, but he slowed even more, not letting me get behind him.

Calvin approached the driver's side window, which Karen had lowered, and bent down to look in the car. If he saw the police scanner, we were going to be in trouble.

"What you doing, little lady?" he asked. His tone was meant to be friendly, but he wasn't a good enough actor to disguise the menace that lurked under the innocuous words.

Skinny Guy stood next to Calvin, a goofy grin on his face, as though that would put us at ease.

I moved around to the passenger side and unlatched the door, ready to climb in if we needed to leave quickly. Calvin shot me a glance that told me he knew exactly what I was up to, and he found it amusing.

The thought didn't make me happy.

"Just waiting for the gal who lives here," she said. "We were supposed to meet her this morning, but it looks like we're a little early." She shrugged, as though being confronted by strangers on a deserted road was an everyday occurrence. She gestured at the thermos bottle in her hand. "Thought we'd just drink our coffee and wait for her."

On the seat beside her, out of Calvin's line of sight, her pocket recorder blinked its tiny red "record" light. She was saving the conversation.

I glanced at the scanner and realized none of the lights were on. In the darkened interior, it was nearly invisible in its holder, and a jacket was tossed carelessly in front of it, the dark navy blue fabric making the radio even less visible.

I was pretty sure the thermos wasn't what Skinny Guy had seen—her phone was in its usual place in the console, but it had been on the dash just a few minutes before.

"What about that phone my pal Donny says you were messing with? Don't think the cell service out here's very good. You might not be getting a signal."

"I wasn't," Karen answered coolly. "Tried to call and find out how long we'd have to wait, but I couldn't get through." She waved at the phone. "Have to try again later, or drive out to the highway or on into Century. But really, she should be here pretty soon."

She waved the thermos again. "Want a cup of coffee? I think I have a couple clean cups here somewhere."

"No thank you, ma'am," Calvin said. I wasn't sure if she'd managed to distract him or not, but I got my answer at once when he said, "But I would trouble you to let me look at the phone. Donny and me, well, we don't cotton to having our pictures took, and I just want to be sure you weren't doing that.

"You wouldn't mind showing me what's on there, now, would you?"

My heart raced at his question. I was certain Karen was taking pictures to go with the recording she was making, and I didn't think either Calvin or Donny was going to look favorably on either activity.

"Well," Karen stretched her hand out for the phone, and began fiddling with it, as though she couldn't quite figure out how to display the photos she'd taken. "Dang! Just a sec, okay? I can't get this darned thing to work."

She fiddled a few more seconds. "Damnation!" Her hand flew up and covered her mouth. "Oh, my! Pardon my French, my mama would purely wash my mouth out with soap for that." She smiled at Calvin. "You won't be telling my mama, will you?"

Under normal circumstances, Karen's Southern belle act would have had me in stitches, but these circumstances weren't in any way normal.

All the while she was talking and smiling coyly at Calvin, she kept fumbling with the phone. Donny jiggled as he waited, nervous energy pouring out in each fidget and shuffle.

Calvin waited stoically, his face impassive, as Karen continued her fussing for another few seconds, drawing out the time as long as she dared.

"Got it!" she crowed triumphantly, just as though she hadn't been able to do exactly what Calvin asked in an instant.

She handed over the phone with a smile. "See, right there? I just took a picture of the cabin. It's the sweetest thing, out here where it's quiet and peaceful, don't you think? I wanted to show it to my boyfriend, 'cause it's just the kind of place I think we'd like to have.

"If I can ever talk him out of living in the city, of course."

Calvin took the phone and nimbly flipped through the images. I couldn't see the pictures from where I stood, but the expression on his face was enough. There weren't any pictures he cared about; certainly none of him or Donny, or anything else that might arouse his suspicions.

He slipped the phone in his pocket, and I saw Karen's right hand clench into a fist, hidden at her side. Outwardly she remained calm, her expression puzzled.

"Why would you take my phone?" She let a hint of outraged innocence color her words. "I *showed* you that there wasn't anything in there that concerned you! You asked me, and I showed you, nice as pie, and then you take my phone. Why would you do that?"

"Just bein' careful, ma'am." Now that he had the phone and was assured there weren't any pictures of him on it, he seemed to dismiss both of us. "Wouldn't want you doing anything foolish before we leave, now would we?"

He stood up and looked over the hood to where I stood on the other side of the vehicle. The door still hung open, but I had hesitated to climb in. I didn't want to be trapped in the car.

He waved toward his still-idling pickup. "Come on up in the truck. We'll carry you up close to the road, and then we'll leave the phone in the mailbox." He pulled it out of his pocket and waved it at her, as though reminding me he still had it. "You can pick it up and bring it back to your friend here."

He looked back down at Karen. "You just wait right here, okay? Your friend will be back in a jiffy, if you just do what we ask." He paused, then added, "Please."

As though that made it all right.

I looked at Karen, and she just stared back, like she was trying to say something. "It'll be fine," she assured me. "I'll wait right here, like they asked, until I hear them on the highway. Then I'll come and get you."

I swallowed hard and nodded. It wasn't like I had any choice.

I followed Calvin to the pickup, Donny bringing up the rear. The hair on the back of my neck stood up, imagining what he was doing where I couldn't see him, but I was afraid to turn around and look.

Calvin climbed into the driver's side, motioning for me to get in the passenger's side ahead of Donny. It would put me between them, a spot I didn't want to be in.

I hesitated.

"You need a boost?" Donny asked from close behind me.

That was enough motivation. I clambered onto the high running board and into the cab of the truck.

To my surprise, when Donny stepped up behind me, Calvin waved him away. "Git in the back, boy," he said. "No reason to crowd the lady here."

Donny didn't argue. He hopped into the bed of the pickup.

Calvin shoved the phone back in his pocket and put the truck in gear. He spun in a circle, sending another cloud of dust over Karen's SUV, and we bounced away down the driveway.

Chapter 27

THE DRIVEWAY SEEMED LONGER THAN I REMEM-
bered as we rumbled along. Adrenaline rushed through me,
a combination of anger and fear. I gripped the armrest, trying
to control the trembling of my hands.

I moved closer to the passenger door, gauging whether I
could jump, and if I did what would happen?

Best case, I'd get away and the two men would give up
and leave us alone. Yeah, and I'd find a pet unicorn and a
pot of gold in the woods.

More likely one of them would go back for Karen while
the other one chased me. I craned my head to look over my
shoulder at Donny in the bed of the pickup. Sure enough,
he was perched on the side and looked like he was ready to
leap out at any moment.

Bad idea.

"Just sit tight," Calvin said. "Couple minutes, you do
what we asked and we're gone, you're back in your fancy
car, and your friend's come home to meet you."

He glanced over at me and I caught something in his eyes. An intellect that didn't quite fit with the rest of him, perhaps. It disappeared so quickly I wasn't sure if it was real or my imagination. I couldn't trust that my mind wasn't playing tricks on me.

We rounded a curve, and I saw the mailbox about ten yards ahead. Calvin stopped the truck and motioned for me to get out. "Just wait there," he said, once I was on the ground.

Donny hopped out of the back and reached for the phone. He stood on the running board, the phone in one hand, the other arm wrapped around the open window frame. He stared at me as the truck pulled slowly down the driveway, a warning not to move.

The truck stopped at the end of the driveway and Donny jumped down. He shoved the phone in the mailbox and ran back to the truck. As soon as the door closed, Calvin gunned the engine.

It coughed once as gas flooded in, then the engine roared, the tires grabbed, and the truck fishtailed onto the dirt road in a cloud of dust.

I immediately ran to the mailbox, grabbed Karen's phone, and headed back toward the cabin at a dead run.

Karen had turned around and come down the driveway to meet me. I threw myself into the passenger side and returned her phone.

I panted, trying to get my breath after the headlong rush back down the driveway. "What *was* that?" I shouted. "*Who* was that?"

Fear bubbled to the surface and I let loose with a string of curses that would have made Bluebeard proud.

Karen stopped the car and stared at me. "Glory?"

"Sorry," I whispered, still trembling. "I just . . ." I tried to laugh, but it came out more like a little sob. "I think Bluebeard might be a bad influence."

Karen punched buttons on her phone, muttering to herself. After several seconds, she gave a triumphant shout. "Got it!"

"Got what?" I asked. I had seen Calvin's reaction to the contents of her phone. There was nothing there to celebrate.

"Confirmation of my upload," she said. "I've got pictures of both those guys—not good ones, they were too far away and I was in a hurry—but I have pictures stored on the station's servers."

"But, I saw you—how?" I couldn't form an actual sentence, but Karen seemed to get my meaning.

"I deleted the pictures from my phone," she said. "But I had already sent them to the server. I wasn't sure, the service really is bad out here, but I checked and they're there."

"We have their pictures."

"So, what now?" I could think of several things. Most of them involved getting the heck out of there.

But what about Beth and Everett?

"And what were those guys doing here in the first place?" My voice was steadier, and my hands had stopped shaking, but I still worried that the two men might come back.

"Seems to me," Karen answered, "that we have two choices. We stay and wait for your friends, or we run away."

She looked over at me and cocked one eyebrow. "Ever known me to run away?"

I shook my head. The only time I had seen Karen run away was when she split up with Riley. Technically she didn't leave, but I considered changing the locks while he was at sea as a way to avoid a confrontation when he came home.

She had always claimed that they had agreed to separate before he left. But I'd seen Riley when he came home, and he sure didn't act like a man who had agreed to a separation. He acted like a man who'd been locked out of his own house.

"Then we're staying." She backed slowly along the driveway, back to the clearing in front of the cabin, and shut off the engine.

In the silence that followed, I listened to the ticking of the engine cooling and the tapping of Karen's fingers on the display of her phone. She made occasional comments, talking to herself as she copied her photos and examined them for clues to the identities of our visitors.

After a few minutes, Karen reached over and flipped the power switch on the scanner. It crackled to life, clicking and squawking as it locked into a frequency, then settled into a low hum of carrier band.

"Those boys didn't want their picture taken, so I could just imagine how they'd have felt about a police scanner," she said.

"Or about having their conversation recorded," I answered.

"You saw that?"

"It was right there on the seat next to you."

"I was hoping you would and they wouldn't. Might have been kind of awkward the other way around." Sometimes Karen was a master of understatement.

I checked the time. Ten-thirty. Beth had said they'd be home by noon. I hoped they would be early.

While we waited, Karen filled me in on what little research she'd been able to do in her search for Anna.

"If my mother would let me," she grumbled, "I could track her down in a couple days. But Mom thinks we should be spending every spare minute together. Which means every minute, since Captain Clint has been tied up on base all day."

"So what you're saying is that this isn't getting you away from your mother after all?"

"No." Karen groaned. "But it gets worse. I think she's trying to wangle an invitation to dinner tonight. She's been dropping hints about wanting to meet my friends—besides you, of course—and getting to know the people that are important to me."

I didn't have any experience myself, but I still ventured an opinion. "That sounds like a pretty normal mom thing," I said.

"It is," she said. Her grudging agreement gave way to

irritation again. "But I don't want to do it this way, to have her and Clint at our Thursday dinner. Especially not the first week they're here. If we do, then they'll expect to be invited every week."

"I hadn't thought of that."

"I have." She groaned again. "And I've given her every excuse I could think of. It's not at my house. I'm not in charge. The hostess isn't expecting extra guests.

"None of it is sinking in. She finally said 'Well, it's Glory hosting. I'm sure she wouldn't mind if we tagged along.'"

"I probably wouldn't," I admitted. "I don't dislike your mother, and I'd include the two of them if it made your life easier."

Heaven knows, right now I would do just about anything that made Karen's life easier and her less of a Bridezilla. But I had an ace in the hole, and I offered it to Karen. "Just tell her that I had an emergency and I couldn't cook." I waved at our surroundings. "It's the truth."

Karen shook her head. "She'd just offer to help."

"Tell her my boyfriend is cooking, and remind her how rude it would be for you to invite them to someone else's home. Someone they don't even know."

Karen thought for a minute and nodded. "Good idea. Especially the part about me being rude. She was always nagging me about my rudeness. Because having an opinion while being female is apparently the definition of rude."

Several minutes later we heard the sound of another vehicle, quieter than the pickup. Adrenaline surged through me, and my heart raced. Beside me, Karen had one hand on the ignition and the other gripped the steering wheel.

We both held our breath, straining to see what was coming at us.

Chapter 28

THIS TIME IT REALLY WAS BETH AND EVERETT. Their usually immaculate hybrid looked dirty and tired, or as Memaw used to say, "Like it'd been rode hard and put away wet."

As soon as I recognized the car, I jumped out of the SUV and waved, making sure they knew it was me. After our latest encounter, I wasn't taking any chances.

The car stopped and Beth dragged herself out from behind the wheel. She looked thinner than when I'd seen her last, and she was already a slender woman. She wore an oversized man's flannel shirt and a long skirt that brushed the ground as she walked. In place of her usual sandals, she had beat-up sneakers, probably a concession to colder weather wherever they had been "up north."

I trotted across the clearing to meet her. "Hi, Beth. Listen, that's my friend that's getting married," I nodded toward Karen, "and she doesn't know anything about the quilt, so don't say anything, okay?"

"Sure, I guess," she said. "But I wish you'd tell us what this is all about."

Everett had climbed out of the passenger seat, rubbing his eyes as though he'd been napping while Beth drove. "Yeah, we kind of need to know what we're getting into."

I wanted to scream. They had insisted I come up here and get them. I hadn't understood their reasons, but I had agreed. And now they were getting cold feet? I fought back the anger at what they had already put me through, and forced myself to smile in what I hoped was a reassuring way.

"I'm really sorry," I said, "but I think the sheriff would rather tell you himself. And I don't think he'd take too kindly to me stepping on his toes like that."

I took Beth's arm and began to gently pull her toward the SUV. Everett followed along, hovering protectively but just out of reach, like he was afraid I was going to grab both of them and force them into the car.

I had to admit, the thought had crossed my mind.

"We probably ought to get going," I said, urging them along. "The sooner we get down to Keyhole Bay and you talk to Sheriff Hardy, the sooner you can come back home and relax."

Beth swiveled her head, taking in the cabin and the surrounding area. A shiver passed over her, just the faintest tremble, as she looked around.

Whatever she was planning when she got home, I could see that relaxing wasn't on the agenda. Both the Youngs were as tense as bowstrings, and it felt like they were close to snapping. I had to get them moving before that happened.

"I did have to close the store to come up here," I said apologetically, "so I do need to get back and open up again. I'm happy to help you out, but I really do need to get going."

I opened the back door of the SUV and helped Beth in, resisting the urge to shove her in and slam the door. Everett let himself in the other side, and I jumped in front, motioning Karen to drive.

She didn't need much urging. In fact, she was already rolling down the driveway while I was still getting my seat belt fastened.

Beth realized we were moving and yelled at me from the backseat. "There's stuff I need to do before we go," she shouted. "Wait!"

But we had already reached the end of the driveway and Karen turned down the narrow dirt road, going as fast as she dared over the washboard surface.

A couple minutes later we turned south on the highway, and I breathed a sigh of relief. We had Beth and Everett in the car, no one was following us, and we were headed for Keyhole Bay at slightly over the posted speed limit.

"This won't take long," I assured Beth, turning around in the front seat to look at her. "We'll go get this taken care of, get it out of the way, and you'll be back home just quick as you please."

I crossed my fingers, but I wasn't really lying. As far as I knew, the sheriff just wanted to ask them a few questions; and when he got their answers, I knew he'd have to let them go. It happened all the time; somebody got caught up in something bad through no fault of their own, and the sheriff got suspicious.

But Boomer was a fair man, and as soon as he believed you were innocent, you would walk away. I knew; I'd done it myself a couple times. This wasn't any different.

It was clear that Beth didn't entirely believe me, but she didn't offer any additional protest. Instead she leaned her head back against the seat and closed her eyes. The message was clear: she was through talking to me.

I was just as happy that she was. I didn't want to argue with her, I didn't want her to spill the beans to Karen about the wedding quilt, and I wasn't going to tell her about the dead bodies on her property. So there really wasn't anything for us to talk about.

The rest of the drive to Boomer's office was even quieter

than the drive to north county had been. I had introduced Karen and the Youngs when we first got on the highway, but they had not spoken to each other once they acknowledged the introduction.

I wondered if Karen still thought this was better than spending the morning with her mother.

Fifty silent minutes later, Karen pulled into the parking lot of the sheriff's station and stopped, but she didn't shut off the engine. "I've got some research I need to do," she said. "Just call me if you get through here before I get back."

I understood what she was doing. She didn't want to walk into the sheriff's station with her recording and her pictures. She would take them and store them away before she came back. And she might actually stop and do some research into Anna while she was at it.

Either way, she was leaving me with the Youngs at the sheriff's station, and she expected me to call her with an update the minute there was any news.

Maybe I should have tried to convince her to turn her possible evidence over to Boomer. It might relate to his case, after all. But I knew without asking that it would be futile.

I got out and waited for Beth and Everett. I pointed them toward the door and followed behind them into the station.

Chapter 29

TAKING THE YOUNGS IN TO THE SHERIFF WAS THE
perfect definition of an anticlimax. After all the drama
that went into getting them there, it was all downhill,
excitement-wise.

I told the deputy at the desk that I had a couple people
who needed to talk to Sheriff Hardy. She took their names
and disappeared for a few minutes.

When she returned, she asked us to take a seat and indicated the row of hard plastic chairs along one wall. I
remembered those chairs from the night Bobby Freed had
been arrested. They were the most uncomfortable furniture ever created.

I stood.

I think Beth and Everett would have left if I hadn't been
there and they hadn't been stranded without transporta-
tion. I could walk home if I had to, or call any one of a
couple dozen people to pick me up. They were nearly an
hour from home, and they didn't know anyone in town.

They waited, and so did I.

Boomer took his own sweet time coming out, like he didn't have a care in the world and he knew the Youngs would wait for however long he took.

He emerged in about ten minutes, looked around, and gestured to the Youngs. "You must be the Youngs," he said, smiling and extending his hand.

Beth took his hand and shook it like she was afraid not to, and Everett did the same. As timid and retiring as Beth was, Everett was even more so. Normally friendly and a little shy, today he was so withdrawn, he was nearly catatonic.

"I apologize for keeping you waiting," he said, gesturing for them to come in the back with him. "I was on the phone and couldn't break away."

He turned back to me and his smile hardened. "I'll talk to you a little later, Miss Martine." I was dismissed.

I watched the door close behind him as he followed the Youngs into the inner sanctum of the station. I was left standing alone in the empty lobby, Boomer's warning ringing in my ears.

I escaped while I could. Boomer hadn't told me to wait for him, and I didn't see any reason to put that restriction on myself. As I saw it, I had done my duty and there wasn't any reason for me to hang around.

I went out the front door, turning north when I reached the sidewalk. A chilly breeze rattled the fronds of the palm trees in the parking lot and raised goose bumps on my arms, reminding me I'd left my jacket in Karen's car. I hurried along for a couple blocks before I pulled out my phone and called Karen.

"You're through already?" She sounded incredulous.

"I am. But Boomer just started with Beth and Everett. He kept us waiting, and then he took them into the back of the station and made it clear I wasn't included."

"Where are you?"

"A couple blocks away, headed toward the library. My

jacket's in your car, and I'd like to get in out of this wind, but I didn't want to hang around the station. Where are you?"

"I'm on my way there now," she said. "I copied the pictures and the audio to my backup. I'm not sure what I'll do with them, but it seems like a good idea to keep them safe."

"Meet you there."

I hung up and covered the last three blocks to the county library at a fast clip. At least it warmed me up a little.

The gray brick building represented the largess of a nineteenth-century philanthropist. It sat in a place of honor in the downtown city park, an unchanged counterpoint to the waves of development that washed across Florida. I ran up the shallow stone steps to the entrance and tugged on the ornate wooden door. It swung open slowly, several hundred pounds of antique wood moving on well-oiled brass hinges.

The original brass coat hooks lined the vestibule. Library regulars, and there were several, had their favorite hooks. I spotted the forest green jacket of Naomi Parks, who ran a small motel out near Frank's Foods, and Linda Miller's favorite Fair Isle cardigan. She must have finished her last fat novel and been in the market for a new one.

Just then Linda herself came through the inner doors, a stack of books in her arms. "Hi, Glory!" She set the books on the shelf above her sweater and gave me a hug. "What are you up to? Shouldn't you be working?"

It would have taken too long to explain, so I just told her I was running a couple errands with Karen and we were supposed to meet back here. She naturally assumed it was wedding related and we chatted for a couple minutes about the upcoming event.

We were soon interrupted by Karen's arrival, and Linda said she'd better get back to the Grog Shop. "Guy will pitch a fit if I don't get back and get his lunch," she said with a chuckle.

We all knew better. More likely, Guy would have her

lunch ready when she returned. After almost thirty years of marriage, that man still adored her.

Karen watched her walk out the door and turned to me. "If Riley and I can do half that well, I'll be happy."

I nodded in agreement.

"So what now?" I asked her. "The Youngs are going to be with the sheriff a while. Beth has my number, so I guess she'll call when they're through." I shook my head. "I don't know what they'll expect me to do.

"They demanded I come and get them, but we didn't talk about how they intend to get home. This is Thursday, and I do have a business to run, and a bunch of other commitments."

My voice rose as I thought about the corner they'd backed me into. "Do they think I am going to just drop everything and run back to north county to take them home? Did they even think about that?"

"Down, girl! We'll figure it out. Maybe they have friends down here they can stay with, or someone else who can drive them home. They're adults, they can take care of themselves. And if they can't, well, that's kind of Boomer's problem, wouldn't you say? He was the one that wanted them here as soon as possible."

She had a point, but I wasn't ready to calm down just yet. "But what if Boomer doesn't take care of it? What then? I'm the one that got them down here."

"You did them a favor, one they asked you to do. There's nothing to gain by worrying about it now." She reached for the inner door. "Now let's go see if we can find something about the elusive Anna before I have to go face my mother."

The library's main room boasted a high ceiling and a mezzanine level, with a third-floor reading room. The children's area took up a corner of the main floor, under the watchful eye of the head librarian. Popular fiction ringed the walls, and low cases for periodicals surrounded the central reading area. Along the back wall, a few computer terminals stood in carrels, available for public use.

As we climbed the dark wood staircase to the second floor, I trailed my hand along the intricately carved banister. The building had stood in this same spot for a hundred years, lovingly tended by a staff who cared about the books and the library itself. The care they took was evident in the condition of each post and rail.

The reference shelves ran all the way around the mezzanine at right angles to the walls, with reading desks spaced along the railing overlooking the first floor.

Karen made a beeline for a shelf halfway along the left side and started running a finger along the spines of high school yearbooks shelved there.

"We know Sly graduated in about 1962, give or take," she said, pulling books off the shelf. "So Anna, whoever she is, is probably no more than two or three years different. Younger, I would guess, wouldn't you?"

She gestured for me to hold my arms out and piled a half dozen yearbooks on them, then took another group off the shelf for herself. I followed her to a reading desk, setting my stack of books alongside hers.

"So we are looking for a white woman named Anna somewhere between 1961 and 1966 at the outside, most likely in '63 or '64." She shifted the stacks, separating the books for '63 and '64.

"One thing you might check," I suggested, "would be the Army enlistments for those two years. Sly did say he enlisted, and I'll bet you could find some records of exactly when."

"That might help narrow down the search."

"It might," Karen agreed as she sorted, "but since I don't have those records here, and these yearbooks *are* here, let's just focus on them for now."

I pulled over a second chair; we each took a book from 1963 and turned to the senior pictures. As I started turning pages, my heart fell. There were hundreds of black-and-white pictures, and that was just in one of the books for that year.

How did we hope to find a single girl among the hundreds of possibilities?

Karen sighed heavily, clearly thinking the same thing.

"We won't have time to go through these more than once," she said, gesturing to the daunting stack in front of us, "so we better have a system."

She pulled a camera from her bag and set it on the table between us. "Anyone named Ann, or Anna, or something similar, just take a picture of the page and move on. Faster than writing it down, and we can worry about sorting through the pictures later."

She set a notepad next to the camera. "We should keep track of which schools and which years we look at," she said. "In case we don't get through them all today."

There was something odd about the pictures, and it took me a couple minutes to realize what it was. "Karen," I whispered. We were alone on the mezzanine, but I still felt the need to whisper in the library.

"Yeah?" She looked up from the page she had just photographed as she turned the page.

"Everyone in these pictures," I continued whispering, "they're, well, *white*. Doesn't that seem odd?"

As soon as the words were out of my mouth, I realized what I was saying. "I just reminded you the other day that the schools were still segregated back then, didn't I? I forget how much has changed. I know we talked about how Sly and Anna couldn't get married, but it almost didn't seem real, you know?"

Karen nodded and gestured to one of the stacks of yearbooks on the desk. "Exactly. If you want to see Sly's picture, he's probably in one of those."

I nodded and went back to scanning the book in front of me. It was amazing how many variations of Ann I found. There was Ann and Anne and Anna, of course, but there were plenty of others. Annabelle, Annabeth, AnnMarie, Mary Ann, Annamaria, and even a Gloryanna. I dutifully photographed each one and moved on, aware of the afternoon slipping away.

I should have turned off the ringer on my cell phone, but I left it on. I expected Beth to call anytime and want a ride home, or something, and I didn't want to miss her call.

Not that I wanted to have to tell her no, but not talking to her was at least as stressful as dealing with the situation and having it done with.

I finished the first yearbook and started to reach for another, then stopped and took the 1961 yearbook off the stack Karen had pointed to. I was curious to see what Sly looked like as a young man.

I flipped to the index and ran my finger along the column of names, stopping at "Benjamin, Sylvester." There were several pages listed, and I turned to the first one. It was a grainy shot, a group of young men—boys, really—standing around a 1940s sedan. The caption said it was the auto shop class and listed their names. Sly's was among them, but the photo was too small and indistinct to make out much.

I looked at two more photos, similarly hard to see, before I found the individual photos in the class listings. I found Sly in the "Junior Class" section. His smile was broad and it was easy to see the man he had become in the picture of the boy he had been.

I put the volume back on the stack and took the 1962 book. He would have been a senior, and his photo would be bigger and easier to see. But I wasn't prepared for just how much I did see.

Chapter 30

I FOUND THE FORMAL SENIOR PORTRAIT, BUT THE young man who seemed to glare at the camera was a far cry from the cheerful boy of the previous year.

His hair was longer and wilder, a defiant burst of dark curls that formed a halo around his head. The broad smile had disappeared, replaced with an intent scowl that spoke of simmering anger. He looked like someone who expected trouble, maybe even welcomed it.

It was a side of Sly I had never seen.

I stared at the picture for several minutes, trying to imagine what had caused the change.

My guess would be the woman we were searching for, and once again I questioned the wisdom of our investigation. Had the intervening years worn away that anger? Or had they merely buried it where it could be resurrected by our interference?

Karen realized I had stopped turning pages. She slid over to see what I'd found. She glanced at the book, then took a second look. She froze for several seconds, staring at the picture, as though finally understanding the implications of what we were doing.

"Oh. My." Her voice was soft, without the usual self-assurance. "Oh," she repeated.

"Exactly," I said. "You still think this is a good idea? Messing around in Sly's life just to provide you with a diversion?"

"I, uh, I'm not sure," she confessed. She stood up and started replacing the books on the shelves. "I need to think about this."

She left the 1962 yearbook, open to Sly's picture, to the last. She closed it gently and placed it back in its appointed spot on the shelf.

Karen gathered up her camera and the notepad, and we left the library in silence. It wasn't until we had buckled ourselves into her SUV that either of us spoke.

"I'll drop you at home," she said. "I've got some things to do, and I have to spend some time with my mother if I want to escape for dinner tonight."

She left me at the front door of Southern Treasures, with a promise that I'd see her and Riley later.

A sign on the door told customers that we were closed for the day. I took advantage of the closure to go next door and check on Chloe.

Lighthouse was busy, a mid-afternoon rush of locals with a few tourists sprinkled in for good measure. Chloe was making coffee drinks and chatting up customers with her usual cheery attitude, and I hung back from the counter and watched until the line of customers had been taken care of.

"How are you doing?" I asked when I reached the counter. From my observation, she was doing very well indeed. But I wanted to know what she thought.

"Good," she said. "We're staying busy, and I have enough stock to last the rest of the day."

I glanced at the case. There were a few pastries left, and

some quiche, as well as several loaves of bread, cake slices, and half a cheesecake.

"I'm impressed that you're staying on top of the baking with Miss Pansy gone." I spoke softly, my words muffled by the soft hum of conversation at the tables around the room. "You know, Bradley gave me her recipes. They're in my safe."

I glanced around. No one was paying any attention to us. "I don't own the place yet, and I didn't feel right about opening them up. But if you need them to keep things going, I'd be happy to give them to you."

Chloe hesitated. She glanced around the shop, then motioned for me to come around the counter.

I followed her to the doorway between the shop and the kitchen, wondering just what she was being so secretive about.

Once she was sure we couldn't be overheard, she looked at me sheepishly and bit her lip.

"I have a confession," she said.

My brain raced. What now? Didn't I have enough on my plate without trouble from my almost-new employee?

I kept my expression neutral and nodded for her to go on.

"I don't need the recipes," she blurted.

I probably looked as surprised as I felt. Pansy had guarded those recipes like they were the gold at Fort Knox. She carried them in her head, not trusting them to be written down where someone else could see them.

"I've been watching her for years," Chloe continued. "She doesn't know, but over time I have managed to figure out most everything she makes. I'd never tell her; the secret recipes mean a lot to her, but so far nobody has noticed any difference."

I thought for a moment. I'd had a couple things from Lighthouse in the days since Pansy went in the hospital. Everything had been excellent, just like always.

"You're right," I said. "I didn't notice, and I knew what was going on."

"See? But you can't tell Miss Pansy! Promise?"

"Of course. I agree completely. That's a very important thing to her. She didn't even let Bradley see the recipes; she gave him a sealed envelope to give to me."

Chloe grinned, relief evident in the lift of her shoulders. "Thanks, Glory. I knew I'd have to tell you and I wasn't real sure how you'd feel about it. I'm glad you're okay with it."

I glanced out to the shop where happy customers were sipping coffee and enjoying the food Chloe had prepared. "I'm more than okay," I told her. "I'm glad to know you can keep things going while we get this sale settled, and I don't have to worry about what kind of food we're putting out in the meantime."

She glanced out at the shop again. A couple of the customers were leaving. "I better get back out there," she said. "If you're really okay?"

I patted her shoulder. "You're doing a great job, Chloe. And I really am okay."

I watched her hurry out front in time to exchange good-byes with the departing customers and wish them a good afternoon. It was what every shopkeeper should do, make their customers feel like valued guests, but not everyone could do it with Chloe's apparent sincerity.

I tried to imagine running Lighthouse without her, and was instantly grateful I didn't have to go there. It would have made the entire enterprise a lot more scary.

Taking advantage of my freedom, I crossed the street to Beach Books. Jake's offer to cook tonight was one big reason I had free time this afternoon, and the least I could do was check in and see if there was anything I could do to help.

Before I went inside, I slipped my phone out of my purse and checked, just in case. Still no word from Beth.

Jake greeted me warmly, reassuring me that dinner was under control. "I decided against Southwest," he said. "Lasagna's ready for the oven, and there's salad and garlic bread. Nothing fancy, but it was a favorite at the firehouse."

In the last few months, Jake had finally started to tell me about his life before Keyhole Bay. He'd been a firefighter and a fire captain in California until his retirement on a partial disability.

Little things, like cooking for the crew, and big things, like the tragedy that killed one of his men and caused the injuries that forced his retirement. It was a sign of our growing connection.

"I can't begin to thank you for that."

He leered at me, and suggested I might find a way. Fortunately we were alone, but I think I blushed anyway.

"So how was your trip up north?" he asked.

The question brought me up short. Had it really only been a few hours since Karen and I had driven up to get Beth and Everett? So much had happened, it seemed like days ago.

"Well, I think we might have met some of the Youngs' neighbors. You'll probably hear the story again tonight, but I know you won't want to wait," I teased.

I launched into the story of Calvin and Donny and our encounter at the cabin. As I talked, Jake's face grew darker, and a frown pulled his eyebrows down.

"And what did Boo—um, Sheriff Hardy—have to say about all this?"

I looked down, not able to meet his gaze. "I didn't tell him," I said quietly.

"What?" Jake acted as though he hadn't heard me.

"Ididn'ttellhim," I mumbled again.

Jake put his fingers under my chin and tilted my head up until he was looking me in the eye. "You did what?" he asked again.

"I didn't tell him."

"Some strange men accost you out in the middle of nowhere, in a place where dead bodies were found just a few days before, they steal Karen's phone, and they force you into their truck"—he paused for a deep breath—"*and you didn't tell the sheriff?*" He shook his head. "Are you two crazy?"

"I didn't get a chance to."

I tried to explain. "They didn't hurt us, just scared us a little. And they didn't even take the phone, they just checked to make sure there weren't any pictures and then gave it back.

"When we got to the station, Karen didn't stick around, and when Boomer finally came out, he just wanted to talk to Beth and Everett, and he made it clear I wasn't invited to join them."

I stood a little taller, and my voice steadied. "By that time, I figured I was better off getting out of there. Besides, what good would it have done? He probably would have made me talk to that self-important woman at the desk, and if she believed me, I would still be sitting there in some tiny room waiting for Boomer to ask me a million questions."

I took a deep breath and went on. "Besides that, they would have demanded that Karen turn over her pictures and the recording she made. I think you know how well that would have gone over."

"You still should have told him. And I thought you said there weren't any pictures. So what was there for Karen to turn over to the sheriff?"

I explained how she had uploaded the pictures to the station's server before removing them from her phone, and about her little digital recorder. "She got everything they said to her."

"Including them forcing you to go with them. That's evidence of at least attempted kidnapping, Glory."

"Maybe."

I didn't want to talk to Boomer, and Jake knew it. He let the subject drop for now, but I knew he'd come back to it later.

Chapter 31

I GOT THE EVIL EYE FROM BLUEBEARD WHEN I finally returned to Southern Treasures. He was used to having company all day, and he made his feelings about being left alone quite clear.

"Out all night, out all day," he chided. "Where have you been? I'm starved!"

He clearly wasn't starved. I had given him a breakfast of fruit and shredded-wheat biscuits before I left, and there were still several of the biscuits in his bowl. What he was, was spoiled.

"No you're not," I told him. I gave him a bit of apple and a piece of banana in penance for my absence. "You can have a treat, but you are not starving."

He muttered as he ate the fruit offering, the words indistinct to anyone who didn't know him as well as I did. "Language, Bluebeard!"

The muttering abated, but it didn't stop. It was part of his game, and I let him have his fun. I had become accustomed to his language and he was usually good when there were customers in the shop. But he expected a reaction and I gave him one.

"Bluebeard!"

He stomped back into his cage, still muttering as he went.

It had been a long and stressful day, and it would be a late night. I started upstairs for a nap.

From below I heard Uncle Louis's voice clearly. "People aren't always who you think they are."

TO MY SURPRISE, I SLEPT SOUNDLY FOR AN HOUR. I had fully expected the phone to ring the minute I closed my eyes. Neither the store phone nor my personal cell showed any missed calls or messages, but I still checked voice mail on both, just in case.

Nothing.

I took a quick shower and dressed in jeans and a polo shirt. I called Jake to double-check if there was anything I could bring for dinner, but he said he had it all under control.

I took him at his word, but I still carefully packed up the pecan pie I'd baked the night before.

Fifteen minutes later, I was at his door. The instant he opened the door, the mingled aromas of tomato, cheese, and herbs hit me. My stomach grumbled, and I realized I hadn't really stopped to eat anything all day.

Jake helped me out of my jacket, and I took it and my purse to the bedroom. I told myself there was no significance to the action—everyone's coats and jackets would end up thrown on the bed when they arrived. But I did put my purse in "my" drawer of the dresser.

Back in the kitchen, Jake was laying out an appetizer of Caprese skewers. Grape tomatoes, mozzarella balls, and fresh basil leaves on frilled toothpicks, sprinkled with olive oil, balsamic vinegar, and a touch of sea salt and black pepper.

I popped one in my mouth and bit down. The tart tomato juice combined with the acid of the vinegar and the earthy flavor of fresh basil, all mellowed by the creamy mozzarella.

My taste buds, and my stomach, thanked me and demanded more. I quickly complied.

"Are those okay?" Jake asked. His back was turned as he pulled a bubbling baking dish from the oven.

"Mmm-hmmm," I answered, my mouth full.

He set the dish on the stove top and turned to look at me. He broke into a grin. "I'll take that as a yes," he said.

I reluctantly left the skewers behind and helped Jake set the table for dinner. When it was just the two of us we ate in the kitchen; but for the Thursday night crew we needed more room than the kitchen table provided.

In the living room, Jake had pushed the furniture back. We pulled the dining table into the middle of the room and opened it up to add a leaf.

"Expecting a crowd?" I asked when Jake added the second leaf, taking it from a square for four to a rectangle that would hold eight comfortably.

"Just six, I think. But you never know."

"What do you mean, 'you never know'?"

"Riley called early this morning. He said his future in-laws were still making noises about joining us for dinner."

"How early?"

"Probably nine, ten o'clock," he said as he headed back into the kitchen to bring the placemats and plates.

I followed him, coming back with silverware and a stack of glasses. "Then I think we have it covered. Karen and I were talking about it, and she was going to play the manners card.

"You know, 'It's just *rude* to invite extra guests to a dinner party without checking with the host first.'

"That's one her mother will understand."

"But Riley did check with me," Jake said. "So that argument won't stand up."

"It will if Riley doesn't *tell* them he called you. And Karen will make sure he doesn't."

Jake shrugged. "Whatever works. I planned on leftovers for the freezer, so there's plenty of food either way. But Riley and I both agreed that it wasn't our place—either of us—to decide who to invite or not invite to Thursday dinners."

I filed that thought away for later discussion. Since Riley and Karen were getting married, and Jake and I were a couple even though we hadn't made any long-term plans, maybe it was time to make our Thursday get-togethers officially the three couples.

We finished setting the table, tossed the salad, and made a quick homemade vinegar-and-oil dressing. We'd just slid the garlic bread under the broiler when the doorbell rang.

As hostess, I answered the door while Jake watched the bread. It was Riley and Karen, without Catherine and Clint.

"Rude was a great idea," Karen said, giving me a hug. "Mom completely understood. Of course that only works for this week, but at least it's something."

"Next week is Felipe's turn," I said, thinking out loud, "and the week after is yours. Maybe you should just suggest that she meet everyone at your house in two weeks."

Karen made a face like she'd just bitten into a lemon.

"You know you're going to have to do it sometime," I said. "You might as well do it on your home turf."

"Maybe," she said. But she didn't sound convinced.

"So, have you heard from Beth?" she asked, turning the conversation away from her mother.

"No, and I'm starting to worry."

"Well, stop it. They're adults. You're not responsible for them. I bet they didn't even say thanks for you coming all the way up there, did they?"

"I don't know if *thanks* was the right response. I shoved them in the car and we carried them down to the sheriff. They didn't seem real grateful at the time."

Riley had disappeared into the kitchen while we were talking, and after we deposited the coats in the bedroom, we went in search of the two men. We found them deep in a serious discussion that stopped abruptly the minute we walked in.

I immediately realized what was going on. Riley wanted to surprise Karen with a honeymoon destination, as she'd told her mother. Riley thought California might be nice, and since Jake had lived most of his life on the West Coast, Riley had asked him for advice.

"Did you think any more about what we found at the library?" I asked Karen, drawing her attention away from the men.

She helped herself to one of the Caprese skewers and then motioned that her mouth was full. It was her way of ducking the question she didn't want to answer.

She was saved by the doorbell.

I went to let Ernie and Felipe in, and Karen followed along, still munching.

There were hugs all around, and exclamations over the smells drifting out from the kitchen. I shooed the new arrivals toward the kitchen while I ferried the last armload of coats to the bedroom.

By the time I returned, the crew was already carrying food to the table: the steaming pan of lasagna, a large bowl of green salad, the Caprese skewers, and a towering platter of garlic bread fresh from the oven.

We settled around the table and Jake brought out a couple bottles of wine. He poured samples for everyone, explaining that these were wines from one of the places he'd lived, a small town north of San Francisco in California's wine country.

I watched Riley's face out of the corner of my eye as Jake talked about the wineries. He was trying to watch Karen without being obvious, looking for her reaction to the talk of wine country. So that was definitely what he was up to.

Jake passed glasses around and answered a couple questions, but he didn't press the point. He'd seen Karen's reaction, and so had I. The idea appealed to her. That was all Riley needed to know.

We spent the next hour talking about food. The Caprese was well received, and I gave away one of Jake's secrets: he'd started a container garden in his sunporch and grown his own basil and grape tomatoes.

"It might not be traditional Southern," I said, "but the basil and tomatoes were grown right here in Keyhole Bay."

Which meant Ernie had to have a tour of the garden. He'd always had a few pots of fresh herbs in his kitchen—any real cook would, he said—but lately he'd been thinking about adding some other plants.

The two of them returned a few minutes later, Ernie looking like a little kid just bursting to unwrap a new toy.

Felipe rolled his eyes as his partner folded his tall frame into his chair. "You're going to want to turn our lanai into a truck garden, aren't you?"

"No, *cher*. Just a few pots of this and that. Really, you'll hardly notice." He squeezed Felipe's arm. "You'll see."

Felipe smiled indulgently. When it came to food, he'd never been able to say no to anything his partner wanted. He enjoyed Ernie's cooking too much.

While they were gone, the conversation had segued from the food to local gossip and personal news. Felipe asked about the Lighthouse plans, and I filled them in on the latest developments.

"Bradley even brought me Miss Pansy's recipes," I said. "She had sealed them in an envelope before she gave them to him, signed her name across the seal, and instructed him to give them directly to me. He looked more relieved to get rid of that envelope than he did about the contracts."

"Have you heard back from the bank?" Ernie asked.

I shook my head. "Buddy McKenna was very positive when he reviewed the proposal." I nodded to Jake and

Ernie. "Thank you both for your help with that. I'm very grateful."

"Anything for you, *ma chère*," Ernie said with an exaggerated New Orleans drawl. "Anything at all." He glanced at Felipe, who was shaking his head. "Well, *almost* anything," he quickly amended, drawing a laugh from everyone at the table.

"So he's going to approve it?" Felipe asked.

"He doesn't have the final say. He said it was a good proposal and the numbers more than justified what I was asking for, but it has to go to the loan committee, and they don't meet until tomorrow.

"And even then, he said I probably won't hear until after the weekend." I was twisting my napkin into knots, and I dropped it on the table. "Not like I'm nervous or anything."

Riley jumped in to reassure me. "Normal reaction, Glory. Do you remember when I was trying to buy *Ocean Breeze*? I about lost my mind waiting to find out about the loan.

"I think that was the time I decked Bobby for some fool thing he did, and my dad said it was his own damned fault for crossing me while that was going on.

"First and last time I got away with thumping on one of my little brothers."

I did remember that. It was before he married Karen the first time, and the complications of buying the boat and setting up his fishing business very nearly scuttled the wedding. Which was part of the reason we'd ended up on the beach with a JP.

I very nearly told him that at least I wasn't planning my own wedding at the same time that I was worrying about the loan. I didn't because it suddenly felt awkward to make a direct reference to my wedding when I was sitting next to Jake, especially after my conversation with Karen last week put the thought in my mind.

Felipe and Ernie repeated their offer of the previous week, and I graciously declined. "There aren't many people

I'd trust, and you're two of them. But I've thought about it and thought about it, and your friendship means too much to me to take a chance that anything could go wrong and damage that."

"It isn't just you guys, either," Jake said. "I've offered, and so has Sly. She's turned us both down."

"Speaking of Sly," Ernie said, "how's he doing? I haven't seen him in a while."

"Seems fine," Jake said. "We had dinner with him Tuesday night. He'd finished a restoration on an old Studebaker, found a part he'd been looking for for years, and wanted to celebrate."

Karen shifted uncomfortably in her chair, and Ernie turned to look at her. "Something wrong, girl?"

"I don't know," she said slowly. "I don't think so, but I started something and now I'm not sure if it's the right thing or not.

"It's kind of a long story, you sure you want to hear it?"

Jake picked up the wine bottle and passed it around the table. "Let's freshen our glasses, and I'll take the plates to the kitchen," he said. "Then we definitely want to hear it."

Ernie helped Jake and me whisk the dirty dishes and leftovers into the kitchen. I knew what was coming, and I told them just to leave everything on the counter. I didn't want to give Karen time to change her mind about sharing her latest investigation.

We returned to the living room, settled into our chairs, and the men turned expectantly to Karen. She looked at me, her expression pleading for my help in explaining what she'd done.

"Go ahead," I said, waving her on. "This was your idea."

"Okay," she said, fidgeting. She didn't know where to begin, and if I didn't give her a little push, we could be there all night.

"Do you all remember," I cut in, "the day Karen and Riley told us they were getting married again? The Fourth of July? Sly was with us that night, and he told us about the girl he almost married."

Nods all around.

"Well, Karen thought we should try to find this woman and find out what happened to her."

They all turned to look at Karen.

"And did you?" Trust Felipe to cut to the chase.

"It hasn't been that easy," Karen said, finally speaking up. "We didn't know much except a first name and a guess as to how old she was. And that she was white, of course."

"But why?" Riley looked genuinely puzzled.

Karen sighed and looked around the table. "My mother was coming, the wedding plans were making me crazy, the station manager decided to do me a big 'favor,'"—she wiggled her fingers, making air quotes around the word—"and give me the month off.

"I wanted a distraction."

"You couldn't read a book?" Ernie drawled.

"I don't know why I came up with this," she said. "All I can say is that it seemed like a good idea at the time. It had nothing to do with me or the wedding. It was just a puzzle that I could try to solve, and maybe if I found out something about her, I could share it with Sly."

She waved her hands in front of her face, brushing away the startled reactions. "Not if it was anything bad," she said quickly. "I wouldn't ever tell him anything unless I thought it would make him feel better about what happened to her."

"I would hope not," Riley said.

"It started out as a lark, just something to do when I needed a break from all the wedding stuff. But then this afternoon, well"—she gestured to me—"you tell them."

"This afternoon we met at the library after I left the Youngs at the sheriff's station."

"Sheriff's station?" Riley said. He turned to Karen. "You didn't tell me anything about going to the sheriff's station."

"I didn't go," she protested. "Glory went."

"And she didn't tell Boomer anything she should have," Jake said darkly. "But we'll come back to that." He waved at me. "Go on."

"Karen suggested we take a look at the yearbook collection, see if we could find anyone fitting what we knew about Sly's girlfriend."

"And did you?" Felipe again.

Karen shook her head. "No. And yes. We found so many possibilities in a single year that it purely overwhelmed us. But that wasn't the real problem."

The four men swiveled back to me, waiting for the rest of the story.

"I found Sly's photo," I said. I knew that wasn't enough of an answer. I took a swig of wine, trying to swallow the lump in my throat at the memory of those pictures.

"Actually, I found several. Some clubs and so on, and his picture from his junior year. He looked a lot like the man we all know; he was smiling and he looked happy. You could see in his eyes that he was the same guy.

"But then I looked at the picture in the next year, when he was a senior. It had to have been taken just a few weeks before he left Keyhole Bay and enlisted; he told me he joined the Army right after he finished high school."

I hesitated, and Jake put his arm around my shoulders. "So what was wrong with that picture? Why does it have you so upset?"

"It was the way he looked, Jake. Angry. Like he was expecting trouble, or maybe even looking for trouble. Something had taken away his smile, but it wasn't just that. He had turned into someone else in the year between those two pictures. Someone we don't even know."

"It wasn't even the anger," Karen said. "It was like he was looking out at the world and daring anyone to tell him what to do."

"And yet that's exactly what he did," Jake said. "He let the world tell him what to do, and he did it and never looked back." He shrugged. "Not to say I wouldn't have done the same thing, given the times."

"How do we know that?" Karen asked. "He might have looked for Anna, he just didn't tell us. And maybe he didn't find anything. He's not a trained investigator or anything. All we know is that he hasn't seen her since he left Keyhole Bay to join the Army."

"What are you going to do about it now?" Riley wrapped a protective arm around her and spoke softly. "Are you going to give up on your search?"

"I really don't know. All I know is that it changed from a diversion for me into something a lot more complicated. It's Sly's life we're talking about, and it isn't my place to interfere.

"The problem now is that after just a few hours of looking, *I'm* real curious to know what happened to Anna. I wonder where she went and what she did, whether she married someone else, and if she even remembers Sly. I don't know how you could forget your first love"—she reached up and squeezed Riley's hand that rested on her shoulder—"but what if she did?"

She sighed. "Whatever I do, it isn't my place to carry any tales to Sly."

Chapter 32

I HELPED JAKE CLEAR THE REST OF DINNER AND serve dessert in the lull that followed Karen's story.

"I didn't plan a fancy dessert," Jake explained as we carried dishes to the table. "Since I was pinch-hitting, I'd planned spumoni ice cream and cookies from Lighthouse. But Glory brought a pecan pie.

"I don't know how well that goes with lasagna and garlic bread, but I know which one I'd rather have."

"You never did explain why you ended up cooking tonight," Ernie said. "Not that I'm complaining, mind you." He patted his stomach and grinned. "That was a mighty fine meal."

"It was my fault," I said, sitting down and taking a bite of pie. "I had an emergency and had to go up north this morning."

"Does this have something to do with the trip to the sheriff's station?" Riley asked, looking at Karen.

She nodded, but left it up to me to explain.

"I told you last week about my suppliers up north that flaked on me. Well, they seem to have gotten themselves in some trouble, and they asked me to help out."

"I don't remember anything about that," Riley said.

"You and Karen were already gone. You had an early trip the next morning, so you left before I told these guys about my problems with my quilt lady." I hoped the explanation would remind the others why I hadn't told the story in front of Karen.

"Turned out they'd gone to visit family. At least that's what they told me. In the meantime, the sheriff found two bodies near their cabin, and he really wanted to talk to the people who lived there.

"I found out about the bodies when I went up there with Karen. Her station manager called while we were at dinner and I just went along for company, but Boomer wasn't inclined to believe me. Especially when he found out I knew them."

"With your history, can you blame him?" Felipe said.

"No, I get it. But I've stayed out of his business for a year and a half. You'd think that would buy me a little credibility.

"Anyway, I talked to Beth. I didn't tell her why she had to talk to Boomer, just that he would track her down if she didn't come back. She said they would, but only if I picked them up. So Karen and I went and picked them up this morning."

I stopped, and Karen didn't add anything, but Jake wasn't letting me off the hook. "There was a bit more than that, Glory." He didn't look happy. "A bit you really ought to share with Boomer."

"We ran into a couple of the neighbors while we were there." Karen jumped in before I could say anything more.

I looked at her. The reason she spoke up was written across her face: she hadn't told Riley about our adventure.

I wasn't about to be the one who told him.

"Yeah," I agreed. "Couple guys pulled up while we

were there. I think they were looking for Everett, but I wasn't real sure. They were only there a few minutes, though."

Jake started to say something, but I caught his hand under the table and squeezed. Hard. I'm not sure he knew why exactly, but he got the message.

"So what's the latest with your mom and the captain?" I asked Karen, eager to change the subject.

She jumped at the change in topic and launched into a long tale of her woes with her mother. "The only saving grace is that Julie and Chloe have got her so distracted with this shower that she forgets to bug me for minutes at a time."

"Doesn't Clint help?" Jake asked, playing along with the change of subject.

Karen shook her head. "Whatever Mother wants, Clint's more than happy to give her. He thinks the sun rises and sets on that woman.

"I suppose I should be happy for her, and I am. I just wish she didn't have to run my life, too. And he's so busy with whatever the Navy's got him doing we hardly see him."

"We are going to have to include them in dinner while they're here," I reminded her. "Maybe we ought to figure that out while we're all together."

It was Felipe who solved our dilemma. "I've been thinking about that," he said. "I know you said you and Riley were spending Thanksgiving with your families, but Ernie and I were thinking of doing a traditional Thanksgiving spread at our place next Thursday, since we're loosening up on the menus. Why don't you invite your mother and her husband to join us then?"

"Really? Are you sure?" Karen's smile of relief nearly split her face in half. "That would be amazing, if you're serious."

Within a few minutes, we planned the meal and Karen texted her mother an invitation. We each offered to bring something, but Ernie turned us all down. "I can't wait to really use all the capacity of my new range," he said. "It's Felipe's turn to cook, but I think we're going to do this one together."

"That actually ties in to something I've been thinking about," I said. "Now that Riley and Karen are getting married, and Jake has proven he can actually cook, maybe we ought to consider officially changing the group from the four of us to the six of us."

I saw Felipe and Ernie nodding, but Jake spoke first. "I'd be honored to be included," he said. "It's a pretty exclusive club, and I would truly appreciate you letting me in."

Ernie reached across the table and shook Jake's hand. "We'd be honored to have you."

"Thanks," Jake said. "How about you, Felipe?"

"After that meal, how could I say anything but yes?"

"I'll gladly ride your coattails," Riley added.

"We're counting on you for fish," I told him. "I still wouldn't know how to cook grouper properly without you."

The evening was winding down, and Jake went to retrieve the coats from the bedroom. Riley offered to help and the two men walked down the hall.

They were gone several minutes, their absence covered by the general chaos as the four of us—the original crew—made quick work of finishing the clearing up.

By the time Jake and Riley returned with coats and jackets, Riley lugging Karen's heavy bag, the dishes were stacked by the sink, the leaves were out of the table and it was pushed back against the wall, and the living room furniture was back in its proper place.

"Leave the dishes," I told Ernie as he started to run hot water in the sink. "Jake and I can take care of them."

Though it went against his tidy nature, Ernie managed to walk away from the chore, and soon we were saying our good-byes.

Once we were alone, I asked Jake what he and Riley had been talking about.

"The honeymoon," Jake said. "As if you didn't know."

"I knew that much." I slid a stack of plates into the hot, soapy water. "I'll wash, since you cooked. But you have to tell me what Riley's planning. Something tells me it involves California wine country."

"That obvious, huh?" He picked up a dish towel and started drying plates as I propped them in the drainer. "You don't think Karen noticed, do you?"

"No." I tried to reassure him. "I only figured it out because I knew you and Riley had been talking about it. I don't think she suspected anything."

"Good. Riley would kill me if he thought I gave it away."

"So *is* that what he's doing?"

"I think so. It's just a matter of timing. It's fun to go during the harvest, though that won't be until late summer. If they go now, it could be chilly, but there's still a lot to see and do. I've been helping him find some fun stuff."

He stacked the dried plates in the cupboard and went to work on the silverware. "Like the B&B made out of train cabooses."

"Cabooses?"

"Yeah. Instead of a bedroom, you get a caboose. They're all separate, so there's lots of privacy, with a central dining room for breakfast.

"It's north of the Bay Area. I got to know the owner when I lived up there. Nice guy, and a heckuva cook."

"That sounds like something that would definitely appeal to Riley, especially the food," I said. "And Karen. She likes things that are a little bit different."

"This definitely is. Anyway, there are a bunch of wineries in the area, so Riley's trying to put together a wine country honeymoon and I'm happy to help him out."

We finished the dishes, and Jake picked up the second wine bottle. "There's enough here for a nightcap," Jake said. "Unless you're in a hurry to get home."

I wasn't.

Chapter 33

I CREPT OUT BEFORE DAWN THE NEXT MORNING, leaving Jake snoring softly. He stirred in his sleep as I took my purse out of the dresser drawer, but he didn't wake up.

I wasn't that successful with Bluebeard.

"Out all night." He wolf whistled. "Again."

I rummaged in the refrigerator and found some cut-up fruit. The faint light of a false dawn wasn't enough to turn off the streetlights that shone through the front windows as I made my way through the shop.

"I brought you some fruit," I said, dumping the berries and melons into his dish. "But I give up on trying to let you sleep."

He gobbled down several pieces of fruit before stopping to give me a beady-eyed stare. "Out all night."

I stared back. "Are you waiting up for me? Is that why you're awake when I come home?"

He turned his head and went back to the fruit. He emptied the bowl in a few seconds, then stomped off into his cage.

"Trying to #&#^*^$% sleep here," he squawked.

"I give up," I said and headed upstairs to make coffee.

Short on sleep, I thought I would have to depend on the coffee to keep me going. Too early to open up, I carried my mug downstairs and checked the website for orders. More Bluebeard T-shirts, some mugs, and one of my regulars inquiring about the new spatterware pieces I'd listed.

I filled orders as the sky lightened from gray to peach to pale blue. By the time the sun was fully up, I had packages ready for pickup, I'd e-mailed confirmations to each customer, and I was ready for another mug of coffee.

When I came back downstairs with my refill, Bluebeard was out of his cage and surveying the world from his perch in the front window.

"Coffee?" he said when he saw me come through the door with a mug in hand.

"No, Bluebeard. You can't have coffee." I kept thinking one day he'd stop asking since he always got the same answer. But given that we'd had this same exact exchange several times a week for the last six or seven years, it didn't seem likely.

I unlocked the front door and turned over the sign. I truly wished I would be able to stay in the shop and have a normal workday. I hadn't had one of those in a while, and the idea appealed to me. A lot.

I was working on my inventory when the computer chimed with an incoming e-mail. I finished the item I was working on and flipped over to the e-mail window. There was a message from Clifford Wilson, with the subject line "Will of Louis Georges."

I thought of Sly's check, still uncashed. It was in the safe, along with Pansy's recipes and the purchase contract for Lighthouse Coffee. All related, and all likely to be influenced by what was in Mr. Wilson's e-mail.

My hand shook slightly as I clicked on the message. It popped up, a lengthy block of text couched in Mr. Wilson's careful legalese. I read it slowly, then read it again to make sure I understood exactly what he said.

He apologized for taking so long, saying he had consulted his original files to be sure he answered completely accurately. There had been several specific bequests, including the ownership of Southern Treasures and the disposition of family heirlooms. My Uncle Andrew had received stock in Back Bay Bank, and the rest of the estate had gone to my mother.

That meant, he explained, that anything that wasn't specifically listed in the will belonged to my mother, and as her only heir, it belonged to me.

Which meant the check in the safe was truly and legally mine. I could do whatever I wanted with it, and Uncle Andrew and Peter had no right to it.

The legal right to the money was settled. But the question remained: what would my conscience let me do with it?

I wrestled with the dilemma as I worked through the morning. Customers came and went. The delivery driver dropped off an order and picked up the outgoing packages. I made another pot of coffee and drank most of it.

And the whole time, I thought about what to do with Sly's check. I could keep it all, or I could give Peter half, or I could give him a smaller portion since I wasn't obligated to give him anything at all.

I could even use it to boost the Buy-Out-Peter Fund, an option I found particularly ironic.

Shortly after noon, Karen showed up at the shop. Her grim expression drove all thoughts of Peter from my mind. "What's wrong?" I said, pulling her into the back of the shop.

"I just came from a press conference with Boomer and Assistant District Attorney Morris." Her voice was controlled, but I knew she was angry. "Morris made a big show out of it, called every news outlet he could get hold of.

"Glory, he's charging Everett Young with the murder of those two moonshiners, and he's charging Beth as an accessory."

I stared at her with my mouth open, too stunned to speak.

"Why?" I asked when I finally regained some semblance of control. "What in the world does he think he's doing?"

"He's gunning for his boss's job," Karen said grimly. "He thinks he's 'cleaning up the county' with this hard line, and thinks that it will appeal to the voters."

"And what happens when the voters find out he's got the wrong guy?"

"He's not thinking that far ahead, Glory. He saw a chance to get some press and he grabbed it. It has nothing to do with what's right or wrong, just what he thinks will advance his career."

I couldn't stand any more. I dashed behind the counter and grabbed my wallet and keys.

"What are you doing?" Karen asked.

"I'm going down there and give Boomer a piece of my mind. Maybe several pieces.

"He got me to talk Beth and Everett into coming back. I even went and carried them to the station—well, you did, but only because I talked them into it—and then he charges them with murder? What kind of a Judas goat does that make me?"

"Don't bother." Karen grabbed my arm and kept me from running out the door. "There's nothing Boomer can do. Once the DA's office files charges, it's out of his hands."

She eased her grip, like she was testing whether I'd run away, but I waited to hear her out. "You said he was there."

"He was. But I got the feeling the whole thing was a surprise to him. And he was not happy about it. He looked like he'd bitten into a sour lemon when that jerk made his big announcement."

"So Boomer doesn't think they did it."

"I didn't say that. I said he was unhappy about the big press conference and the announcement. Knowing Boomer, at the very least he's waiting for more evidence before he makes up his mind."

"That's not what you said when he arrested Bobby," I reminded her.

"No, and I still think he jumped the gun on that one. But he had the feds breathing down his neck. I think he was trying to keep Bobby in Keyhole Bay, and that was the only way he could think of to do it."

"What do we do now?" I asked.

"Nothing," Karen replied. "It's hard for me to admit that, but there isn't a thing we can do right now. The ADA says there will be an arraignment and a bail hearing this afternoon, but he's already made it clear he'll oppose bail. He says they don't have any 'ties to the community' and that makes them a flight risk."

"Right," I said bitterly. "Especially since they just came back from wherever they were of their own accord."

"You know what he really meant."

"I do. He's reminding everybody that they aren't from around here. They're outsiders, so they can't be trusted." I threw my keys back on the counter in frustration. "Sometimes I hate this place!"

"He's wrong, Glory. We both know that, and I think Boomer knows it, too. This will eventually sort itself out, but there isn't anything we can do today.

"Tomorrow, after the dust settles a little, you can go down and see if Boomer will allow you to visit Beth. I doubt you'll get to see Everett, but he might at least let you talk to her."

"And say what? 'Sorry I got you arrested'? How do you think she's going to react to that?"

"You could offer to find her a lawyer, or whatever else we can do to help."

"We?"

"Yeah." Karen looked sheepish. "The truth is, I feel like I'm responsible, too. I went up there with you, and I was part of the plan to get them back here. So, yeah. I want to help."

Karen's offer, well intentioned though it was, only served to depress me more. Usually she knew what to do, who to call, where to apply pressure to get what she wanted. This time all she could say was "Wait," and waiting wasn't one of my better skills.

"What about the pictures you took? And the recording? Isn't that evidence? Those guys were out there, sniffing around the place." Against my better judgment, I made a suggestion. "Maybe we should take them to Boomer and get him to follow up."

"And just how do we explain that we didn't report it when it happened?" Karen was always reluctant to turn over anything to the sheriff; I shouldn't have expected this to be any different. "Besides, all it shows is that a couple guys confronted us while *we* were sniffing around instead of calling to tell the sheriff that Beth and Everett were coming back. I couldn't really see faces or vehicles or anything useful, and no matter what they show on TV the sheriff doesn't have a magic computer that can change that."

We talked for a few minutes longer, both of us trying to come up with something positive we could do, to no avail. Karen left, saying she had to cover the bail hearing, and she promised to call me if she heard anything more.

I was still reeling from the news when Jake showed up an hour later. He flashed me a big grin as he came through the door.

"You didn't have to leave so early," he said as he walked toward the counter. "I was going to cook breakfast."

"You were sleeping so soundly," I said. "I woke up way early and remembered that the loan committee was supposed to meet today. After that, there was no way I could get back to sleep. I didn't want to wake you up with my tossing and turning, so I decided to get back here and get some things done."

"I'm always happy to wake up if you're there."

He looked at me, a frown creasing his forehead. "Glory, what's wrong? They said you wouldn't hear about the loan until after the weekend. Did they call?"

I shook my head. "It's Beth and Everett. Karen was here a little bit ago. They're being charged in the deaths of those two moonshiners Boomer found up on their property."

"That's ridiculous! What is Boomer thinking?"

"It's not Boomer." I sighed. "It's some assistant DA who's out to make a name for himself. Karen says he's trying to take over his boss's job, and he jumped on this case as a way to make some headlines."

"What an idiot! He's going to get plenty of attention, sure. But he'll get even more when he has to let them go. Especially if a smart lawyer gets hold of them and they decide to sue the county."

"Wow, I hadn't even thought of that."

"One of the joys of being a civil servant."

I was sure there was a story behind that remark, one that I wouldn't like any more than Jake did. But this wasn't the time, and I made a mental note to ask him about it later.

"Karen said there isn't anything we can do today, not until after the bail hearing and the arraignment. Apparently this guy isn't letting any grass grow under his feet. Karen's gone to the courthouse to report on whatever he does.

"She'll call when she knows anything."

The phone rang and I grabbed it, expecting to hear Karen's outraged report on the latest machinations of Assistant DA Morris.

Instead I got Peter.

"Are you okay, Glory?" he asked as soon as I said hello.

"Yes. Why wouldn't I be?"

"Mother just called me," he said. "She wanted to know if I had talked to you, if you were all right."

Peter's mother, Melissa, was a prune-faced gossip who delighted in borrowing trouble. Aunt Missy—it rhymed with prissy for a reason—took every snippet of bad news she heard and made it her mission to share it far and wide. I had no idea what her latest rumor was, and I certainly wasn't in the mood to be patient with Peter's ill-concealed glee at my potential misfortune.

"I can't imagine why she thought I wouldn't be," I snapped.

"She heard about the murders, Glory. There were two men killed right there in your county, and she was worried that you might know them." His tone grew increasingly patronizing as he went on, "You know, you do have something of a reputation for getting yourself into trouble, Gloryanna. You've had several run-ins with the law, and Mother says you've had your name in the paper far more than any lady ought."

"Peter," I lowered my voice and spoke slowly, a tactic that usually stopped him. "I am fine. Those two people were found miles away from me, practically across the border into Alabama. They were probably closer to you than they were to me."

"Maybe so, but I haven't been in trouble with the law, now have I?"

"Peter," I growled.

This time he didn't catch the warning in my voice, and he plowed ahead. "You have to realize we worry about you, Glory. You're down there all alone, without any advice from your family, and we worry about you."

Under normal circumstances, this was the point at which I would start counting to ten. But I had barely gotten to one when Peter made the worst mistake of his life.

"I know you need my help with the store, and I'm sorry that I can't just leave my job and come down and help you, but—"

"Shut up!"

"What?" Peter's indignant shout answered my angry one.

"Just shut up, Peter. Right this very minute.

"Stop talking and listen to me. Very carefully, because I am only going to say this once, and if you ever bring it up again—ever!—I will never speak to you for as long as I live."

I waited for an instant of stunned silence and then continued. "Are you listening?"

"Yes, but—" The whining had started.

"No buts. Just listen.

"You have one chance, right now, to apologize for your attitude. I run this place, I work hard, and I do a good job. Your insistence on offering me advice will stop, as of now, because I am going to buy your interest in the store.

"You have always complained that your 'investment' in Southern Treasures doesn't provide an adequate return." I stopped short of reminding him that he hadn't *invested* a penny in Southern Treasures; he'd inherited it, just as I had. The difference was I'd spent years working in the store.

"Well, this is your chance to take that 'investment' and put it somewhere you think is better." I wanted to tell him where he could put his investment, but I resisted. There were some limits on my anger. "Put it someplace where you can make the kind of return you think you deserve."

"You can't do that!"

"Oh, yes I can. I will. You *will* sell to me, Peter."

"No," he said scornfully, defiance replacing the whine. "You can't buy me out because you can't possibly have enough to pay me what my share is worth."

I thought about the money I'd been saving, and the fund Jake had put aside to help me make Southern Treasures all mine.

Sly's check was still in the safe, and I no longer had any dilemma about its ownership. It was mine, and I was going to use it to do the one thing I wanted most in the world.

"Peter," my voice didn't waver, though my insides were shaking like a bowl of jelly, "I recently had the bank assess the value of Southern Treasures, and I know *exactly* what your share is worth. To the penny. I'll be glad to send you the report they gave me, along with a cashier's check for forty-five percent of the total on that report.

"In return, I want full ownership of Southern Treasures."

Peter began to sputter incoherently.

"Take it or leave it," I said coldly. "But the longer you make me wait, the lower my offer will go. My banker tells me that all those years of below-market wages should make my value much higher than the fifty-five percent I inherited. The longer I have to think about this, the more I think I just might have to take his advice.

"Call me back when you decide."

My hands were shaking so badly I couldn't hang up the phone. Jake took it from me and placed it back in its cradle, then helped me into the tall chair behind the counter as my legs threatened to give way and topple me to the ground.

"Bravo!" From across the shop, Uncle Louis's voice shouted his approval, whistling and flapping his wings. "Bravo!"

I looked up at Jake as the reality of what I'd said hit me.

"What have I done?"

Chapter 34

"EXACTLY THE RIGHT THING," JAKE SAID. "BLUE-beard thinks so too, don't you, old man?"

The parrot had left his perch and made his way across the shop to sit on the counter in front of me. "Absolutely."

"Thanks," I said, addressing both of them. "I think I scared him a little. I know I scared me."

"Heck, you scared me," Jake said with a laugh. "Remind me not to ever make you mad."

"I've put up with so much from him, I just couldn't take any more. Especially when he told me I couldn't possibly have the money to buy him out."

"But that wasn't what started this, was it?"

"No. What started it was him telling me I needed his help with the store. He has never understood what goes on here, and he's made no effort to actually learn. I just had to get him out of here. I'll deal with the fallout later."

Jake offered to stay a while longer, but I shooed him out

and sent him back to take care of his own business. I did promise to call him if I heard any news.

Eventually Karen called. As she'd predicted, the assistant DA had argued against bail, and the judge agreed. Beth and Everett were in jail for the foreseeable future.

"They didn't even have a lawyer," Karen told me. "Oh, some young public defender showed up about halfway through, but he didn't even know what the charges were, much less anything about his supposed clients.

"It was all just for show."

We agreed to meet the following morning and try to see Beth at the jail, in the hope there would be something we could do. I didn't realize I hadn't told her about Peter until after I hung up. No matter, it could wait.

When I finally closed up for the night, I was feeling restless. I hadn't been home much in the last few days, and I'd been looking forward to an evening alone, but I wasn't ready to settle down quite yet.

I needed to move. I grabbed a jacket, stuck my wallet, phone, and keys in the pockets, and picked up a bag full of reusable grocery sacks. A walk to Frank's Foods and back would take care of my restlessness and alleviate the problem of my empty refrigerator.

One of the downsides of having Jake cover my Thursday dinner was the lack of leftovers. Usually I could count on enough food to carry me through the weekend after one of my Thursday nights. But this time the food was in Jake's freezer, not mine.

It was only a few blocks to Frank's, just far enough to work some of the tension out of my back and shoulders. I was feeling more relaxed by the time I reached the market, glad I'd decided to walk instead of drive. I might not be able to carry as many groceries, but that wasn't even the point.

I wandered through the store, trying to decide what I wanted for dinner. It was just me tonight and I wanted comfort food, something warm and familiar.

I went for an old favorite: canned chicken noodle soup and grilled cheese sandwiches. I needed a couple cans of soup, a package of cheese slices, and a loaf of white bread. Nothing fancy, tonight's dinner was more about familiarity than fancy.

I wandered through the produce section, selecting fruit and vegetables to share with Bluebeard, careful limit myself to what I could readily carry home.

After the turmoil of the last few days, it felt good to do something normal, and I made a leisurely circuit of the entire store. I ran into Cheryl, Frank's wife, next to the dairy case as I searched for the proper sandwich cheese.

We talked for a few minutes, catching up on the things normal people talk about. I didn't have to talk about murder or arrests or meddling partners. I didn't have to think about who might hear us, or what tales they might carry back to the sheriff.

Normal.

Frank rang up my groceries and I swiped my debit card and punched in my PIN. We chatted as he filled my shopping bags, arguing lightheartedly about whether tomato or chicken noodle was best to accompany a grilled cheese sandwich.

It was exactly the kind of outing I needed, and when I left the store, I was carrying a couple heavy grocery sacks, but my mood was considerably lighter.

The trip also reminded me why I loved living in a small town. I'd run into friends in the store, stopped for a minute to say hello and exchange pleasantries. There hadn't been a single conversation that was terribly important, but they were all important; every one was a reminder of the connections we all shared.

Bluebeard greeted me with his usual litany of complaints about being gone, but it quickly turned to wheedling when he realized I was carrying grocery bags.

I let him carry on, trying to guess what was in the bags and what might be for him, but I still brought the full bags up the stairs to my apartment. As I put away the groceries and cut up some fresh vegetables for him, I could hear a steady stream of pleading and sweet talk floating up from the shop below.

I finished prepping the produce and took several small containers to the downstairs refrigerator. I could have kept everything upstairs, but I liked the convenience of having Bluebeard's food close at hand.

I gave him his treats, taking time to reassure him I wasn't going out. "I just want a quiet night at home," I told him as I scratched his head. "I want to have dinner, maybe read a book, and turn in early. I don't want to think about any problems, or worry about anyone except you and me."

"No worry," he echoed back. "Don't borrow trouble."

Someone else had said the same thing just a few days ago, and I searched my brain for the memory that hovered just out of reach. I was in a car, north of town, so it had to be Karen or Jake. But trouble had already found me when I was with Karen.

Jake. Jake had said the same thing to me when Beth and Everett weren't home.

"Great advice," I said. "But it didn't work out so great the last time."

I shut down the lights, checked the alarms, and went upstairs to grill a cheese sandwich, heat some soup, and lose myself in a made-up world for a couple hours.

JULIE WAS IN EARLY THE NEXT MORNING, AND I filled her in on the last few days as we got the store ready to open.

"How's your mom?" I asked.

"Getting better," she said. "Doctor told her they caught it early, and she's responding really well to the medication. She even said she could keep Rose Ann all day today, though I think that might be a bit much for her."

I nodded. "I'm going with Karen first thing this morning, but I should be back before noon. If you need to get home and relieve your mom, it shouldn't be a problem."

"Thanks. More wedding stuff?"

"I wish."

Julie did a double take at my answer. I had made it clear that Karen's constant wedding errands and projects were trying my patience, so if I would rather be doing wedding preparations, something was seriously out of whack.

I quickly explained about Beth and Everett, and the turmoil that I'd been drawn into. I was just finishing up when Karen arrived.

"I have something to tell you both," I announced and waited until I had their full attention.

They looked at me expectantly.

"I had a call from Peter yesterday," I went on, my voice squeaking with the remembered tension of the phone call.

"Spit it out, Martine," Karen commanded. "We haven't got all day."

I swallowed hard and concentrated on speaking calmly. "I told him I was buying him out, that I wanted full ownership of Southern Treasures."

"Sure did!" Bluebeard chimed in from across the room. "Told him good!"

Julie glanced over at Bluebeard. "I swear, that bird has a bigger vocabulary than some people I know." She turned back to me. "What did he say?"

"He didn't take it well. He said a lot of things, but the worst was that I couldn't have enough money to buy him out." I felt my anger rising again, just thinking about how smug he'd been. "Like he knows anything about my finances! He might spend every penny he makes, but I've been saving for a long time, and I do have enough."

Julie had taken a half step back, and Karen was holding out her hand, her palm toward me. "Down, girl!" she said. "I just hope you gave him a dose of that."

"Oh, I did. Believe me, I really did. And I told him the longer he waited to accept my terms, the worse they would get for him."

"Good for you!" Karen beamed her approval, then glanced at the clock and back at me. "We better get going," she said. "Boomer agreed we could have a few minutes with Beth, but I got the distinct impression that he didn't think the ADA would look too kindly on our visit.

"We need to get over there before Morris gets wind of it and tries to keep us out."

Chapter 35

AT THE SHERIFF'S STATION, DEPUTY FUENTES, A solid woman with dark eyes and slicked back black hair, checked our IDs and then led us into the back. She ran a wand over both of us. "Standard procedure," she explained, and locked Karen's bag and my purse in a secure bin and handed us the key to claim our property on our way out.

She showed us to a small room with two narrow, barred windows and a sturdy table bolted to the floor. Two chairs sat on each side of the table, with a large mirror behind one set of chairs. I was sure the mirror was placed to allow someone in an adjoining space to observe the room, but there wasn't much we could do if Boomer had decided to eavesdrop on our conversation with Beth.

"Sheriff Hardy is out this morning," Deputy Fuentes said, "but he left instructions that you were to be allowed ten minutes with the prisoner. No more. I'll bring Mrs. Young in and lock the door." She showed us a button on the underside of the table. "If you need help, just push that and an alarm will sound. Otherwise, if you want anything before I come back for you, use the call box by the door."

She had said this was all the usual process for visits, and for the first time I really understood that Beth was in jail charged with a crime, and being treated like an accused criminal instead of an innocent bystander.

"Do you understand everything I told you?" Fuentes asked before opening the door.

Karen and I both nodded.

"Good," she said. She opened the door and went out. It closed behind her with a solid *thunk* as the latch clicked into place.

I have never been claustrophobic, but when that door shut with the sound that made it very clear we were locked in, I had to battle a momentary feeling of panic.

For one brief moment I felt as though I were the prisoner and I might never get back out.

I looked at Karen and it was obvious she had the same reaction. "It's creepy, being locked in here," she said, as if talking about her fears would make them less powerful.

I just nodded, not trusting my tightened throat to speak.

A minute later the door opened and Beth Young came in. She wore a shapeless gray jumpsuit and slip-on plastic sandals. The jumpsuit was that marvel of modern clothing, one size fits all. Just not very well. I supposed her undergarments would be the same poor fit, but after another glance, I was pretty sure they simply didn't exist.

That was the first thing on my checklist then. Some clothes that fit, maybe even some of her own, if it could be arranged.

We said our wary hellos and took seats at the table, Karen and I on one side facing the mirror, and Beth with her back to it. Judging by the way she studiously ignored the mirror, I could guess that she'd been through this once already and been forced to sit on our side of the table.

Karen fiddled with her tablet. Fuentes had checked it

over thoroughly and allowed her to keep the device instead of a pen or pencil. There was no outside connection available, but she could use it for notes.

Beth didn't look happy to see us.

"Are you okay?" I asked. It was a stupid question. The woman was in jail and her husband was charged with murder. How could she be okay?

"I've been better."

I fumbled for the right words, finally settling for the simplest. "Beth, I am really sorry. I had no idea Boomer would do this, or I wouldn't have been so eager to get you back here. I really thought you would answer a few questions and he'd send you home. I never imagined this would happen."

I didn't think she was going to accept my apology, and I could see that she didn't think she would, either. But I hadn't reckoned with Karen's power of persuasion.

"Beth, we all got taken in by this. I won't say they lied to us"—I noticed that she didn't specify *who* lied—"but we were certainly misled.

"I don't expect you to necessarily believe that; I certainly wouldn't if I was in your position. I don't really expect you to trust us, either. But I hope you will let us help you if we can."

She tapped the pad and started typing. "I'm going to make a list of what you need so we can try to figure out what needs doing first, okay?"

Beth nodded, still skeptical, but at least she was listening.

"First off, did you get a lawyer?"

Beth shrugged. "There was a public defender at the hearing thingie yesterday."

"I was there. I saw him," she said. Her tone left no doubt of her opinion of his legal skills. "They assigned you some kid who just got out of law school and has probably never tried a case, much less a serious felony.

"No, what I meant was, have you been able to find a *good* attorney?"

Beth shook her head. "We don't know any lawyers down here. Haven't had any need of one. And even if we knew a good one, we couldn't afford him anyway."

"Doesn't matter," Karen said firmly. "You'll get a public defender, but they have to provide you adequate counsel, which that bozo certainly is not.

"I know a couple people," she went on. "I'm sure they can see to it that you get someone qualified to represent you."

Beth didn't look convinced, but I knew better. Karen wasn't the type to tell you she "knew people" just to impress you. It wasn't her style.

But she did have contacts. Not always the top dog, but always someone with knowledge and influence, the kind of person who sometimes found it useful to let information "leak" to the press. She was honest and she was discreet. It made her friends in high places.

"I'm not promising you any special favors or preferential treatment," she went on, choosing her words carefully for the benefit of whoever might be watching. "I'm just saying some of my friends will be interested in making sure you have a proper defense; that no one cuts any corners or stacks the deck.

"This is a serious case, and they're going to take it very seriously."

"Is there anything you need in here?" I asked. "If we brought you some of your own clothes, something that fit, do you think Boomer would let you have them?"

"I don't know," Beth said. "He did tell me that he didn't have any women's sizes, I had to take the smallest men's size he had. It's a bit large."

That was an understatement. The baggy garment hung off her and the pant legs were rolled up several times to keep them from dragging along the ground.

"I can bring you some jeans and a couple T-shirts," I said. "I think you're a bit smaller than me, but they should be a better fit than that jumpsuit."

"A hairbrush," she said quietly, running her fingers through her long, straight hair. "All they have here are flimsy plastic combs. And a clip, or some rubber bands, something to tie it back a little."

"Okay," Karen typed her instructions. "We can get that here, unless you'd rather we went up to the cabin and brought you your own things."

"No," she said. Her voice changed from hesitant to authoritative. "That's such a long way to go."

"What about the cabin?" I asked. "Is there someone to take care of things while you're gone?"

"Don't worry about that," she said firmly. "Really. I know you're trying to help, but there just isn't that much that needs doing. I've already called Granny, and she said she'll take care of things."

She rose from her chair, and it was clear our visit was at an end. "I think I'll go back now," she said. "Could you call Deputy Fuentes, please?"

We were back in the car with our reclaimed property when Karen spotted a sharply dressed man parking in one of the reserved spaces at the front of the lot.

She slid down in her seat and turned away from him. "Is he going into the building?" she asked me.

I turned my head, but she snapped at me, "Don't look at him, just tell me if he pays any attention to us."

"And how do I do that without looking at him?" I asked. I kept facing forward, straining my eyes to the side to see if I could follow his movements.

"He's going in," I said, relaxing my neck a little as the man turned his back to us. All I could see was an expensive suit, a BMW with custom plates, and the back of a haircut he definitely didn't get in Keyhole Bay.

In Keyhole Bay, you went to the barbershop that had

been in the same spot with the same barber since the '70s, or you went to the beauty school in what used to be the five-and-dime. A haircut like that came from a much bigger city with pricey salons.

"Is that Morris?" I asked.

"I think so," Karen said. "I didn't get a good look, but I didn't want him to see me."

"You two have a history?" Karen had friends in high places that could prove valuable, but she also had friends in low places, and that sometimes brought her into conflict with the authorities.

"Not yet." She started the car and backed out, pulling slowly past the Beemer on her way out of the lot. "That's his car, all right. Look at the license plate."

I read the letters aloud. "M-O-R-L-A-W. Charming. He certainly doesn't have any problem telling you who he is."

"Or what he stands for," Karen said, pulling into the light Saturday morning traffic. "Except he doesn't stand for much, of course."

"But you said he was using this case to go after his boss's job; doesn't that mean he's one of those 'tough on crime' guys?"

"Not necessarily. I did a little research on ADA Morris, talked to a couple people who have lots of business in the courthouse." By which she meant local bail bondsmen, though she'd never say so publicly. "He's new to the area—"

"I wondered," I cut in. "I didn't recognize the name."

"No, he moved here a couple years ago from down near Orlando. Politically very ambitious, and the field down there was crowded, so he grabbed at the chance to be a big fish in a small pond, and maybe snatch a few headlines in the process. Wanted to raise his profile for a run at something bigger.

"Word is he's being groomed for a Senate run at some point, and this will look good on the CV."

"CV?" It wasn't a term I was familiar with.

"Curriculum vitae. It's kind of like a specialized résumé, with lots of additional information. But lately it seems like the politicians are using the term, incorrectly I might add, to make themselves sound more important."

"So this is a guy from five hundred miles away, trying to make headlines by charging Everett with murder, basically saying he's guilty because he's 'not from around here,'"—I drew in a deep breath—"and he's not even from around here himself?! Is that about the size of it?"

Karen nodded, her mouth in a grim line. "That's about the size of it," she agreed. "The guy's an opportunist. He's part of a big family firm down south that specializes in estates and trusts and real estate investing. No criminal work, unless one of their regular clients gets caught with his hand in the company cookie jar. And no civil work either, except when some millionaire wants to jettison his wife for a newer model."

"And you wonder why people hate lawyers."

"I don't wonder," Karen replied. "I know."

I let it drop. "Have you found out anything from the pictures you took?"

She shook her head. "Zip. I showed them to a few people I know, but nobody recognized either of them. As I said, the quality is so poor that I don't think they'd be any help to Boomer."

"How about the recording?"

"Garbled," she answered. "All that trouble, and we got nothing."

We pulled up in front of the shop and she let me out. "Got time for coffee?" I asked.

"Wish I did. Mother's waiting for me to go shopping with her. She insists I need clothes for the honeymoon, even though I have no idea where I'm going or what I'm doing."

I didn't take the bait. I wasn't about to even give her a

hint of Riley's plans. "Just take whatever advice she gives you," I told her. "I'm sure Riley gave her some guidelines."

Karen rolled her eyes. "You know how much I love taking fashion advice from my mother. We're two completely different body types; she hates everything I like, and vice versa. And you want me to take her word for what I need to pack?"

I shrugged. "Suit yourself. But I do think she's talked to Riley and will know what kind of things you need."

"It's a vacation," she said. "Jeans. Sneakers. A couple T-shirts and maybe a bathing suit. What's so hard about that?"

I didn't argue. Actually, from what I'd heard so far, she was probably right. But Riley was determined to make this trip special, and I suspected she'd need something a little more fancy than T-shirts and jeans. Either way, I'd leave that fight to her mother.

Chapter 36

BUSINESS WAS BRISK ON SUNDAY, A NICE CHANGE from the slow days. Several times I had customers lined up at the counter, while Bluebeard did his best to entertain those who were still browsing the aisles.

I noticed two clean-cut men who came in, wandered for a few minutes, and then left without buying anything. Not that that was unusual—I got my fair share of lookie-lous— but these two weren't locals, and they didn't fit any of the usual tourist categories.

There was something about them that drew my attention, perhaps because they seemed intent on not being noticed. I even wondered if they were a couple, but not openly so. I rejected the idea; Felipe had taught me to recognize far more than most people did.

It occurred to me that they might be shoplifters, casing the place to see if it was a worthwhile target, which it wasn't. I kept most of the smaller valuables in the locked case up front, and everything else was either too big or too inexpensive to be worth stealing.

That seemed the most likely explanation, and as soon as I could I made a call that would start the phone chain, alerting other merchants in town in case the duo found someplace that looked more enticing. It might be nothing, but a reminder to be extra vigilant just might save a friend from losing inventory.

When I closed for the night, the register held a nice stack of bills, and I'd rung enough credit card sales to see me through the next week. Combined with the online sales, it made for a good week in spite of all the distractions.

I settled Bluebeard for the night and set the alarm. I felt uneasy as I checked and double-checked the sensors, like someone was watching me. I told myself it was just a reaction to the two strangers and the stress of my visit to Beth. Still, I checked the alarms a third time before heading next door for a six-pack of microbrew.

"Hot date?" Linda teased as she rang up the beer.

"With Sly," I told her. "Which reminds me. I need a couple pieces of beef jerky"—I pointed to the case next to the register. "Low sodium, please. It's for Bobo."

Linda put two pieces of jerky in a small bag and handed them to me. "For Bobo, no charge," she said, and sighed. "I wish we could have a dog, but Guy's right: we're in the store all day and it wouldn't be fair to the dog to be left alone like that."

"You could always bring him in with you."

She shook her head. "Not here. Too many people and no place to hide. At least Bluebeard can get up out of reach of little hands if he needs to."

I took the beer and jerky and cut through the storeroom and out the back to my truck. One of the advantages of being friends with the owners.

It was nearly dark as I drove to Sly's, streetlights winking on as the light drained from the sky, and I saw few other vehicles on the short drive. The empty roads and the deepening twilight made me feel like the last person on earth.

I pulled into Fowler's parking lot and drove around the back to the gate in the chain-link fence. Sly had left the gate open and I pulled through into the junkyard.

I was climbing out of the truck when Bobo bounded out to greet me. After the eerie feeling of emptiness, I welcomed his joyful greeting.

I patted his head and scratched behind his ears, and he rewarded me with a yelp of pure doggy joy. He was too polite to jump up, Sly would never allow that. But he leaned into me and rubbed his head against my leg.

How different from our initial meeting. I had come upon him unexpectedly the first time I ventured into the junkyard. He had appeared out of nowhere, alert for the sound of an intruder. I'd frozen, staring at an immense black dog with a head the size of a basketball. If basketballs had a mouth full of sharp teeth.

Bobo was Sly's early warning system when strangers came in the yard, and he was usually all that was needed to keep out those who didn't belong there.

Fortunately for me, I belonged.

Sly was a few steps behind Bobo. He greeted me with a hug and grinned at the beer in my hand. "You sure know how to make an old man happy," he said, leading the way back to the cinder-block house, hidden among the rows of cars and trucks that filled his yard.

"You're not that old," I chided him as I followed along. I did some quick mental arithmetic, based on the pictures we'd found in the library. "Heck, I'll bet you aren't even seventy yet, are you?"

"Few months away. Like I said, an old man, old enough to be your grandpa."

"That's not that old. And you're barely older than my dad would have been, nowhere near old enough to be my grandpa." It was only a slight exaggeration.

Sly didn't have an answer to that, and I accepted my win with gracious silence.

From the outside, his house looked like a plain block-wall structure, with a few windows and a nondescript, wooden front door. The kind of place you would expect to find a not-so-old bachelor and his dog.

But once inside, the décor of the house was completely unexpected. Wicker and chintz and lots of plants. Every time I came in, I was struck by the contrast between the cozy, comfortable interior and the harsh exterior. Sort of like Sly and Bobo.

A small fire crackled in a Franklin stove and the front room was warm, in spite of the evening chill. A medley of homey aromas drifted in from the kitchen.

I took my usual seat on a wicker settee and Sly lowered himself into the leather recliner that was his favorite spot, with Bobo at his feet.

We had fallen into a routine over the last several months. Every few weeks, Sly would invite me to dinner. Usually we'd eat at his place, unlike our celebration at the Bay House; I'd bring the beer and a treat for Bobo, and we would spend a quiet evening catching up on whatever we were doing. I wasn't exactly checking up on him, but I was the nearest thing to family he had, and I cherished that role.

"Meatloaf and potatoes in the oven," he said. "And succotash simmering. Should be about ten minutes, we'll be ready to eat."

I took the small plastic bag out of my purse and handed it to Sly. "For Bobo," I said. "I made sure to get low-salt."

Bobo was instantly alert, his sensitive nose picking up the smell of the jerky the moment Sly opened the bag. "You know you only get a little bit." He shredded one piece of jerky into several smaller pieces.

"Sit."

Bobo obeyed instantly, his eyes glued to the bit of dried beef. Sly lowered it to the floor in front of the dog. Bobo remained still, though I could see the effort it took for him to maintain control.

"Okay."

The word was barely out of Sly's mouth before the meat disappeared into the mass of teeth. A second later, Bobo looked up in anticipation of more beefy goodness.

Sly put Bobo through his paces, giving him several small pieces of jerky before sealing up the bag. "That's all you get for now," he said. He patted Bobo's broad back and put the remaining jerky in the drawer of a small side table.

"No sense tempting him by leaving it out. He's a good dog, but even a good dog has his limits."

"Sort of like people." He gave me a look that said he was waiting for me to tell him what was going on.

"What?" I sounded defensive, even to myself.

"Somethin's up with you, girl. You're all tensed up, like you been pushed past your breaking point. So what gives?"

"How can you tell that? I haven't said or done anything since I got here except drink a little beer and watch you give Bobo treats."

"Mostly because you're looking like this is the first time you've relaxed in quite a while. Which means you've got something on your mind. So tell me what it is."

A timer rang in the kitchen, and I was literally saved by the bell. But not for long.

In just a few minutes, we were seated at the kitchen table with our dinners in front of us.

Sly speared a bite of meatloaf and looked up at me before he put it in his mouth. "Now, tell me what's going on."

Some of it was easy, and some he had even heard already. He knew about Beth and Everett being charged, and he had already heard all about Morris. "He may be from down south," Sly said between bites, "but he's still no better than a carpetbagger."

I nodded in agreement, my mouth full. I swallowed and continued my story. I told him about going to the jail, and how adamant Beth had been about our not going up to the cabin. "It wasn't like we were going to snoop," I said. "Okay, well, maybe a little, but only to try and find evidence that would help clear them of these bogus charges."

"And she didn't trust you to do that? Were you really surprised? You were the one who handed her over to the sheriff. I can see where that would make a body a mite unhappy with you."

"But I didn't know he was going to arrest her. I know she didn't do it, and I would swear Boomer knew that, too. I figured if they came back on their own, that would make it easy on everyone involved. Besides, you know how cranky Boomer gets when people don't want to talk to him."

"Yep." The single word implied far more than it said.

I gave him a sharp look. "Have you been talking to Jake?"

"Ain't saying I did, ain't saying I didn't."

"Which means you did.

"I know I should have told Boomer about those men, but he never gave me a chance. He didn't want me around while he was questioning Beth and Everett—didn't even thank me for going up to north county and carrying them back—so I left, and I haven't had a chance to talk to him since."

"Have you tried?"

"I was at the station just yesterday. He wasn't even there." It was a weak argument, but it was all I had.

"And you didn't try very hard to see him."

I shook my head in surrender. "I know I should talk to him, but now that the ADA's already filed, nobody's going to want to hear what I have to say anyway."

Bobo barked at the front door, and Sly excused himself to let the dog out. "Something got him riled," Sly said when he returned. "Likely a possum or a raccoon. He doesn't much care for other critters in his space."

"There was something else I wanted to talk to you

about," I said, taking the opportunity to change the subject. "It's that check you gave me."

"Nothing to talk about. It's yours, fair and square. I told you that."

"Yes, you did. But I wasn't sure what to do with it. Seemed to me like maybe it didn't all belong to me, that part of it should go to Uncle Andrew, or to Peter."

"Those two don't have any claim on that money," Sly interrupted. "They got their share years ago."

"Well, I had to make sure of that. Just for my own peace of mind. And I did. I heard from Clifford Wilson on Friday. He told me the terms of Uncle Louis's will, and that anything that would have gone to my mother would come to me."

"Good. So cash the dang thing and do something good with the money. Something you'll enjoy."

"Actually"—I paused, drawing out my announcement— "I already have. I'm doing the one thing I want most in the entire world."

Sly looked impressed. "Good for you! What did you do?"

"Well . . ." I backpedaled. "I haven't done it yet, but I am working on it.

"I told Peter I'm buying him out. And that check will make a huge difference in paying him off and getting him out of my hair."

Sly grinned so wide, I though his face might split in half. "That is about the best news I have heard in a month of Sundays," he said. "Mr. Louis would be so happy to know you did that."

"Oh, he was." I told Sly about Peter's call, and about Bluebeard's approval. "Jake said I did the right thing, and Bluebeard said 'Absolutely,' so I think he was pretty happy."

Sly got a faraway look on his face. "He was a great man, your Uncle Louis. I never met a more righteous man in my life, aside from my own dad, God rest his soul."

We talked through the rest of dinner, and over the peach tarts Sly had baked for dessert.

"What about Lighthouse, you haven't told me where that deal stands. Have you heard from the bank yet?"

I shook my head. "Buddy told me the loan committee would meet on Friday, but not to expect an answer until after the weekend. He said I had a great business plan and it should go through just fine, but it's hard not to worry."

"Nothing to worry about. I'm glad to help you out if there's any problem." He thought for a minute. "I could probably just make you the loan myself and get more than what the bank's paying on my savings."

I sat back, startled. Sly had offered to guarantee my loan, even offered the yard as collateral. That I understood. But to make the loan himself, he had to have a lot more money put away than I thought.

"I don't need much," he said with a shrug. "My daddy left me this place free and clear, and business been good over the years. I started putting something aside every week.

"It adds up."

I let out a low whistle. "I guess. I appreciate it, Sly. And I'll keep it in mind. But I really have to believe what Buddy said. I won't need it.

"Besides, what would happen if you needed it? If you wanted to take a trip, or buy another car? Or a boat?" Boats were popular around Keyhole Bay, all kinds and sizes.

Sly picked up the plates from the table and stacked them in the sink. "Don't need none of that. Got me plenty of cars, and if I want to fish, there's a perfectly good pier." He started the water running, his back to me. "As for travelin'," he said in a voice so low I could barely hear him over the rush of the water, "I did plenty of that with Uncle Sam. Now everything I want is right here at home."

Somehow I didn't quite believe that last part. There were things he still wanted, but he'd made peace with not having them. It was an uncomfortable reminder of the pictures I'd seen at the library.

For Sly, peace had come at a cost.

Bobo scratched at the door, wanting in. Sly glanced over at Bobo's usual resting place as though just realizing the dog was still outside.

"He must have found something that purely needed chasing," he said. He opened the door and Bobo came in. His fur was matted, and he had a couple scratches. Clearly he had tangled with something while he was out, though we hadn't heard any sounds of a fight.

Sly grabbed a towel and cleaned him up, though Bobo didn't seem at all concerned with his condition. He endured the cleaning with a nonchalance that clearly said, "You oughta see the other guy."

"What have I told you," Sly said to the dog as he took a tube of ointment out of a drawer and applied it to the scratches, "about fighting above your weight class? What?

"I told you don't do it. I said fight someone your own size. But did you listen? You did not. And who gets to clean you up when you do this? I do."

Sly capped the ointment and patted Bobo's head. "I swear," he said, turning back to me. "That dog would take on a Florida panther if one wandered into the yard."

Considering that there hadn't been a panther sighting in the Panhandle in my lifetime, I didn't think it was something to worry about.

There was still plenty of wildlife that was common, though, and he'd obviously encountered something.

Chapter 37

I WAS STILL THINKING ABOUT WHAT MIGHT BE OUT in the yard when Sly walked me to my truck a little while later. Bobo had tried to follow me out, but Sly ordered him to stay and closed the door behind us. "No sense letting him run off and find something else to mess with tonight."

I could imagine unseen eyes watching us in the dark, tracking our progress by the beam of Sly's flashlight and the perimeter lights.

I thanked Sly for dinner and clambered quickly into the cab of the truck. "I'll lock the gate," I offered, but Sly turned me down.

"I'd just have to come out and check it later," he said. "Can't sleep unless I make sure everything's closed up proper."

I drove out through the gate in the chain-link, secretly relieved that I didn't have to get back out of the truck in the dark. It was silly, but after Bobo's encounter, it felt as though the night was full of eyes, all watching me.

The feeling intensified on the drive home, finally spooking

me to the point that I parked under the streetlight in front of the store instead of pulling around to my usual spot in the back.

I could move the truck in the morning. In the daylight.

Bluebeard woke up the instant I put the key in the front door. "Who's there?" he called loudly. "Who's there?"

"It's just me, Bluebeard," I answered. I locked the door and reset the alarm. "I'm home."

I understood his agitation. Changes in routine distressed him, and normally when I went out at night, I would park in back and come in through the warehouse door. The only time I used the front door was when someone else dropped me off.

"Don't do that," he said.

I didn't bother to ask him to explain; he never did. Instead I murmured something noncommittal that he could take as agreement if he wanted to, and went about my business.

I wasn't ready to settle down, and I thought I would do a little work downstairs.

The minute I turned on the overhead light, however, I felt exposed. The large front windows afforded anyone passing by a view of the store and a view of me. Combined with the eerie sensation that someone was watching me, I quickly became too uncomfortable to stay in the store.

That, too, would have to wait for daylight.

BY MORNING MY FEARS SEEMED AS FOOLISH AS they had seemed real the night before. Jake came by early, with lattes from Lighthouse Coffee and a biscuit for Bluebeard.

"How was your dinner with Sly?"

I accepted the coffee gratefully. "Good." I sipped the sweet drink and felt the warmth slide down my throat. "You know, I'm going to lose a steady customer once I buy this place." I gestured with the cup. "I won't be able to have you buy me coffee anymore."

I took another sip. "Which will be soon, I hope."

Jake grinned. "Well then, enjoy it while you can."

"You know, Sly did say something that caught me by surprise. He told me he could loan me the money to buy Lighthouse, and he'd make more off the loan than the bank was paying him."

Jake whistled, impressed. Whether by the offer itself or by the amount of money involved, I wasn't sure.

"He said he'd inherited his place free and clear, and when I suggested he might want to spend some on himself, maybe even travel, he said he already had everything he wanted right here."

"I know how he feels," Jake said.

"Really?" I was headed into dangerous territory, but caution wasn't on my agenda lately.

Jake nodded and counted off on his fingers: "A job I love, a great volunteer unit to belong to, a comfortable house, wonderful friends, amazing weather all year . . ." He paused as though trying to remember what else. "Oh, yeah! And you."

It made me laugh. I gave him a hug, happy that he had included me in the list of everything he wanted.

"But that's why I don't believe him completely," I explained. "He says he has everything he wants, but he's all alone. And don't tell me he has Bobo. It's not the same thing."

Jake was quiet for a minute, thinking. When he spoke again, his voice was low and I had to strain to hear him.

"You resign yourself to certain things, and you learn to be okay with them. Over time, okay becomes content, and eventually you are almost happy. And you tell yourself your life is just fine.

"And that works until you meet somebody that changes everything." He leaned down and kissed me lightly.

"Hey, break it up!" Bluebeard's squawk interrupted the moment, and we both jumped.

"Yes, sir!" Jake snapped, tossing a salute in the direction of Bluebeard's perch. "At once, sir!"

Bluebeard cackled, the high-pitched laugh that imitated Rose Ann's toddler giggle, and preened, reminding us that here at least it was all about the parrot.

Jake said he needed to get back to work, and I walked out with him to move the truck around to the back.

"I wondered what this was doing at the curb," Jake said as I unlocked the door.

"I got spooked last night. It was dark and the street was deserted. I didn't want to park around back in the dark, so I left it out front. But I need to move it before the parking patrol comes around."

When the highway is also the main drag, parking is sometimes at a premium. As a result, the Merchants' Association funded a year-round position for a parking enforcement officer.

We didn't call her a meter maid—for one thing, we didn't have any parking meters in Keyhole Bay, and she took her job seriously. Very. Seriously. Enforcement would start in half an hour. If the truck was still in front an hour after that, there would be a warning, complete with instructions to the municipal lot a block off Main Street; and in another hour, I'd find a pricey parking ticket on the windshield.

"Maybe we should think about putting a high-intensity floodlight on your parking area," Jake suggested. "With a motion sensor, you wouldn't have to leave it on all night."

"Good idea," I said. "There's one on the back of Lighthouse since Pansy comes in so early." I stopped and corrected myself. "Chloe comes in so early." I shook my head. "That's gonna take some getting used to."

"I'll watch the door until you get back," Jake said. He stood on the sidewalk, sipping his latte while I drove around the block, parked the truck in my spot at the back, and came back through the warehouse to the front of the shop.

I waved through the window and he waved back, glanced up and down the quiet street, and crossed back over to Beach Books.

Just another autumn Monday in Keyhole Bay.

I normally wasn't much of one for watching the clock, but nothing was normal for me right now.

I didn't know what was going on with Beth, hadn't heard anything from her since our visit on Saturday, even though Karen had dropped off a small bundle of clothes at the jail on Sunday afternoon.

The bank was supposed to call today, but I had no idea when.

And then there was the question of Peter. He could go in any direction, from complete cooperation to complete obstruction, and I honestly couldn't guess what he might do.

I got my answer shortly after lunchtime, when Peter's phone number showed up on my caller ID.

I wasn't sure I wanted to talk to him, but I knew we were going to have to resolve the issue. And as much as I might not want to talk to him, I wanted this settled more.

"Southern Treasures, how may I help you?"

"You can stop acting like you don't know who this is." Peter's superior tone instantly raised my hackles, but I waited him out, and he finally continued. "I really don't think there's anything you can do to help me."

I literally bit my tongue, holding it gently between my teeth, to avoid telling him I knew he was beyond help. I realized that was quite the opposite of what he meant, but it didn't stop me from putting my own spin on his jibe.

"But there is something I can do for you." He sounded a little deflated, as though he was trying to goad me into an argument and I was refusing to play. "I've been thinking about our last conversation, and I think it's time I pulled my investment out of Southern Treasures and put it some-where more lucrative. Put it into something that will pro-vide an adequate return for my family.

"I'm sure you'll understand that, won't you?"

I understood all right. I understood that Peter was taking what I'd said, taking my demands that he sell me his share of the business, and acting as though it was all his idea.

My brain said *I understand you are once again dismiss-ing my concerns as though they are of no value.* But what my mouth said was, "Of course. I'll have my attorney draw up a contract for the sale. At fair market value, of course, with a consideration for my services over the last three years.

"I'm sure you'll understand."

The yelp at the other end of the line told me Peter understood exactly what I'd just said. I allowed myself a moment of "gotcha" before I explained. "He tells me I've been undervalued about twenty thousand dollars a year for several years. But that seems like such a huge amount, how about we say five thousand a year for the last three?"

It was all an elaborate bluff. Buddy had advised me that my proposed salary in my business plan, consistent with my current earnings, was well below the market and I should be drawing a much larger salary. I'd used that infor-mation as leverage in my battle with Peter.

And it worked.

"Fine," he snapped. "Market value, less fifteen grand. But I want a copy of that appraisal. My financial advisor will need it to plan for the tax consequences of the sale."

My brain said *I'm not impressed*, but my mouth agreed to send a copy of the appraisal.

I ended the conversation and hung up the phone before my brain took control of my mouth and said several things that would probably kill the whole deal.

I reminded myself that I really didn't care all that much what Peter said or thought, as long as he sold.

Bottom line? That was all I needed.

Southern Treasures was all mine. And I had a long list of things that I had to do immediately.

But first I had to tell Uncle Louis.

Bluebeard had been napping in his cage when the phone rang and hadn't bothered to come check on my conversation. But when I called his name, he hopped out, looking around for the cause of the commotion.

"We did it! Peter's selling!"

Bluebeard leaped from his perch and flew to the top of the ceiling, moving around the hanging fluorescent fixtures. There really wasn't room for him to fly inside the shop, and his movements were ungainly, but there was no other way for him to express his excitement. He shrieked and squawked as he dodged obstacles in his flight path, finally coming to rest on the counter where he did a little hoppity dance, bobbing his head and spreading his wings.

I gave him some pets, then put a couple almonds and a pecan in his cage as a treat. He hopped across the racks and into the cage, happily settling down to the challenge of opening the nuts for the tasty treat inside.

It was his favorite way to celebrate.

I e-mailed Clifford Wilson and asked him to draw up another sales contract, this one for my purchase of Peter's interest in the business. I outlined the terms, including the fifteen thousand as consideration for my work in the shop, and asked him to let me know as soon as the papers were available. I wanted to move as quickly as possible, before Peter changed his mind.

I also e-mailed Peter a confirmation of our conversation and reiterated the terms we had agreed on. I might have even implied that I had a recording of the phone call, though that was certainly subject to interpretation.

I called Karen, but only got her voice mail. I glanced at the clock and confirmed my suspicion—it was time for her regular news broadcast. I left a message, telling her Peter had agreed to sell, and to call me when she had time.

There were other people I needed to call, and many more details to tend to, but one person deserved to know more than anyone. I locked the door behind me and dashed across the empty street to Beach Books.

Jake looked up as I burst in the door, caught sight of the giant grin on my face, and ran over to give me a hug.

"They approved your loan!"

I hugged him back, then disentangled myself and stepped back. "Even better!"

Jake looked puzzled. "What could be better than that? Did you win the lottery?"

I laughed out loud. "It feels that way."

"So, what? Come on, you've got me dying of curiosity."

"Peter just called. He agreed to sell me his share of Southern Treasures. And I got him to agree to a fifteen thousand dollar kicker to make up for all the years I've worked."

Jake's eyebrows shot up and he gave me another hug. "Fifteen grand? You actually got him to go for that? Man, you are good!

"We need to celebrate!"

"Wish I could, but I'm still waiting on word from the bank. But I had to tell you, since you're going to have some of your money in this deal."

"I consider it a sound investment," Jake said, his voice shifting from jubilant to serious. "You'll make it worth my while to invest in Southern Treasures."

"And you won't try to tell me how to run my business," I reminded him.

"No way. I've seen what happens when a man tries that."

"Just remember that," I teased as I headed for the door. I waved as I walked out. "I'll talk to you a little later."

I went back to the shop, intending to make a few more

calls. I certainly wanted to tell Sly, and Guy and Linda. Julie would need to know as well.

But before I could pick up the phone, an older woman came in and marched up to the counter.

"Are you Gloryanna?" she asked. Her direct approach marked her as a Yankee as surely as her flat Midwestern accent.

"Yeeees," I drew the word out, tentative.

"I need to talk to you." She stuck out her hand. "I'm Althea Stevenson, Beth's granny."

Chapter 38

"GLORYANNA MARTINE. I'M GLAD TO MEET YOU," I said, shaking her hand. The skin on the back of her hand was loose, as though it was too big for the tiny bones underneath, but her grip was as firm as her voice. She might be a small woman, but she had enough grit for a linebacker.

I liked her immediately.

"What can I do for you, Mrs. Stevenson?"

"For starters, you can explain to me what kind of trouble that granddaughter of mine and the fool she married have gotten themselves into. And how we're going to get them out of it."

I started to protest that I barely knew Beth and Everett, but she continued talking a mile a minute. "No question whether he did it or not. Boy couldn't hurt a fly. I mean *really* couldn't hurt a fly. I've seen him carry one outside and let it go instead of swatting it like he ought to. The only way he could kill someone is to talk them to death."

I'd never thought of Everett as much of a talker, and my skepticism must have shown on my face.

"I know, I know. Normally the boy won't say *boo*. But every once in a while, he decides something is real important, and then he won't shut up about it. Talk 'til you think you're going to die of boredom."

"He is charged with murder," I said.

"Charged isn't convicted," she said. "And I'm telling you, I know he couldn't do it."

"You know it. I know it. But there's an assistant district attorney that says he did."

I saw Bluebeard peek out of his cage, then retreat back inside, like a turtle pulling into his shell. Sometimes he preferred the role of an unseen observer.

"Then he's a fool, or a liar," Mrs. Stevenson shot back. "Or both. If he's a politician, I'd say both."

I couldn't argue with the truth.

"So this fool charges Everett with murder, based on what? The fact that the two guys were found near his house? He wasn't even home. He and Bethie were at my house."

"Where is your house? I don't think Beth ever said."

"Dearborn. Outside Detroit. It's almost a thousand miles." She winced and her tough exterior cracked for a minute. "And right now I am feeling every one of them."

I excused myself and ducked into the back to get the coffeepot and a couple mugs. "You look like you could use a cup of coffee," I said, offering her a mug.

"That I could. It was a long trip." She took the mug and held it out for me to fill. "Black's fine," she said, anticipating my next question.

"You fly?" I asked. I poured myself a mug and took a sip.

"Drove. Didn't have time to mess with schedules and rental cars and all the rest. Beth and I tossed our bags in the car and drove all night."

"Beth?"

"Sorry." She gulped coffee. "My sister-in-law. My granddaughter was named for her. Never had any kids of her own, so my Meg named her youngest after her favorite aunt."

She drained the mug and set it on the counter. "So what do we do?" she asked.

I told her there wasn't much we could do. Karen was already working her magic where the public defender was concerned, and once they had a competent lawyer, he could petition for another bail hearing.

"About the best thing would be to find out who really did it. But that's not really a job for amateurs," I said, conveniently failing to mention that I'd been involved in several investigations that were solved by an amateur, namely me.

I wondered if my history had anything to do with Mrs. Stevenson's visit. "Why did you come to me, anyway?"

"Because Bethie said you wanted to help. You were the only person she knew down here, and she said you'd been kind to her.

"Thanks, by the way, for the clothes. She told me she hadn't even realized how much that jumpsuit depressed her until she was able to take it off. We'll replace everything, of course."

"No need. I have a whole wardrobe of jeans and T-shirts, so plenty to spare." I remembered how defeated the baggy jumpsuit had made Beth look. "She just looked like she could use some regular clothes. So you're welcome."

It struck me that she'd come in alone, but she'd said her sister-in-law had driven down with her. "Where is the other Beth?" I asked. "Isn't she with you?"

"She's back at the motel. She did a lot more of the driving, so I told her I'd come see you and let her get a little nap before we went back to see Bethie.

"She used to live around here when she was a kid, and I think she's a little overwhelmed. Lots of things she recognized, but lots that's changed, too."

She snapped her fingers. "One other thing Bethie asked

me to tell you. That quilt of yours is still at the cabin, far as she knows, but even if she could get it, the sheriff wouldn't let her have the tools she would need to finish it off.

"Beth and I are both pretty fair quilters, that's where Bethie learned it, so we'll go get it and finish it up in time for your friend's wedding."

It was a generous offer, considering how much this woman had on her plate already. "I would appreciate that," I told her. "But I know that you have a lot of important things demanding your attention right now, and I would understand if you can't get it done."

She huffed impatiently. "It needs to be done. We'll do it. It's how it has to be.

"Now I need to be going. Lots to do." She tapped the mug. "Thanks for the coffee. I'll be in touch."

She was gone as abruptly as she had appeared.

THE FINAL PIECE OF MY MONDAY FELL INTO PLACE shortly before closing time.

Buddy McKenna called me. We exchanged greetings, but for once I did away with the required pleasantries. It was apparently my day for blunt conversations.

"I have news," Buddy said.

I lowered myself into the tall chair behind the counter. I didn't trust my legs to hold me up.

"Go on."

"You're approved. Your application sailed through the loan committee, one of the easiest I've ever seen, and we got confirmation on all the reports this afternoon.

"It will take a couple days to fund and there will be some papers to sign, but the money is yours.

"Congratulations, Gloryanna. You just bought a coffee shop."

I thanked him and managed to hang up the phone

before I got the shakes. Between Peter and Buddy, this was one of the most dramatic days of my life.

I picked up the phone again and dialed Jake's number.

When he answered, I said, "*Now* we can celebrate."

"I'll be right there."

"No," I said. "Meet me at Lighthouse. I can't wait to tell Chloe. And Bradley."

Chapter 39

"WE GOT US A COFFEE SHOP," I TOLD BLUEBEARD before I left. "I have to go tell Chloe I'm her new boss!"

Next door I found Jake, waiting for me on the sidewalk. He looked like he was about to burst. "I didn't dare go in," he said, reaching for the door. "This is your news to share, and I would have totally blown it."

I laughed, giddy with the excitement of the day.

Once inside, I struggled to maintain my composure as Chloe waited on a couple stragglers, picking up bread and dessert at the end of the day.

I managed to tamp down my excitement until we were alone, but then I couldn't contain myself any longer. "I got it!" I hollered to Chloe. "I got the loan!"

Chloe rushed around the counter and grabbed me in a congratulatory bear hug, then just as quickly she released me and stepped back in confusion.

"I totally want to congratulate you, and you know I'm kind of a huggy person, but now that you're my boss, I think that's totally inappropriate, isn't it?" She struggled with the thought for a few seconds, then leaped forward and hugged me again. "But just this once," she said, nearly squeezing the breath out of me. "I can't help myself."

Bradley Whittaker came out from the bakery, a puzzled look on his face. "What's all the commotion?"

Chloe released me and turned to Bradley. "Glory got the loan, and she'd going to buy Lighthouse."

Bradley's smile was a mix of relief and regret. "That's good," he said. He offered me his hand. "Congratulations, Miss Glory. I know Mother will be happy, too."

"I hope so," I said. I shook his hand with both of mine, glad we had reached this point so quickly. "It will be a couple days for the funds to come through at the bank, but we can sign the final offer and acceptance any time, and you'll have your money by the end of the week."

We made a date for Wednesday afternoon. I offered to come to the house, but Bradley said his mom wanted to come back in, to say good-bye to the place. It was even possible I would have my money by then.

Chloe promised to keep up as she had been. "We can work out schedules and so on next week," she said. "After the dust settles a bit."

I sighed, a deep breath of relief that dissolved into happy giggles. "And I can finally open that envelope of recipes with a clear conscience."

Bradley looked at me, shocked. "You haven't opened the envelope? Then how?" He stared at Chloe. "How did you?"

She looked sheepish, like a kid caught with her hand in the cookie jar. "You must never, *ever* tell your mother," she said solemnly. "She would be crushed, and I would never hurt her. But I have been coming in early for years to help her with the baking, and I've learned how to make most everything in that time." An anxious frown creased her forehead. "You won't tell her, will you? Promise you won't."

Bradley smiled. "I couldn't. You're right, it would upset her terribly." He raised his right hand, index finger pointed toward himself, and drew an X across his chest. "Cross my heart."

I double-checked our meeting time on Wednesday, and Jake and I went back to Southern Treasures.

"This really does call for a celebration," Jake said. "What would you like to do? Anything you want."

I pretended to think over his offer. "Anything? How about dinner in Paris?"

"Too late," he said. "It's already after midnight there. But we might be able to make it in time for breakfast. Is your passport current?"

I held up my hands in a gesture of surrender. "You got me. Paris is out. I guess I have to think of something else."

Jake waited as I considered my options. There were a couple decent dinner places in town, and Pensacola was only a short drive away. Even the glossy casinos of Biloxi were just a couple hours away.

And I didn't want any of it. Not while Beth and Everett were still in jail. It would feel wrong to celebrate my good fortune when they were stuck behind bars, and I had helped put them there.

"Do you mind if we just stay home?" I asked. "We can call Neil's for a pizza, or get some drive-thru burgers, or I can cook for us, but I want something quiet tonight. Just us."

Jake nodded. "I wouldn't mind at all. But are you sure you don't want to call the rest of the gang over?"

He had good reason to be skeptical. I was usually the one who pulled together impromptu dinner parties and picnics, who organized events for our little group, and who always wanted to include my new friends when I got together with my old friends.

But tonight was different. Tonight, if I admitted the truth, I was afraid. I didn't want a celebration, I wanted comfort and reassurance.

I nodded. "I'm sure." I wasn't sure I could explain why, so I fell back on a reasonable, if less complete, explanation.

"I'm just tired. This has been an unbelievable roller coaster the last few days, and I need a break. Besides, there will be plenty of time to celebrate on Thursday night."

I stretched and wiggled my shoulders, feeling some of the tension of the last week fall away. "I'll call people tomorrow. This was supposed to be our early Thanksgiving, and I will truly have a lot to be thankful for."

We climbed the stairs to my apartment and rummaged in the cupboards and refrigerator, coming up with the ingredients for a tuna-noodle casserole.

The creamy, hearty casserole was exactly the kind of comfort food I wanted. We found an old movie on television and settled down on the sofa with our feet propped up and plates on our laps.

Perfect.

Jake insisted on helping with the cleanup when we finished the movie. He scrubbed vigorously at the sticky bits in the baking dish, until I finally stopped him. "Let it soak," I said. "Otherwise you could be here until morning."

"Would that be such a bad idea?" It was a serious question, and he let it linger unanswered for several seconds. "Of course, you might think I was just after you for your money, now that you're the successful owner of two businesses."

"I don't know about successful," I said. I slid a small bowl of leftover casserole into the refrigerator. It could be dinner the next night. "And I only own one-and-a-half businesses. I still have a partner in the other one." I nodded at him, acknowledging his stake in buying out Peter's share of Southern Treasures.

"Not a partner," he said. "An investor. I put my money into a business I think will earn me more money, and I let you run it your way. That's the difference between an investor and a partner, to my way of thinking.

"I give you my money to do what you do best—run a gift shop. In return, you give me back part of the profits. It's the lazy man's way to make money."

I could talk about Jake all day and the word "lazy" would never be spoken. He worked harder than most men I knew, volunteered with the fire department several shifts a week, and helped run occasional disaster preparedness classes.

"So you're saying this isn't going to work for you."

"Of course it works for me. Why wouldn't it?"

"Because"—I waved my hand around the kitchen, now immaculate after Jake's attention—"you are clearly not a lazy man."

"I aspire to be. Isn't that good enough? I would be very happy to sit around reading books and drinking coffee all day."

"No you wouldn't. You barely made it through the movie, and it was less than two hours. When was the last time you sat in one place all day? I bet you can't even remember."

He had a ready answer, actually named a date, and he had an explanation. "You were in the hospital. Again. I spent two days there, most of it in the chair next to your bed."

"Okay," I said, quickly conceding the point. "So you can sit still for longer than an hour. Under duress. But you know that isn't what I meant.

"You're not the sitting-around type. You're a guy who gets up out of his chair and does things. You will never be content to be a lazy man, however you define it."

"So I will just have to keep myself busy with my own work, and keep my nose out of yours. I promise I will not interfere unless you ask me for my help."

"And no unsolicited advice?" I prodded.

"No unsolicited advice.

"We can do this, Glory. I really believe we can do this and still be friends. Because I respect what you have accomplished, and believe in what you will accomplish.

"And because you will always be more important than any amount of money."

Now how is a girl supposed to resist a declaration like that?

Chapter 40

I TOOK ADVANTAGE OF JULIE'S PRESENCE ON TUES-day morning to get out of the shop for a little while without feeling guilty.

After coming to an agreement with Peter and getting approval from the bank, there were a ton of details to think about.

I managed to get a few minutes with Clifford Wilson, but only because I sat in his waiting room for forty minutes and snuck in between clients.

Mr. Wilson was his usual gracious self, but I knew he was short on time and I condensed my agreement with Peter to a couple sentences, giving Mr. Wilson a sheet with the figures on it for reference.

"He agreed to those terms," I said when I handed over the paper. "I just need that turned into an ironclad purchase agreement. I'll have a cashier's check drawn to go with it as soon as you have it ready."

"You have that much in cash?" He cocked his head in a tiny salute. "You're doing better than I expected."

"I had an unexpected windfall, and a friend is investing some cash. Put that together with my savings—and that fifteen thousand dollar bonus—and I have enough."

"That windfall wouldn't have anything to do with the question you asked about Mr. Louis's will, would it?"

"It would. I know you have another client due any minute, so I'm going to get along. I'll tell you the whole story when we have a little more time."

I made my exit, waving at the receptionist on my way through the outer office.

Ten minutes later, I was sitting across the desk from Buddy McKenna, talking about his boys while we waited for the loan documents to finish printing.

"I'm going home in three weeks," he said. "For good. The new, permanent manager should be starting on Thursday, and I'll be showing him around town, introducing him to our business customers. I'll give you a call early next week to set up a time, if that's okay."

"Certainly, though I'll hate to see you go. I was kind of hoping you'd get to stay on, and bring your family to Keyhole Bay with you."

He shook his head. "We have a nice house in a wonderful neighborhood. Most of our family's in the Twin Cities. It's home for us, and eventually I'll move back to a desk job where I get to go home every night instead of one week a month."

"Well, before you go, be sure you stop by the store. Now that you won't be manager here, I'd like to give you those Bluebeard shirts for the kids as a gift."

"Thanks." He glanced over my head and I turned to look. The senior loan officer, a new man brought in during the transition, was headed our way with a stack of papers. Barbara, the bank's on-site notary, was next to him, her book and stamp in her hands.

The ritual of signing loan papers always took longer

than anyone would expect. There was something about the act of signing a document promising to repay a staggering amount of money that made time slow down.

I signed my name about a million times, and signed Barbara's book a million more. I wrote slowly, carefully forming each letter, as though I expected to be graded on my penmanship when we were through, all under the watchful eyes of the senior loan officer.

When the signing was done, the loan officer shuffled the papers into several piles and assembled the piles into groups. He placed one set in a large envelope and offered it to me. "These are your copies," he explained unnecessarily. "Keep them in a safe place. I would suggest, if you don't have somewhere secure on your premises, that you talk to Mr. McKenna about a safe deposit box."

"I have a safe," I said. "I think it will be adequate."

"A pleasure to meet you, Miss Martine." He gathered up his remaining papers and rose from his chair. "If there's anything else I can do, please don't hesitate to call."

After he was gone, I turned to Buddy. "Is that it?" I whispered. "Am I through?"

Buddy nodded. "I'll call you as soon as the funds clear," he said. "And I'll see you sometime next week with the new manager."

Pleased with my productive morning, I moved on to the next thing on my list: checking in on Beth. I had sent over clothes and talked with her granny. But I hadn't talked to her directly since that first meeting on Saturday morning.

I'd packed a small bag with a few toiletries and some chocolate for her. Deputy Fuentes took the bag, glanced inside, and made a face. "Mostly we're not supposed to let prisoners have outside supplies," she said. "But since we don't really have provisions for females, I am going to let this pass. If anyone asks, I'll tell them it was just 'woman stuff,' and they'll shut up so fast you'll feel the breeze when their jaw snaps shut."

"How is she?" I asked. "Can she have visitors?"

"Her granny's back there with her, and they're limiting her visitors to family and her lawyer for today, so I'm afraid not. In fact"—she checked the clock on the wall—"her granny's time is almost up. You know, if you want to check on her, you could just wait until Mrs. Stevenson comes out and ask her."

I took her suggestion, but chose to stand rather than sit in those miserable plastic chairs. I would rather do almost anything than sit in those chairs.

Ten minutes passed, then twenty. I went back to the desk and asked Deputy Fuentes how much longer.

"They're in the middle of a conference with the lawyer, so I have to let them have all the time they want. I didn't realize he was in there with them when I told you to wait. I'm really sorry."

"It's okay. I'd appreciate if you let Beth know I came to see her, though. And if you could, tell Mrs. Stevenson to give me a call. I would like to know how it's going."

"After you had to hang around because of my mistake?" Fuentes said. "You got it."

JULIE AND CHLOE WERE IN THE SHOP TOGETHER when I got back, bent over pages of paper spread across the back counter.

"Hi, boss!" Chloe said. "I came over on my day off so Julie and I could settle some of the stuff for the shower."

"Get everything squared away with Bradley after I left?"

She rolled her eyes at me. "He was totally fine. Said he had wondered how I'd managed. Thought maybe Miss Pansy made up some mixes for me, or had batters or something stashed in the freezer.

"As if we would ever serve anything that wasn't made fresh from scratch that day! I told him his mother would never have done any such thing, and I wasn't about to change that."

"Has anyone talked to the relief barista?" I asked. "I hardly know the girl, but I expect I'll keep her on. Actually"—I pointed to Chloe—"that will be your decision as manager."

"I did tell her Miss Pansy was selling, and that you'd told me you weren't making any changes. But that was all I said. I just wanted to tell her before the rumors started flying and she heard about it from somebody else."

"Good idea. Just keep me posted on what you decide." I turned back to Julie and the lists. "So what kind of trouble are you two cooking up for me?"

"We talked to Karen and her mom, separately and together. At first Karen said she didn't want a shower, they had everything they needed, most of it two times over. Her mother said the shower was a lovely idea and she should let her friends spoil her a little. They went back and forth for a while, and we just tried to stay out of it.

"Karen finally agreed to a party, but she was insistent on no gifts. We're still trying to come up with something that we can do for her, but we haven't got any ideas we like yet."

"The other thing we haven't settled yet," Chloe said, "is the food. I told Julie I could do most of the food, but we have to decide if we're going with tea and sweets, or cocktails and savory. I'm more a cocktail kind of girl, but I don't know about the rest of you. Or Karen."

"Of the two, I'd say Karen's more cocktail than tea. But not by very much. And a lot depends on who you want to invite. There are a few people around here who won't attend if they know we're serving alcohol."

"And a few that won't show up if we aren't," Julie muttered. Like every small town, Keyhole Bay had its very own problem drinkers, and I suspected at least a couple of those were on their guest list.

"Which is another reason to go with the tea and sweets." I looked from Julie to Chloe and back again. "I think we'd all vote for cocktails and savory finger foods, but I would not be able to relax and enjoy it, knowing the potential for problems." They nodded their understanding. "So we're agreed? Sweet?"

"Yeah."

"You're right."

The replies weren't wildly enthusiastic, but at least we had an agreement.

I left them to their planning and went back to work. It didn't seem to matter how few or how many people came through the store, there was always something out of place, a shelf that needed restocking, or merchandise that had to be priced or re-priced. It was a constant process, one that was never really finished, and I could always find something that needed fixing.

And it would only get worse when I took over Lighthouse.

Althea Stevenson showed up a couple hours later with another woman. She was a sturdier version of Mrs. Stevenson, her dark hair showing the first faint streaks of gray, and dark eyes that missed nothing.

"This is Beth Stevenson, my sister-in-law," Mrs. Stevenson introduced her companion. "The one I told you Bethie was named for. Beth, this is Bethie's friend Gloryanna. She's the one who sent her the blue jeans."

"Thank you so much for doing that, Miss Gloryanna. It was very thoughtful of you."

I thought I detected a hint of the South in her soft voice and the way she slipped into calling me Miss Gloryanna, and remembered that Mrs. Stevenson had said she'd grown up in the area.

"I am glad I was able to help in a small way," I said. "I hope you'll let me know if there is anything else I can do.

"Just how is Beth doing, Mrs. Stevenson? And Everett, is he holding up okay?"

The two women both started to answer me, then stopped and looked at each other. "Please, call me Althea."

"And me Beth. It's just easier."

"Then you must call me Glory." I smiled at Beth as I said it.

"We've been dealing with this for decades," Althea said. "Our husbands were brothers and they spent a lot of time together. We decided long ago that first names were better than confusion, even if it didn't fit Beth's idea of proper manners."

I had to smile. "I understand how you feel, Miss Beth. If my mama was still with us, she would purely skin me alive if she heard me call one of my elders by their Christian name."

Althea blinked and turned to Beth. "You weren't kidding, were you? All these years you told me stories like that, and I always thought you were exaggerating."

"Told you," Beth said. She was looking around the store, almost as if it was familiar to her. I wondered if she had ever been in before; Althea had said she lived here as a child.

"You've never been down here before?" I asked Althea.

She shook her head. "Beth came up north and married Milt's brother Will, but somehow we never came down here for a visit. Always some reason or another."

"To be fair," Beth said, her attention pulled back from her inspection of the store, "Mama and Daddy preferred to visit up north anyway. Always looked forward to coming up to our place."

"But you *did* grow up around here?"

"Lordy, yes. That's how Bethie and Everett got that place to live on. My daddy bought bits and pieces of land all over. Said it was a solid investment. Laughed at his own joke every time he said it, too.

"Anyway, when they said they wanted to try living off the land, I offered to let them stay in the cabin. Didn't think they'd last very long—no offense, Thea."

"None taken. I didn't expect them to make it a month." Not exactly the warm and fuzzy kind of grandma I'd envisioned, but her candor was part of her charm.

"Deputy Fuentes told me you were in with the lawyer," I said. "Was this one better than the first one, I hope?"

We'd lost Beth to an inspection of the store again, but Althea answered me immediately.

"You better believe it. He had read the charges, knew what the problems were, and he asked good questions. He's not going to get Everett released right away, but at least he's working on it." She glanced around, looking for Beth. "We better get going," she said, addressing Beth more than me. "Still a lot to do this afternoon, and not much afternoon to do it in."

After they left, Julie, who had kept a discreet distance while we talked, came up to my side. "That one gal sure took an interest in the place," she said.

"She grew up somewhere around here," I told her. "Probably just reminds her of someplace she used to go."

Her interest reminded me of the two men I'd seen in the store a few days earlier. I'd been meaning to ask Julie if they'd come in again, but when I asked, she said she hadn't seen anyone that looked like who I described.

We hadn't had any calls from the merchant alert links either, but I still couldn't shake the feeling someone was watching the store.

Chapter 41

ALTHEA STEVENSON TOOK ME AT MY WORD AND called late the next morning to ask a favor.

"We're going up to the cabin," she said. "We're going to stay up there, even if it means a long drive to see Bethie. Our motel isn't all that cheap, and we'd rather save our money for important things, like lawyers.

"The problem is that we haven't been over to the jail yet today, we still have several errands to take care of here, and I think once we get up there, we will be too busy to drive back down this afternoon. But I hate to leave Bethie alone, with no one to check on her.

"I know you have a business to run, but is it possible you could go over for just a little while and check in on her?"

"I'd be glad to," I said, and meant it. It would only take a few minutes, and I still carried the guilt of my part in getting Beth and Everett put in jail. It hardly atoned for what I'd done, but at least it was something.

I locked up shortly after noon and hung the clock sign

in the window with the hands pointing to one o'clock. I hoped I would be back well before then, but I always erred on the side of caution.

I parked in the lot, taking a wary look around for the Beemer with the custom plates. It wasn't in any of the reserved spaces at the front of the lot, and I couldn't imagine someone who drove a car like that passing up the opportunity to flaunt his success.

Deputy Fuentes wasn't at the desk, but she came in while I was talking to a Deputy Hicks, according to his nameplate.

"She's on the sheriff's approved list," Fuentes said, waving at me. "Ten minutes. I'll take her back."

I checked my bag and followed Deputy Fuentes to the same interview room where we'd met Beth on Saturday. She locked me in like before and promised to return with Beth in a couple minutes. "She might want to freshen up to see a visitor," Fuentes explained.

While I waited, I thought about Deputy Fuentes's behavior. She hadn't asked permission, or waited for someone to give her the authority to act. She had done what any other deputy—correction, what any *male* deputy—would have done. She assumed she already had the authority and acted on it.

It was a little thing, one that could easily have gone unnoticed. But I was always wondering where our next group of leaders was coming from, where we would find the people who would replace the good ol' boys network.

Fuentes was somebody to watch.

Beth was surprised to see me. "When the deputy said I had a visitor, I expected it was Granny."

She looked very different than she had at our first visit. For starters, she was wearing clothes that fit.

"She asked me to stop by. She and your aunt Beth were busy, and then they were going up to the cabin, so she wanted me to make sure you were okay." I suddenly felt very self-conscious, not sure what to say. "I, uh, is there anything you need? Anything I can do?"

She shook her head. "Not unless you know how to get me out of here. Otherwise there isn't much anyone can do.

"What are they going up to the cabin for, anyway?"

"You didn't know?"

She shook her head. "They didn't say anything."

"I just assumed you knew. They checked out of their motel this morning. They're planning to stay up at your cabin, well, your Aunt Beth's cabin, I guess. Said the motel wasn't all that great and it was costing too much."

"They can't stay there!" Beth jumped up from the chair she had been sitting in and pounded on the locked door. "You have to let me out!" she yelled. "I have to stop them!"

She whirled around to look at me. "You have to make them come back. They can't stay there. It isn't safe!"

"What do you mean, it isn't safe?"

"There are some bad people up there. If they can't scare you off, they find other ways to get rid of you. Please, Glory, please go get them."

"Tell the sheriff what you know, Beth. He can send deputies after them."

"My lawyer told me not to."

I started to ask her what was more important, her granny's safety or what her lawyer told her to do, but the stricken look on her face told me she'd already thought of it on her own.

"I'll talk to him," she said, "but I don't know if he'll listen to me, or believe me."

She hung her head. "I couldn't blame him if he didn't; I didn't tell him the truth to begin with.

"But you could talk Granny into coming back here before anything happens, couldn't you? Just tell her I need her. I just need a little time to convince the sheriff.

"Besides, they only just left, didn't they? Maybe you could even catch up to them before they get there." Desperation and hope battled for control of her voice. "You have to stop them!"

She whirled back to look at the door. "Where are they?" she demanded. "They should be here by now!"

I reached under the table and pressed the alarm button Deputy Fuentes had shown me on my first visit.

Instantly the room was filled with the deafening blare of a Klaxon horn. Within seconds the door burst open.

The Klaxon cut off abruptly when the door opened.

Fuentes crouched in the doorway, her service revolver steady in her hand as she swept it across the room. Behind her, Hicks stood, his weapon also at the ready.

"It's okay!" I shouted. "But Beth needs to talk to the sheriff. Now! She's got something to tell him."

Fuentes made one more visual sweep of the room. I hadn't moved from my chair, my hands in plain sight on top of the table. Beth stood on the other side, her hands over her head.

Fuentes signaled Hicks to stand down. He backed up, still covering her as she slowly holstered her weapon, keeping a watchful eye on both of us. "You sure you're okay, Miss Martine?"

"Absolutely. I just needed to get someone for Mrs. Young. Like I said, she needs to talk to the sheriff right away."

"Wait here," she pointed at Beth. "You"—she gestured to me—"come with me."

I followed her into the hall. Hicks closed the door behind us and moved down the hall where he could still watch us.

As soon as Hicks backed away, Fuentes whirled around. Her eyes flashed with anger, but she kept her voice and demeanor under control. "I showed you that button for emergencies. Not for every whim that a prisoner takes it into their head to act out."

"Believe me, she was truly agitated. I thought she was

calming down, but she was about that close"—I held up my thumb and forefinger a hair's breadth apart—"to a complete meltdown.

"She's afraid her grandmother and aunt may be in danger, and she's willing to spill everything she knows, or even thinks she knows, to protect them.

"Get Sheriff Hardy in there while she still wants to talk."

Wariness had replaced anger in her expression. "I can try," she said. "But the sheriff is out of the office and I'll have to track him down. I'll get her back to her cell—they're usually calmer there than in interrogation—and try to get him back here as quick as I can.

"In the meantime, I think it would be wise for you to leave."

On that we agreed 100 percent.

Back in the truck, I considered my options.

I could do nothing, and wait for Boomer to handle the situation. If Althea and Beth were actually in danger, his men would be the best qualified to deal with it.

I could wait and see if Boomer showed up quickly. If he didn't, then I could decide if I needed to do something myself.

Or I could do the thing I knew I was going to do as soon as Beth said it. I could drive like a bat out of hell to north county and hope I caught up with Althea and Beth before they got to the cabin.

I started the engine and pulled out of the parking lot.

If I hurried, I should be able to get back in time for my meeting with Miss Pansy.

Chapter 42

NORMALLY, A MISSION LIKE THIS NEEDS AN ACCOM-
plice. And normally, my accomplice would be Karen. But
since this all started with her wedding quilt—and since I
still hoped to salvage that surprise out of this disaster—I
couldn't call her.

I could call Jake, but it wouldn't be right to ask him to
close Beach Books and go on a wild-goose chase with me.

That's all it was. The panic-fueled imagination of a
frightened woman. But I'd do it because it might help calm
Beth's fears.

I had pretty well resigned myself to making the trip
alone when I thought of one person who might be up for a
little adventure.

I turned toward the junkyard behind Fowler's. Even if
Sly couldn't go, it only took me a couple minutes out of
the way.

To my surprise, Sly not only agreed to go with me, he
offered to drive. "Bobo loves car rides," he said. "If we

take one of my cars, there's plenty of room for him to go along."

He climbed in the cab and directed me through the yard to one of the garages hidden deep in the maze of vehicles and parts. Bobo was already there, waiting for us with undisguised doggy glee.

Sly opened the garage door and gestured for me to pull the truck inside.

The inside of the garage, like the inside of Sly's house, was completely at odds with the exterior. Two vintage muscle cars were parked side by side behind the other two doors on a concrete floor that looked as clean as if it had been freshly poured. Rolling tool chests that would have put Fowler's service department to shame stood against the walls, and a series of hooks near the doors held an array of crisp coveralls.

Sly grinned knowingly at the stunned look that passed over my face. "I'd say that's how most folks would react, if I let folks in here. But you're only about the third person's ever seen my workshop."

"I'm honored," I said. "This is truly amazing."

"That there's the spot where your truck lived for a lot of years 'fore I sold her to you. We'll just leave her in her old space while we're gone."

He flipped a couple of switches and the garage door closed and another garage door opened, this one behind the sleek black Mustang. I wasn't sure of the year, but I would have bet it was in the 1960s.

Sly opened the car door and Bobo streaked for the opening. He leaped inside, planting his rump in the middle of the backseat. He was ready for whatever adventure lay ahead.

Sly got behind the wheel, I slid into the bucket seat on the passenger side, and soon we were on the highway heading north.

Sly slid the Mustang through traffic with a deftness born of long practice and an intimate knowledge of his vehicle. He had a light touch on the clutch and brake, a heavier foot on the accelerator. We quickly left the traffic behind and had the road to ourselves.

He grinned and opened up the throttle a bit more. The engine went from a purr to a roar in the blink of an eye. His grin grew bigger, the look of a man who purely enjoyed what he was doing.

In the backseat, Bobo yelped happily and mashed his nose against the tiny open slit at the top of the window. This wasn't the first time these two had done this, and Bobo seemed to be enjoying it just as much as Sly.

Sly held his speed for another couple minutes, then let off the gas and coasted back to within shouting distance of the speed limit.

"A car like this needs to open up once in a while," he said. "But I know if I keep that up for very long, I'll end up having a little chat with one of Keyhole Bay's finest."

We continued north at a little over the speed limit. While Sly drove, I filled him in on all the latest developments.

"I was going to save the news for tomorrow night, to tell you all at once. But really I've been dying to tell you since we got in the car."

I told him about Peter's phone call, and how I had bluffed him into taking less money.

He laughed. "You did good. You been working in that store a long time and he's been getting the benefit. 'Bout time he made up for that."

"Thanks. But that isn't all the news. The bank called Monday afternoon and my loan was approved. That's one of the reasons I'm in a hurry. I have an appointment this afternoon to meet Miss Pansy at Lighthouse and sign the final papers."

"You want me to go a little faster?" he offered with a wide grin. "I could, you know."

"I'd love it," I said, and meant it. The car hugged the

road through long, sweeping curves and purred along the straight stretches, hinting at barely contained power. I would love to see it let loose. "But getting a ticket would take more time than staying close to the limit."

Sly nodded in agreement. "So why exactly are you going up here?" he asked. "You just told me you needed to go to north county and you wanted company. It don't make no never mind, but I'm curious what's so important."

I explained Beth's fear for her granny and aunt, and how agitated she'd become. "I don't think there's anything to be worried about. But I said I'd come in the hope it would calm her down. It didn't fix things, but it helped. And once I said I'd do it, I couldn't go back on my word."

"You won't have to. We'll get you up there, you can talk Beth's granny into coming back, and we'll be back in time to meet Miss Pansy. Now I might just have to go direct to Lighthouse.

"Just to get you there in time, of course," he added innocently.

"Suuuure."

"You just keep watch and tell me when I need to turn."

"It's hard to miss." I described the brightly painted fence and the narrow road leading off the highway.

I looked around, getting my bearings. "In fact, we're almost there."

Chapter 43

SLY SPOTTED THE FENCE ABOUT THE SAME TIME I did and signaled the turn at the same time I pointed it out.

"Take it easy through here," I cautioned as he left the pavement for the hard-packed dirt. "It's so narrow that if another car comes along, one of us will have to pull into a driveway to let the other one pass. And it's not a very good road."

As if to underscore my words, the Mustang bumped through a deep pothole, bouncing us in our seats.

Sly grimaced at the insult to his pristine ride. He slowed even more and tried to steer around the worst of the ruts and divots in the roadway.

Fortunately, we didn't meet any other cars on our trip down the tree-lined road. This area had been logged once, and it likely would be again, but the fast-growing hackberry and oaks had filled in along the road, shielding the cabins and mobile homes that dotted the roadside. I was certain the privacy provided by the trees was no accident of nature. These were people who wanted to be left alone.

I described Beth's mailbox as we bounced along. "Should be just a little ways up here, on the right." I spotted the carved post and patterned box.

"Right there."

Sly made the turn and we crawled down the driveway. I recalled the last time I'd been down this driveway, in Karen's SUV, then coming back out in Calvin's massive pickup truck.

A shiver passed through me.

"You still think it's nothing?" Sly said.

"Yes," I said with more conviction than I felt. "I'm just spooked from my last visit out here."

Beth and Everett's hybrid was still there. A dusty compact was parked next to the porch, the Michigan plates a clear signal that Althea and Beth had arrived.

Now all I had to do was convince them to come back to Keyhole Bay.

We climbed out of the car, and Sly left the window down for Bobo. "Stay," he said when Bobo crawled into the front seat. "No sense letting him scare the ladies," he explained. "You remember how you felt the first time you saw him."

"I was in his territory," I reminded him. "He had every right to object. But I get your point." I reached through the window and gave Bobo a pat. "We'll be right back."

We climbed the steps to the large porch and I knocked on the door.

From somewhere inside, an exasperated voice shouted, "I told you they weren't here. Go away!"

"Althea," I called out, "it's me, Gloryanna. Beth asked me to come up here."

I glanced nervously around the clearing, wondering if the other visitors, whoever they were, had decided to hang around. The feeling of being watched returned full force, and I stepped closer to the door, as though looking for shelter from the prying eyes I imagined were watching from the woods.

The door swung open, taking me by surprise. I stumbled, then caught my balance.

Althea snapped, "Are you coming in or aren't you?" She swiveled to look Sly up and down before she included him in her brusque invitation. "I guess you better come in, too, if you're with her." She stomped away, leaving the door open.

"How could we say no?" I whispered to Sly, and led the way into the cabin.

I'd been here before, when I'd come to pick up quilts and small pieces of furniture. They had filled their home with handmade pieces from Everett's wood shop and wall hangings from Beth's collection of vintage quilts and needlework. The house was always tidy when I arrived, even when freshly baked cookies or bread showed they had been working in the kitchen shortly before.

Today the place was a mess. Furniture out of place, wall hangings crooked or knocked to the ground, dishes strewn across the table and counters, clothes spilled from drawers and closets.

It looked like someone had ripped the place apart.

We followed Althea to the bedroom, and I felt a knot in my stomach. If someone had robbed the place, it was likely the cedar chest had been rifled. The wedding quilt was, in all likelihood, gone for good.

From the doorway, I could see that the lid of the chest was closed. I took a step closer and spied deep gouge marks on the front, around the lock. But the chest appeared to be intact, the contents safe.

It was small consolation in light of the destruction.

Sly lingered in the doorway when I entered the room, as though he was uncomfortable invading the private space of the couple who lived here.

As I surveyed the damage, he made an odd, strangled sound, like his vocal cords had ceased to function.

I whipped around, worried that he might be ill.

He stared straight ahead, his eyes wide. He looked like he had seen a ghost.

"Anna?" he whispered, unable to get enough breath to speak.

Maybe he had seen a ghost.

I spun around, looking in the same direction.

Beth Stevenson stood in the doorway of the closet, her arms filled with a tangle of clothes and hangers, her mouth frozen in a tiny O.

"Anna?" Sly said again, his voice still soft, "Annabeth?"

I looked from one to the other. The pieces clicked into place, and I remembered one of the pictures we'd seen in the high school yearbooks. A girl with barely contained dark curls and a sweet smile. We'd snapped a photo and moved on.

A girl named Annabeth.

A girl who had stopped being Anna and become Beth.

"Sylvester?"

Her question answered all of mine. Somehow, without intending to, we had found Anna.

Chapter 44

THE TWO OF THEM STARED A MOMENT LONGER AS Althea and I stood rooted in place, too stunned to speak.

"You know him?" Althea asked, breaking the silence.

"That's Anna?" I asked a split second behind her.

"Yes."

"Yes."

Althea looked at me for an explanation I wasn't prepared to give her. It wasn't my story to tell.

When no one volunteered to explain, she shook her head and went back to work. "If we're going to stay here, we need to get this place cleaned up." She gave a disgusted grunt. "If this is my granddaughter's idea of keeping house . . ." Her voice trailed off into another grunt.

"It isn't." I jumped in, grateful for something to fill the awkward silence. "The house is usually tidy, everything put away, everything in its place.

"I don't think Beth left it this way."

"They did leave in a hurry," Beth said softly.

"No," I said. I forced back the panic that had been clawing at my insides since I first walked in. "They wouldn't have left this kind of a mess, no matter how big a hurry they were in.

"Someone's been here. They were looking for something." I gestured to the spilled clothes and the marks on the chest. "I don't know if they found it, or if they got scared off, but I don't think we should hang around.

"That's what Beth sent me up here for," I said to Althea. "She wants you and her aunt Beth to come back to Keyhole Bay. She doesn't think you're safe up here."

I looked around the room. "I thought she was exaggerating, until about five minutes ago. Now I don't know. But I do know we shouldn't take any chances.

"Let's get what we need and get out of here. You can talk to Beth and decide if you want to come back."

I looked back to Sly. He and Beth—Anna—had moved within a few feet of each other and were talking quietly, haltingly, oblivious to the rest of us.

I wanted to give them their privacy, but I didn't want to stay in that house a second longer than we had to.

"Sly, Beth, um, Anna, um, whatever your name is." I was snapping, rushing, adrenaline making my voice sharp and stretching my nerves tight. "We need to go. Now."

Sly turned to me, hurt in his eyes. "I'm sorry," I said, instantly contrite. "I think I caught Beth's case of nerves. But I really think we should get out of here."

"And I think you ought to stay a while."

The voice, deep and gravelly, came from the hall outside the bedroom. Heavy boots clomped on the bare wood floor, and two men stood in the doorway.

Sly shot a look at me that clearly asked, "Are these the guys that gave you trouble?" I shook my head just a fraction of an inch. I didn't know either of them.

They stood one behind the other, each nearly as wide as the doorway. The man in back was slightly taller, but other than that, they were nearly identical—heavily muscled, stern-faced, bandanas covering their hair.

Worn black leather pants and jackets made them look like bikers. I hadn't heard motorcycles, but that meant nothing.

Sunglasses wrapped around their faces, hiding their eyes. I could imagine the cruelty in those eyes that went along with the voice, but I couldn't see them.

It was, if anything, even more frightening.

I tried to think, to find a way out. We outnumbered them, but three senior citizens and I didn't seem like much of a match for the two muscular men who were, I imagined, staring us down.

Besides, they had us trapped. There was a single, small window in the bedroom. But even if I could get to it and get it open, there was no way four of us could escape before the men could get across the room and grab us.

I could see Sly making the same calculations and coming to the same conclusions. I knew he should naturally be the leader; he was the toughest and strongest, but I wanted the two men to underestimate him.

Which they would do if a woman seemed to be in charge.

"What do you want?" I demanded. I was pleased my voice didn't waver, though my insides were quaking. "We just came to pick up some clothes and we found the place trashed.

"Did you do that?"

"What if we did?" The shorter man swaggered forward a couple steps, making room for the taller one to follow him into the room.

It had been crowded before with four of us in there. The addition of two more, large men at that, made it nearly impossible to move.

But if we couldn't move, neither could they. And we were smaller. Two of us could fit through a gap that would stop either of them.

I saw Anna clasp her hands behind her back. I wasn't

sure what she was doing, but she seemed to be concentrating on something.

Althea moved close to her sister-in-law and laid her head against Anna's shoulder. The women whispered to each other and the tall man growled at them. "Nobody said you could talk."

"She's scared," Althea said in a submissive voice I had not heard from her. "We all are. I was just trying to keep her calm, poor thing."

"Women," he spat the word. "Just shut up. Nobody talks." He pointed at me. "Except her."

Okay. I was the spokesman. Spokeswoman. Whatever happened was going to be up to me.

"Tell us what you want," I said. "Maybe we can help you find it. Or help you find out if it's even here. It's a small place, it shouldn't take long.

"You get what you want, you're on your way, and everyone's fine and happy. You don't find it, at least you know it isn't here. Either way, nobody has to get scared or hurt."

I thought of Calvin and Donny, how they had done exactly that. I hoped these two were as reasonable.

"It's not a *what*," the big man said. "It's a *who*. We need to know where those two hippie-dippy freaks went, and we need to talk to them.

"Think you can fix that?"

Didn't these guys watch TV, or listen to Karen's newscasts, or read a newspaper? I dismissed the newspaper, but I still found it hard to believe they hadn't heard of Beth and Everett's arrest.

I had to turn that to our advantage.

I looked from one man to the other, trying to keep their attention on me. Whatever Anna and Althea were up to, I wanted to give them every advantage.

"Look, whatever happened out there"—I gestured to the woods beyond the cabin—"two guys ended up dead. Or hadn't you heard?" I was pretty sure they knew exactly what had happened, but I wasn't about to let them know what I was thinking.

"You think those two would stick around? My guess is, they hightailed it out of town about two steps ahead of the sheriff.

"These two old gals came to me, said the girl who lived here promised them some old clothes for some charity project," I rolled my eyes, "and they wanted me to help them get the stuff from the house.

"I'm a nice lady, I try to help, and this is where it gets me? I don't know where those two went, and I doubt anyone in this room does. But we'll help you search for clues."

I gestured to the other three, huddled together against the wall nearest the door. "Won't we?"

They all murmured their assurances.

"Where do you want us to start?"

The two men looked at each other, and I took the opportunity to sneak a peek at my companions. They had moved closer to the door while I distracted the men, maybe close enough to make a run for it.

Go, I mouthed and made a tiny shooing motion with my hands.

Sly looked as though he wanted to argue. I glared at him.

He was responsible for Althea and Anna. I could take care of myself.

I hoped he got the message.

"Well?" I challenged the men, drawing their attention back to me. "Where do we start? In here?"

I moved toward the closet. My path took me directly toward the window, and I made a show of pausing in front of it.

I got what I wanted.

Both men moved toward me, the smaller one taking a shortcut across the bed. He didn't realize the hippie-dippies still had a waterbed. It didn't make for solid footing.

He slipped, sprawling face-first across the bed.

The taller one grabbed me by the arm and pulled me against him. "What are you trying to pull?" he shouted, his face inches from mine.

I couldn't look at my friends, couldn't draw attention to them. I hoped they had used the distraction to escape.

A scream of pain from the bed told me otherwise.

The biker and I both turned.

Sprawled across the bed, the shorter man was staked to the gushing water bed with a metal rod driven through his leg and into the mattress.

Water and blood welled around him, sloshing onto the floor as he thrashed around, trying to pull the spike out of his leg.

My brain finally registered what had happened.

A wire coat hanger.

A flash of memory, Annabeth with her arms full of clothes. And hangers.

The biker dropped me and reached to pull the hanger from his accomplice's leg.

I sprinted for the door, following my friends' mad dash toward the cars.

A hand grabbed my arm, tossing me to the ground. A heavy boot filled my vision and I had a moment of sick clarity, knowing it would land in my midsection, and knowing more blows would follow.

In the distance I heard Sly's shout. "Bobo! Cantaloupe!"

A black blur streaked across the dirt.

The boot hovered for an instant.

It moved out of my sight, accompanied by a thud that shook the ground.

Hands grabbed my arms, pulling me toward the car. Tiny hands with loose skin.

I was shoved into the backseat of the Mustang and we roared out of the yard and bounced over the washboard driveway.

As I sorted out the jumble of arms and legs, I realized

Althea and Annabeth had managed to shove me in the back seat between them, with Sly at the wheel.

"Bobo!" I screamed at Sly. "Where's Bobo?"

"He'll find us," Sly said between clenched teeth.

He threw the car around a tight curve without slowing down. In the back, the three of us tumbled together, another tangle of arms and legs.

"Anyone behind us?" Sly shouted over the roar of the engine.

"Not yet," Althea shouted back. "But I can't see around the curves in the road."

"Not far to the highway," Sly answered grimly. "They won't be able to catch this baby once we're on pavement."

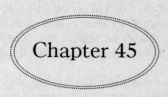

Chapter 45

WE ROUNDED ANOTHER CURVE AND FOUND A DARK SUV coming straight at us. It reminded me of the car I'd seen Captain Clint climb into at the airport, and for one insane moment I imagined Karen's stepfather charging to our rescue.

A siren shrieked, and Sly spun his head, looking for a driveway. He slewed to the left, across the path of the oncoming vehicle, and slammed to a stop in a clearing barely big enough for the car.

I cringed as I heard branches scratch the sides of the Mustang. I hoped the damage could be repaired.

Two more SUVs sped past, followed by a patrol car.

Sly backed out and headed back the way we'd come, once again taking it easy over the bad road.

We slowly wound around the curves, Sly watching warily for vehicles coming our way.

"Bobo's gonna be looking for us," he said.

We eventually caught up to the SUVs, stopped in the middle of the road, angled every which way, and completely blocking the road. The sheriff's cruiser was pulled in behind them.

Sly stopped, then backed up until he was able to park the Mustang in a pullout about twenty yards away.

We waited, though we weren't sure what for. Within a few minutes, Bobo came trotting down the road, looking unharmed.

I would have sworn that dog was grinning.

He gave a happy yelp when he spotted the car and covered the rest of the distance at a dead run. Sly reached over and swung the passenger door open. Bobo leaped inside and greeted Sly with a big doggy kiss, obviously happy and excited to see his master.

Sly looked far more relieved than his casual assurance that Bobo would find us would have indicated. I knew how he felt.

We couldn't see much beyond the cluster of SUVs, and I wanted to know what was going on. I clambered over Althea and pushed my way out of the car.

"I'm going to walk a little closer," I told Sly.

"Not alone, you aren't," he said. He climbed out of the car, then turned back to his other passengers. "You ladies just stay here where it's safe," he said.

He looked at Bobo. "Guard," he commanded. The big dog yipped in reply.

"Let's go."

We took our time approaching the cluster of vehicles, making sure we were visible. We kept our hands in plain sight and our posture as relaxed as possible.

Even so, we were stopped by a stern-faced man with a crew cut and a badge that he flashed so quickly we couldn't read it. "This is a crime scene," he growled. "Authorized personnel only."

From behind him I heard an exasperated, "Martine! What the hell are you doing here? Pardon my French, but why can't you stay away from my crime scenes?"

"Hey, Sheriff. Mr. Benjamin and I just came up here to help Beth's granny get some things." I smiled, all innocence.

"Well, you just get right back to your vehicle." He took us each by the arm and started marching us back toward the car. In the distance I could hear voices shouting for somebody to "Stay down" and "Show me your hands."

I was pretty sure I knew who they were talking to.

"You are going to come to the station and answer some questions, and you are going to do it right now," he said. "There are a couple messed-up boys back there. One of them looks like he's been bit." He glanced over at Sly. "You know anything about that, Mr. Benjamin?"

"I believe I might, Sheriff."

"Then you don't want to talk to anyone but me," Boomer said. "You get in your car and you head for the station. I will be right behind you, just to make sure you don't get lost. You hear?"

Sly smiled and nodded. "Sure do, Sheriff." He looked over at me. "Miss Glory, I do think it would be in our best interest to do as the sheriff asks, don't you?"

"Sure."

We climbed in the car, rearranging ourselves so Annabeth could ride up front with Sly. Bobo settled down between me and Althea, worn out from all his adventures, and we drove back to the highway.

True to his word, Boomer's car soon fell in behind us. Sly held the Mustang to the speed limit as we headed south with our escort.

"You know my car is still parked up there," Althea said at one point.

"Don't worry about it," Sly said over his shoulder. "I

would be happy to take you ladies back up to get it when you're through."

The conversation reminded me of Karen driving Beth and Everett to meet with Sheriff Hardy. Except they hadn't come back for their vehicle; they'd gone to jail.

I kept that thought to myself.

Chapter 46

I MISSED MY APPOINTMENT WITH MISS PANSY. Bradley was alarmed when I told him I was at the sheriff's station, but I reassured him I was just a witness and would be home soon. We agreed to meet the next afternoon.

"How is Miss Pansy doing?" I asked. "Was it difficult for her to be back in the shop, knowing she wasn't going back to work?"

To my surprise Bradley just laughed. "She's already got a million projects started at home. Says she doesn't know how she ever found time to work so much. I think she's going to handle retirement just fine."

I hung up, relieved. I had been afraid that somehow missing the appointment would mean Miss Pansy would change her mind.

Boomer kept me cooling my heels in one of those blasted plastic chairs while he talked to each of the other witnesses, making me wait until last.

When he finally called me in, it was completely dark

outside and the sodium vapor lamps in the parking lot cast a dull yellow glow over the cars parked there.

"Sit down," Boomer said wearily. I took the chair across from his desk, grateful at least that we were in his office, not the stark interview room where I'd talked to Beth that morning.

"Just tell me your version of the story," he said. "I've heard what the others have to say."

I started with my visit to Beth that morning. "I said I'd go because I thought it would calm her down. I really didn't expect any trouble. Sly, Mr. Benjamin, offered to drive, and I took him up on it. Almost wished I hadn't; I think his car got pretty banged up."

"He says he can fix it pretty easy," Boomer said with a dismissive wave. "Go on."

"We got there, went in to talk to Mrs. Stevenson and Mrs. Stevenson"—it sounded funny to say it that way, but neither one of us even cracked a smile. "Then those two guys busted in, demanding to know where the two hippie-dippies were."

Boomer's mouth twitched at the description.

I shrugged. "Didn't sound like they knew Beth and Everett had been arrested, so I tried to distract them so the others could get away.

"I was the youngest and probably the fastest. Figured my companions might need a head start."

Another twitch. Maybe Boomer was starting to relax. Maybe he even believed me.

"Anyway, it worked. Mostly. They got away, but the big guy caught up to me." I shuddered at the memory of a huge motorcycle boot suspended over my body. "I think he was going to stomp me, when Bobo attacked him."

From there the memories were a jumble, but I told him as much as I remembered. "We parked the car and started back to see what was going on, and that's when the crew cut guy stopped us, and then you told us to come to the station.

"And here we are."

I sat quietly for a minute as Boomer scowled at a legal pad in front of him. "Anything else?"

I shook my head. "No. But what were you doing up there? And who were all those other guys, the ones with the SUVs?"

"Now, Miss Glory," Boomer started, then stopped. He tossed his pen on the desk and leaned across it, looking me in the eye. "Just who do you *think* they were? Big black SUVs. Crew cuts and knife-crease khakis. What does that look like to you?"

"Military," I shot back. I'd lived my whole life close to several bases. I knew what a military man looked like, and I knew what military investigators looked like. "But why?"

"I don't know. Officially. But the rumor is that several of the boys down at one of the bases, not saying it was the Navy, you understand. Several of those boys got themselves real sick on moonshine."

"They get shore leave, they get liquored up. Nothing new."

"This wasn't the usual," Boomer said. "Now mind you, this is only a rumor, right?"

"Of course," I answered. I resisted the urge to give him a big wink.

"The booze was bad, cut with something that poisoned some of those boys. I've heard that one of 'em died, and I've heard they just got real sick. Those Navy boys—oops!—those military boys can be real closemouthed."

"But what does any of this have to do with us? What does it have to do with Beth and Everett?"

"That's why I was there. After your little pal threw her fit in interrogation, Deputy Fuentes called me. Convinced me I needed to talk to Mrs. Young.

"She talked her head off, and I believed her. Put out a BOLO for your truck so we could stop you."

I thought of the patrol car that had passed us on the

road. "I wasn't driving," I said. "We were in Sly's Mustang."

Boomer nodded. "I know that now. Anyway, Mrs. Young said they chased some moonshiners off the property when they first moved here. The husband even helped them move their still, if you can believe that. Those boys showed up a couple weeks back, trying to warn them off the place. Said a new crew was moving in, trying to take over, and the new guys were likely to come around looking for them. Asked them not to tell 'em where they'd moved the still.

"The way they described them to her, they sound like those two you met today.

"She says they heard a bunch of yelling in the woods later that day, got scared, and ran off back to Michigan."

He paused and glanced around like he was looking for eavesdroppers. "She identified the two victims as the men who warned them."

"That explains what you were doing there. But what about the other guys?"

"I think they were watching the place. I can't be sure, but it's the only way they could have been there that fast."

He sat back and steepled his fingers over his stomach. "I don't think those boys in the SUVs are going to be interested in anything you four have to say about what happened this afternoon. In fact, I am almost sure they would prefer you just forget everything that happened out there."

"Out where?" I asked with feigned innocence.

"Exactly," Boomer answered.

He nodded at me. "One more thing. Is it true that little gal, the one named Beth, is it true she stabbed one of them guys with a coat hanger?"

It was my turn to nod.

"That's a woman I wouldn't want to cross."

"Me neither." I stood up and stretched. "Is that all? Can I go home now?"

"Go," he said. "You know, you got lucky today. At least

this time I'm not talking to you in a hospital bed, which is an improvement. But it would be even better if I didn't have to talk to you at all. If you get my meaning."

I nodded and walked out.

Jake was waiting in the lobby, looking worried. "Sly called me," he said. He wrapped his arms around me and pulled me close. He looked down and said, "At least I'm not picking you up at the hospital this time."

I wondered if he'd been talking to Boomer.

Chapter 47

BY THE MIDDLE OF THURSDAY, I HAD A CASHIER'S check for the purchase price of Lighthouse Coffee. The amount was the largest single transaction of my life, even larger than the check I had written for Peter that morning.

Jake met me at Lighthouse when Miss Pansy came back in, and we gathered around a table: Miss Pansy, Bradley, Chloe, Julie, Jake, and me.

The little ceremony of signing the sales contract and handing over the check was a solemn moment. It represented a major change for all of us, including the two young women who served as witnesses.

"Thank you," Miss Pansy said when I handed over the check. "I am so happy to know the place is in good hands."

"That would be Chloe," I told her. "You taught her well, and I am lucky to have her. Thank you."

When the paperwork was done, I handed Miss Pansy a plastic card. It was one of the gift cards from Lighthouse

Coffee. "It's good forever," I told her. "Anything you want, any time you want, you're my guest."

"I pay my own way," she said crisply.

"Yes, you do. And you've earned this fair and square. You take it. It's my way of making sure you come by now and then and say hello."

"Well, when you put it that way"—she slipped the card in her pocketbook. "Bradley, we need to get home. I've got work to do."

"Yes, ma'am." Bradley was on his feet instantly, escorting his mother out to the car parked at the curb.

We watched her go, and I doubt there was a dry eye in the place. I know mine weren't.

I turned to Chloe. "All right, you are officially in charge. I'll stop by in the morning to check in, but it's up to you now."

Jake promised to pick me up at six thirty for dinner, and I went back to Southern Treasures. Julie stayed behind to talk to Chloe for a few minutes.

I walked into Southern Treasures and stopped, looking around. It was exactly the same store it had been this morning, and yesterday, and last week and last year.

And yet it was completely different.

It was all mine now, along with the shop next door. And someday Guy and Linda would retire and I would buy the Grog Shop. It was what I was meant to do, I was sure of it.

Bluebeard whistled at me from his perch. "You did it, girlie. You by gum did it!"

"I did, didn't I?" I walked over and scratched his head, ruffling his feathers. "We're going to be retail moguls, you and me. This calls for a celebration."

"Coffee?"

I laughed. "You know better. How about a banana?"

I was still floating when Jake knocked on the front door. I let him in and we said good night to Bluebeard.

"I'm taking your best girl out to celebrate," Jake said.

"Your best girl," Bluebeard repeated.

Jake tilted his head like he was thinking, a gesture so like Bluebeard it was comical. "You're right," he said, taking my hand. "She is my best girl."

WHEN ERNIE ANSWERED THE DOOR, HE GRABBED me in a hug that took my breath away. "I heard you had another one of your adventures," he said. "Girl, this has *got* to stop!"

"It's not like I try to get into these things," I protested. "Stuff just happens to me."

He waved away my defense. "Well, it had better stop happening, is all I'm saying."

We followed him into the kitchen. Felipe was stirring gravy, and a perfectly roasted turkey sat on the counter, resting.

The table was already set for eight, with a cornucopia centerpiece that was as period as the sleek table. It looked like a centerfold from a 1950s *Better Homes and Gardens*.

"Eight?"

"Captain Clint and Catherine, remember?" Ernie said. "We called Sly, but he said he was busy, catching up with an old friend. Might you know anything about that?" He arched an eyebrow at me, clearly expecting me to know everything.

I did my best to look innocent.

I waited for Karen and Riley to arrive with Captain Clint and Catherine. Some kind of detente appeared to have been achieved, and the two couples seemed to be getting along better.

Or maybe they were just better actors than I gave them credit for. Clint was cordial and pleasant, though he kept disappearing to take urgent calls on his cell phone.

"Something's going on down at the base," Catherine explained. "We almost had to cancel. Which would have been a crying shame, to miss a meal like this."

She was right about that. Ernie, with Felipe's help I'm sure, had filled the table with a traditional Thanksgiving feast. It was all there, from turkey to oyster dressing to cranberry relish.

Clint came back from his latest phone call and I caught him staring at me. Something in his expression told me he knew more about my little incident with the crew cuts than I thought.

Might not be the time to tell everyone the details of that little adventure.

There was plenty of other news to share, and I managed to keep the conversation on my business dealings and off my latest run-in with the law.

"What about your pals in the hoosegow?" Riley asked. "Karen said she heard they were released late this afternoon. What's up with that?"

"I guess they caught the right guys," I said lightly. Clint caught my eye. I smiled sweetly. "I don't know any more than you do. In fact, I hadn't even heard they'd been released." I glanced at Karen. "Did they have a big press conference? Did Morris announce their release?"

"Ha! He hasn't shown his face in public since the word came down that the charges were being dismissed. I tried to reach him for a comment, but his office says he's 'unavailable' and won't be back in until after the holiday.

"They're claiming he had a family vacation scheduled for this week, but nobody believes a word of it. He's likely hiding out somewhere, trying to figure out just how badly he's tanked his career." She smiled, and it wasn't a pretty sight. "Karma can be cruel."

"I do have one other bit of news," I said. "If we're through talking about dear Mr. Morris."

"With any luck," Karen said, "I will never have to talk about Mr. Morris again for the rest of my career."

"From your lips to God's ears," Felipe said, crossing himself. He'd been raised a Catholic, and old habits die hard.

"So spill already, Martine," Karen said impatiently.

I looked at Jake and he nodded. He already knew. "I know who Anna is."

Stunned silence, broken at last by Ernie. "Is that what Sly meant by 'an old friend'?"

"Yes. Beth Young's granny came down here with her brother-in-law's widow. The two of them are pretty much best friends. Aunt Beth is the one who owns the property where Beth was living. And yes, it is incredibly confusing for both of them to be named Beth. Also for both of the women to be Mrs. Stevenson.

"Anyway, when Sly and I ran into the two of them, he recognized her and she recognized him. They've got fifty years to catch up on, so I think that might take a while."

"How did Sly take it?" Karen asked. "Is he okay?"

"He seemed genuinely pleased to see her, and it looked to me like she felt the same way. I got to talk to her a little bit. Did you know how they met? She came into Southern Treasures while he was there doing odd jobs for Uncle Louis. She told me they used to meet there and just talk when they couldn't be seen together anywhere else in town.

"I don't know how things will go, but at least they each know what happened to the other, and I think that's a good thing."

I looked around the table, at the family I'd made out of my favorite people. "Yeah," I said. "Today I have a lot to be thankful for."

Chapter 48

I STOOD IN THE CHURCH VESTIBULE, DARK GREEN satin skimming over my body and brushing the toes of my high heels.

I was steadier than I'd been a few weeks ago, thanks to hours of practice, walking around my apartment, feeling foolish in stiletto heels and blue jeans. But at least I knew I could make it down the aisle without tripping over my own feet.

Jake stood next to me, keeping me distracted until the bridal march began and he had to take his place with the groomsmen. As maid of honor, I would walk with Bobby, Riley's brother and best man.

I fidgeted, unable to stand still.

"It'll be fine," Jake said, wrapping his arm around my shoulders. "Everyone knows what to do. And in very short order, Karen and Riley will be married again and headed for their honeymoon."

"Did you get everything worked out?" I asked him for about the thousandth time.

"Plane tickets to Las Vegas, hotel reservations, rental car reserved, hotel reservations in wine country, and a flight home Christmas Eve. It's all set.

"Are you sure she doesn't suspect?"

I shook my head. "She's still fussing over what to pack, but with Catherine and Julie's help, I managed to get everything she might possibly need."

I sighed and shifted again, trying to stay balanced in the narrow heels. "Though I really think we could have started with the plane tickets several months ago, and skipped all this."

The church was full of people. Friends of the bride. Friends of the groom. Friends of their parents. Riley's people alone filled several pews; he had a big family.

Karen's side didn't have many relatives, but the pews were packed with her friends and co-workers. In the front pew, Clint sat patiently, waiting for the best man to escort Catherine to her seat.

Two uniformed Navy officers came in and one of the ushers stepped forward. "Friends of the bride's family," the taller one said. The voice was familiar, though I couldn't immediately place it. "The Captain is expecting us."

The usher, one of Riley's brothers, nodded. "He told us a couple of his team would be here. Asked me to seat you near him."

"Thank you."

I gasped, finally placing the voice. The tall officer turned, looking for the source of the sound. A tiny grin lifted the corners of his mouth for a fraction of a second.

"You all right, ma'am?" Calvin asked before he and Donny followed the usher to their seats.

In the small office at the side of the vestibule, Karen waited with her escort. She had asked Sly to walk her down the aisle. Her father had been MIA a long time, and she wasn't close with any of the stepdads.

She was getting to know and like Clint, and had even

offered to switch. It was a peace offering to her mother, but Clint was a pretty smart guy. He declined, saying she should have her old friend do the honors, if she just saved one dance for her new stepdad.

Next to Clint, Anna waited for Sly. She'd delivered the finished quilt on one of her many trips down from Beth and Everett's place, where she'd been staying the last few weeks.

The organist ended the number she was playing, and then the opening notes of a Baroque canon drifted softly from her instrument.

That was our cue.

"See you soon," Jake said and kissed me good-bye.

He took his place in line, linked his arm with one of the bridesmaids, and followed the procession down the aisle. Moments later, I linked arms with Bobby and followed along.

We reached the front of the church where Riley waited, then turned to watch Karen make her entrance.

She was a beautiful bride.

I'd promised myself I wouldn't cry, but I'd known when I did that it was impossible. Two of my best friends were getting married. Again.

Sly and Karen reached the front of the church. He took Karen's hand from his arm and placed it in Riley's outstretched hand, then kissed her lightly on the cheek and stepped back to join Annabeth in the front pew.

As he passed Clint, the captain stuck out his hand and shook Sly's. I could see him form a silent "Thank you."

I took Karen's bouquet, holding it as she held Riley's hands and focused on his face.

The minister began his speech and the first part of the vows. I swallowed hard around the lump in my throat, knowing I had one more part to play.

The minister had come to the point where he asked, "Who gives this woman in marriage?"

On this point Karen had been adamant. She was a grown woman who had already been married to Riley once.

"I do," she said.

She expected the ceremony to proceed, but her family and friends had other ideas. With Riley's approval, we'd added one more item.

"And who comes to support this gift?"

Across the church, people stood. Sly and Anna. Felipe and Ernie. Chloe. Julie, holding Rose Ann. Catherine and Clint. Linda and Guy. Riley's parents and brothers.

We spoke in unison.

"We do."

Menus and Recipes

Ernie's Cajun Roots

CHICKEN, SAUSAGE, SEAFOOD GUMBO

Gumbo, like so many home-cooked dishes, varies with each cook. As Ernie said, it often depends on what kind of fish or shellfish or sausage was available. The heart of the gumbo is the roux, and the trinity (onion, bell pepper, and celery) and okra are staples of every gumbo recipe. From there you can pick and choose the meats and seasonings you prefer, adding hot sauce, herbs, and spices to please your palate. Ernie's recipe is a good place to start.

1 pound boneless skinless chicken breast
1 pound smoked sausage, sliced ¼ inch thick
¼ cup vegetable oil
½ cup flour
5 tablespoons margarine
1 large onion, chopped
8 cloves garlic, minced
1 green bell pepper, chopped
3 stalks celery, chopped
¼ cup Worcestershire sauce
2 teaspoons salt

½ teaspoon black pepper

½ teaspoon dried thyme

2 teaspoons filé powder

½ teaspoon Cajun seasoning blend

¼ bunch flat leaf parsley, coarsely chopped

4 cups hot water

5 beef bouillon cubes

14 ounce can stewed tomatoes, with juice

1 pound sliced okra, fresh or frozen

4 green onions, sliced

1 pound cooked shrimp

1 pound lump crabmeat

Season chicken with salt and pepper. In a heavy skillet, heat oil over medium-high heat. Cook chicken just until browned on both sides; it will not be cooked through, but will finish cooking in the broth. Remove from pan. Brown sausage and remove from pan.

Reduce heat to medium, sift the flour over the hot oil, add 2 tablespoons margarine and stir continuously until mixture is brown. This takes about 10 minutes, and constant stirring is essential. Set the roux aside to cool.

In a Dutch oven, melt remaining margarine over low heat. Cook onion, garlic, bell pepper, and celery in margarine 10 minutes. Add Worcestershire, seasonings, and parsley. Cook another 10 minutes, stirring frequently.

Add hot water and bouillon cubes to vegetables, whisking constantly until mixed. Bring to a boil, add chicken and sausage to broth, reduce heat, cover, and simmer 45 minutes. Add tomatoes and okra, replace cover, and continue simmering for 1 hour.

Add green onions, shrimp, and crabmeat. Cook just until shellfish are heated through. Garnish with chopped parsley and green onion and serve over steamed rice. Serves 8–10.

BOUDIN BALLS

Boudin is a spicy pork sausage, especially popular in Louisiana. You can buy it ready-made (at least you can if your store carries it), or you can make your own. Either way, it's a great way to start your evening.

1 pound boudin sausage, homemade or purchased
1 cup cracker meal or crushed crackers
2 eggs
½ cup milk
1 teaspoon salt
½ teaspoon black pepper
¼ teaspoon cayenne pepper
Oil for frying

Form sausage into golf ball–size balls, set aside.

Mix the cracker meal (or finely crushed crackers) with seasonings and divide into two shallow bowls. In another bowl whisk together the eggs and milk. Roll the sausage balls in the first bowl of crumb mixture, coat with egg mixture and roll in the second bowl of crumb mixture.

Refrigerate prepared balls for 1 to 2 hours before frying.

Heat the oil to 350 degrees in a deep fry pan (or use a deep fryer) and fry until golden brown. Drain on paper towels and serve warm with remoulade or tartar dipping sauce.

Boudin

1 ¼ pounds pork butt, cubed
½ pound pork liver
1 quart water
½ chopped onion
¼ cup each chopped green bell pepper, chopped celery
1 teaspoon chopped garlic

2 teaspoons salt
1 teaspoon cayenne pepper
¾ teaspoon ground black pepper
½ cup finely chopped parsley
½ cup chopped green onion (green part only)
3 cups cooked medium grain rice

Place water in a large saucepan. Add pork butt and liver, onion, bell pepper, celery, garlic, 1 teaspoon salt, ¼ teaspoon cayenne, and ¼ teaspoon black pepper. Bring to a boil. Reduce heat and simmer 1 ¼ to 1 ½ hours, until meats are tender.

Remove from heat. Drain, reserving the broth.

Using a food processor or meat grinder, process the pork mixture with parsley and green onion. Combine meat mixture and rice in a large bowl with remaining salt, black pepper, and cayenne. Mix in ½ cup broth. Continue adding broth in ½ cup increments until mixture is a firm paste. Be sure all ingredients are mixed thoroughly.

Rest the mixture until it cools enough to handle, and proceed as above.

FRIED OKRA

Fried okra is as common as French fries in Southern restaurants, and maybe even more popular. These bite-sized pieces will disappear as fast as you can fry them up.

1 pound fresh okra pods
1 cup milk
½ cup flour
½ cup corn meal
1 teaspoon salt

½ teaspoon black pepper
Oil for frying

Clean okra pods, remove stems, and slice into approximately 1" pieces. Put the milk in a bowl and set the okra pieces to soak. Sift the last 4 ingredients together and put in a paper sack (a plastic bag or a bowl will work as well).

Working with a few pieces at a time, shake the okra pieces in the bag to coat with the flour mixture. When you have finished shaking all the pieces shake them a second time to ensure a good coating.

Heat the oil to 350 degrees in a deep fry pan (or use a deep fryer) and fry the okra in small batches until golden brown. Drain on paper towels, sprinkle with salt, and enjoy!

BREAD PUDDING WITH CARAMEL SAUCE

Bread pudding is a great way to use bread that's slightly stale, and some recipes even suggest drying fresh bread before starting your pudding. The custardy goodness topped with warm caramel sauce can be topped with whipped cream or ice cream, but it's also delicious all by itself.

7 cups white bread or egg bread, cut into 1 ½ inch cubes
½ cup golden raisins
½ cup melted butter
4 whole eggs
1 cup granulated sugar
¼ cup light brown sugar
1 teaspoon grated nutmeg

2 teaspoons vanilla extract
2 cups half and half
2 cups whole milk

Caramel Sauce

½ cup butter
1 cup light brown sugar
¼ teaspoon salt
1 teaspoon vanilla
½ cup evaporated milk

In a buttered 13" x 9" pan, place bread cubes topped with raisins. Drizzle with melted butter, but do not stir.

In a large bowl beat eggs and blend in sugars, nutmeg, milk, and half and half. Pour egg mixture over bread and let it soak in. Gently push bread down into liquid if it tries to float. Sprinkle with additional nutmeg, if desired.

Bake at 350 degrees for 40–50 minutes, until puffy and golden. If it browns too quickly, cover loosely with foil. Cool.

Melt butter in a saucepan and add brown sugar. Bring to a boil, remove from heat, and whisk in remaining ingredients. Serve warm over squares of cooled pudding.

GLORY'S PECAN PIE

What can I say about pecan pie? It is, quite simply, the quintessential Southern dessert. Rich, buttery, filled with the dark, nutty goodness of pecans, a small slice will satisfy any sweet tooth. Glory's kitchen is small, so she often resorts to refrigerated crusts for convenience and time savings, and you can do the same. The pecans are the star of this show, so make sure they're the best you can find.

4 eggs
1 cup sugar
1 cup corn syrup
1 teaspoon vanilla
Dash salt
1 stick butter, melted and cooled
2 cups chopped pecans
9" pie shell

In a bowl, whisk eggs. Add sugar, corn syrup, vanilla, salt, and butter. Mix well. Stir in pecans.

Prepare your favorite pie crust, or use a ready-made pie shell.

Pour filling into unbaked crust and place on a baking sheet to guard against spills. Bake at 375 degrees for 35 minutes, or until a knife inserted 1 inch from the edge comes out clean.

Cool before serving. Refrigerate leftovers (as if there are going to be any!).

From the Secret Files of Miss Pansy and Lighthouse Coffee

QUICHE

A quiche can be just about anything you can dream up. Eggs and cream create a rich custard base for whatever savory add-ins you can imagine. The meat and vegetable combinations are limited only by your imagination. And it's a great way to use up those leftovers that aren't quite enough to be a meal on their own. Start with this basic ham and cheese, and see where you wind up! As with the pecan pie, use your favorite pie crust recipe, or buy a ready-to-bake shell—though Miss Pansy would never allow such a thing in her kitchen!

9" unbaked pie shell
1 ½ cups shredded cheese (any variety, use your favorite)
½ cup chopped cooked ham
4 large eggs
2 cups heavy cream, or half and half
¼ teaspoon salt
¼ teaspoon pepper

Spread cheese and ham in bottom of unbaked pie shell. In a medium bowl, beat eggs with cream, salt, and pepper. Pour over ham and cheese. Bake at 325 degrees for 45–50 minutes, until knife inserted in center comes out clean. Let stand 10 minutes before cutting and serving.

SCONES

Scones come in many varieties, but Miss Pansy's favorites are the traditional biscuit-like ones. They can be plain, served with berry preserves, flavored with lemon or orange zest, or baked with a handful of currants or dried cranberries added.

2 cups flour
4 teaspoons baking powder
¾ teaspoon salt
⅓ cup sugar
4 tablespoons butter
2 tablespoons shortening
¾ cup cream
1 egg, beaten

Combine dry ingredients in a large bowl, mixing well. Cut in butter and shortening, using a pastry cutter or a fork.

In a second bowl combine beaten egg and cream. Add to dry ingredients and stir.

Turn dough out on a floured board and knead 10–12 times. Pat dough into a circle and cut in wedges. Bake at 375 degrees until brown, about 15 minutes.

Serve warm with berry preserves.

PECAN TASSIES

These tiny tarts are like miniature pecan pies, and they fly
out of Miss Pansy's pastry case every time she bakes them.

Cream Cheese Pastry

2 ounces cream cheese
⅔ cup butter
¾ cup sifted flour

Filling

1 ½ cups brown sugar
2 tablespoons soft butter
2 teaspoons grated orange peel
1 teaspoon orange extract
Dash salt
2 eggs, beaten
1 ⅓ cup coarsely broken pecans

In food processor, process flour, cream cheese, and butter
until it forms into a ball. Flatten into a disk, wrap in plastic
and refrigerate for at least 1 hour.

Remove chilled dough from refrigerator and divide into
24 portions. Flatten each portion into a circle and line
ungreased mini muffin cups, pressing into bottom and sides.

Set aside half of the pecans. Place remaining half
equally in pastry-lined cups. Mix remaining filling ingredients thoroughly and fill each cup about ⅔ full. Top with
reserved pecans.

Bake at 350 degrees for about 25 minutes, or until set.

Cool, remove from pans, and serve.